Fake in Love

BAILEY HART

They told you that you weren't good enough.
They lied.

Playlist

"Anti-Hero" — Taylor Swift

"Best of You" — Foo Fighters

"Unstoppable" — Sia

"Bette Davis Eyes" — Kim Carnes

"Ironic" — Alanis Morisette

"I'm On Fire" — Bruce Springsteen

"Kiss It Better" — Rihanna

"Agora Hills" — Doja Cat

"Middle of the Night" — Elley Duhé

"Water Under the Bridge" — Adele

Scan in app to listen:

Content Warning

This story contains topics that readers might find upsetting. I've done my best to handle them with grace and sensitivity.

Please visit www.baileyhartromance.com/filcw or scan the QR CODE below for more details.

One

MARCI

A SIREN WHOOPS BEHIND ME, and I glance in the rearview mirror.

"Oh, balls."

One of the sheriff's lackeys is on my tail. I'm not over the speed limit. In fact, this is a leisurely drive by anyone's standards, even mine, but the cops in this town love to mess with me, and they'll take every opportunity they can get.

I pull over and put my brand new cherry red Hyundai in park, tapping my fingers on the steering wheel, my eyes narrowing.

There are two things I hate in this world.

Authority figures and books with third-act breakups. The first, because of *reasons*, and the second because they're going to get together in the end. Save me the heartbreak and throw in an extra spicy scene instead. I haven't gotten any in literal years, so I need that smut, like I need rechargeable batteries.

A door slams and Jesse Taylor gets out of the patrol car behind me.

Make that *three* things I despise.

I huff out a breath as he saunters over to my window and stops, removing his sunglasses from his stupidly handsome face and peering at me with those Taylor blue-blue eyes. Blue as a poison dart frog.

Jesse taps on my window, and I stare at him, stubborn as hell.

"Open the window," he says.

I inhale through my nose and release a breath. Because this asshole is the last person I want to see today. Out of all the deputies in this town who could pull me over, he's the one who I want to talk to the least.

"Come on, Angel," he says.

"Don't call me that," I snap.

Jesse smirks at me. I've known him since we were kids because I'm friends with his little sister, Hannah, and with June, who's dating his younger brother, Cash.

I press a button, and the window descends, allowing in more of his presence and that fuck boy cologne he wears. Spicy, cinnamon, vanilla, a little smoke. I'm a sensory person, and I hate that he smells good.

"License and registration, Angel."

"Have you no shame?" I ask. "You realize you're wearing a body cam, right? So anyone who reviews that footage will hear you calling me that."

"That's an added bonus."

"You're right. What a dumb question," I say. "You have zero shame and never have."

"Glad we're on the same page." He leans his tan,

muscular arms on the top of my car door, his uniform straining over his biceps. "License and registration."

I hold his gaze for a second longer, unwilling to back down.

This asshole and I have *history*. Jesse Taylor has caused my family literal trauma.

That devilish grin doesn't leave his face as I lean over and open the glovebox. I hand over my license and registration, then fold my arms and stare out at the street. I barely get time for myself these days. Between running the diner and dealing with my brother, Billy, I'm usually swamped. This morning's drive is part self-care, part errand.

"Is there a reason you pulled me over?" I ask. "Because I've got to get to work."

I'm not usually this rude, but Jesse brings out the brat in me.

He's frowning, his blue eyes flitting to focus on my face and then back to my license.

"Was I speeding?" I ask.

Jesse straightens. "Stay here. I'll be right back."

I open my mouth to argue, but he's already walking toward his squad, and I squeeze the wheel, my palms growing slick. What could this be about? I haven't broken any laws. Billy is on probation, though, and if he does anything, it's going to cause a world of pain for our family. Nothing matters more to me than the diner, and my family—my besties included. And with business dwindling during the fall and winter months, I need a win. I thought this car was it.

My pulse notches up as Jesse walks back toward my window.

It can't be about Billy. He wouldn't stop me if it was about Billy.

Jesse sighs. "Miss Walsh, I need you to step out of the vehicle."

"Oh, now I'm Miss Walsh? Miracles do happen."

"Out of the vehicle."

"Why?"

"Do you always answer a command with a question?"

"You're realizing this now? My specialty is answering questions with questions."

Anything I can do to piss him off is great in my book.

"Step out of the vehicle."

I get out, leaving my car door open so that I can slide back in.

"What are you doing, Taylor?" I ask. "I don't have time for this." I gesture to the box of baked goods on the passenger seat. "I'm on the way to the homeless shelter to drop these off. I can't—"

"This is a stolen car," Jesse says.

"What?" My jaw drops. "That's impossible. It's brand new. I got this car yesterday."

"Where did you buy it?" Jesse asks, handing my license and registration back.

I tuck them into my back pocket. "I didn't buy it. My brother—"

The words die on my lips.

"Your brother gave it to you?" Jesse asks.

I clamp my lips together.

"Angel?"

The nickname is quiet but dangerous.

He's called me that for years, thanks to one of my many run-ins with him. I'd called him the devil in a uniform. He'd laughed and asked me what I was, then mocked me and called me Angel for the rest of the night.

Jesse lets out a second breath, moving a hand through his dark hair and then dropping it to his side.

"Turn around and put your hands on the car."

"You're kidding, right?"

"This is a stolen car. I'm going to detain you until we can figure out exactly what's happened here and—"

"No," I say. "No, no. I swear, it's not stolen."

I hate the panicked quality of my voice. I hate showing I'm rattled when he's already caused so much damage. I squeeze my eyes shut.

I should have asked Billy where he'd gotten the car from, but I'd trusted him. I'd trusted that what he'd said about finally getting on the straight and narrow was true. And if this is a stolen car and not a ploy by Jesse to torture my family, then that has to be a lie.

Keep it together.

I'm not going to collapse under pressure. I refuse.

"It's not a stolen car," I say. "I didn't steal it."

"But you got it from your brother."

"Am I under arrest?"

"You're being detained," Jesse says. "Turn around. Hands on the roof of the car."

My breaths come quickly. Blood rushes to my ears. This is my worst nightmare. Getting arrested will suck, but Jesse Taylor being the one who does the arresting? Stick a fork in me. I'm not done, I'm overcooked.

"If you don't follow my commands, I'll make you."

I'm tempted to see if he'll follow through with the threat, but even I'm not that stubborn. I turn around and place my hands on the roof of the car.

"I need to pat you down. You want me to call a female police officer to the scene?" Jesse asks.

"No."

He clears his throat. "Do you have any weapons I should know about?"

"No."

Jesse places his hands on my waist for the briefest moment, circling them like he's holding me for real, and my skin prickles, my breath catching. His tan hands move over the back pockets of my jeans, removing the license and registration and placing them on the roof of the car beside me.

He pats my legs gently, and I widen my stance. Jesse's hands sweep over the insides of my thighs, moving lower to my calves and then my ankles, then up again and around to the front of my jeans. He dips his fingers into my pockets, tugging gently, so I'm pulled toward him.

I can barely breathe, and I hate it.

Jesse's hands shouldn't do anything to my pulse, or my skin, or my breath.

He straightens and brushes over my arms and finally across my breasts and back down to my waist, leaving a wake of goosebumps.

I bite down on the inside of my cheek.

"Get your fill?" I murmur.

"Hardly."

The word is said quietly.

"What?"

"Hands behind your back," he says.

I do it. He slips cuffs onto my wrists and tightens them. Not too tight. Loose enough that they don't hurt too much.

Jesse *knows* I don't steal cars. I've lived in Heatstroke

my entire life. I've run the diner ever since my dad passed. I'm a law-abiding citizen, albeit a wild one, so in what world does he think I'd steal a car?

The rational part of my brain mentions it's his job, but I don't care. I'm too angry. Angry at myself and Billy, and the whole goddamn situation.

"You have ten seconds to get these cuffs off me, Taylor," I say, my frustration finally getting the better of me.

He takes hold of my upper arm and I misstep and collide with him. He steadies me, his breath hot on my ear.

"I'm going to take all the time I need, Angel."

Jesse walks me to his car. The logo for the Wait County Sheriff's Department is printed across the side.

"You've finally lost your last brain cell," I say. "I haven't done anything wrong."

He opens the back door and sits me down in the back on the hard plastic seat, protecting my head with his hand, but doesn't belt me in.

Jesse stares at me, hard.

"I'll make sure the food gets to the homeless shelter. Stay here while I search your car and get your things."

I sit there and seethe, my cheeks coloring and heating as regulars at my diner drive by, staring out their car windows at us. I'm around the corner from Main Street, and even though the tourist season is ending, this street is plenty busy.

Jesse comes back holding my purse.

"I'm going to impound the car," he says.

And then he does something that I don't expect.

He reaches up and taps the body cam so that it shuts off. Wordlessly, he removes me from the back of the squad and takes the cuffs off, fingers light against my wrists. Jesse hands me my purse.

"I'll be in touch. You're free to go."

"What do you—?"

But Jesse Taylor has already dismissed me. He's walking back toward the Hyundai, talking on his radio, and I'm left shaken, wondering what kind of mind game this is. And why I care.

Two

WHENEVER MARCI WALSH IS INVOLVED, I make dumb decisions. My ears are hot from the verbal ass-whooping the sheriff gave me once I got back to the department.

I want to regret it. I don't.

My squad rattles on the dirt road that leads up to the quarry. It's a family dinner night at Cash's place, at least for the siblings.

Cash bought this place for June, or Jayjay as I like to call her, in a romantic gesture that had the wives in Heatstroke nudging their husbands in the ribs and pursing their lips. But that's Cash's style. Grand gestures. Concerts. Celebrity moves.

I squeeze the steering wheel, tension banding across my shoulders. Tonight's the night I tell them. Maybe. If I can bring myself to do it. Fuck.

A flash of light grabs my attention as I'm taking the turn away from the quarry road toward the main house, and I tap the brakes, frowning.

There's someone out by the quarry in the dark. While Cash has pretty much kept this place open to tourists and locals during the day, even though it's technically private property, the quarry is closed at night.

This won't be the first time some rebellious teens have come out here to party.

I smile and slam the squad into reverse.

I'm not a ballbuster. I don't like ruining people's fun—I remember what it was like to be a kid, doing shit you weren't meant to be doing—but the quarry's dangerous at night, and this is my brother's property.

The quarry is deep, the water a midnight blue, reflecting the stars in the night sky. I put my car in park and then jump out, grabbing my flashlight, but keeping it off.

Waves lap the shore, and the moon is so full tonight that the ripples on the water's surface are visible. I search for the trespassers, but there's no one around. True, they probably saw the car coming and scrambled into the trees that ring the water, but no noise whatsoever? No evidence that they were here?

I open my mouth to call out, but stop when movement at Diver's Point, far above, catches my attention.

A naked woman has climbed over the railing of the lookout spot, and my pulse picks up.

"Fuck."

I take a step forward, bringing my flashlight up, my finger sweeping toward the button, and then stop.

Because the woman takes another step forward, and her silken red hair comes into view, waves of it falling past her shoulders. The moon casts light over her features, the slightly upturned nose, the pouty, rosebud mouth that's spreading into a slow, joyous smile.

Marci brushes her hands over her arms, shaking, and I can't fucking move.

Not a muscle.

Not a thought.

She's stunning.

Mind-numbingly perfect. The dips and curves, from her hips to the plane of her pale stomach to the full breasts that bounce as she rubs her hands together and claps them.

Wake up, asshole!

Marci knows the quarry. She knows it's dangerous, so why the hell is she up there, naked, taking the risk? Is she out of her fucking mind?

I click on the flashlight and point it at her.

"Freeze!"

I make sure the beam is pointing below her eye line, so she's not blinded by it, but the look on her face is fucking priceless.

Bewildered and then angry, her eyes widening as she realizes the gravity of the situation. Instead of shielding her breasts from view, she takes another step forward.

"I said freeze," I yell at her. "That's an order."

"Oh, Taylor," she says. "You mistake me for giving a shit."

And then she whoops and dives off the lookout.

I try to track her in the water with my flashlight, my mind imagining the worst possible outcome. Water splashes, and I find her a second later, bobbing in the quarry and treading water. She sweeps her hair back from her forehead, her eyes sparkling emerald, and glares at me.

"Why is it," she asks. "that you always show up to ruin my fun?"

"It's adorable that you think I'm going out of my way to find you doing dumb shit," I say. "Do less, and you'll see me less, Angel."

She narrows her eyes at me, and I fucking love it. I love how angry that nickname makes her. It's made her stamp her feet, try to stomp on my toes, ball her fists, and lash out verbally at me. She despises it, and I'm the man-child who loves watching her lose control for me. Even if it's through anger.

"You're trespassing on private property," I say, mostly to piss her off.

Marci's always at Taylor family events. She's friends with my sister, Han, and with June, too. My grandmother loves her.

"You're harshing my vibe," she says.

"One of these things is illegal. The other is not."

"Get real, Taylor, I'm here for the same reason as you. So why don't you cut the crap and leave me the hell alone?"

"Can't do that."

"Why not?"

Because I like watching your cheeks go pink when I'm around.

"Because if I do, you're going to go back up there and dive back down again."

"And what if I do? Why do you care?"

She breast strokes closer toward the shore.

My body tenses at the thought of her rising from the water, dripping wet. Fuck, my cock is already at half-mast because of a brief eyeful. I don't need Marci aware of what she does to me. That mental image of her naked is going into my shame-fueled spank bank.

"Let's see," I say, tapping my chin once. "Why do I care? Huh. Maybe because you've caused enough trouble for one day? Or maybe because I'm off-duty, and I don't feel like cleaning up when you smash yourself to pieces on the rocks?"

"Such a gentleman."

"Only when it comes to you, Angel."

"I'm coming out," she says.

I turn my back on her so she can have some privacy. I might have enjoyed the view when she was up there, but I'm not about to creep on her purposefully. Still, the sounds of her moving around on the shoreline nearby send my thoughts in a *specific* direction.

"Where are your clothes?" I ask. "You got a towel?"

"I need your help like I need a heart attack."

I laugh under my breath.

"Decent?"

Marci strides past me without a word, barefoot, wearing cut-off jeans and a top that rolls up around her stomach.

Sexy as hell.

Trouble.

If Marci didn't hate me so damn much, or if I believed in long-term relationships, I would have made a move long ago. But I'm a realist, and she's a firecracker who doesn't want a man and deserves better than a one-night stand. Besides, she's too loyal to her lowlife brother.

I follow her, moving toward my squad, but she strides right past it.

"You going to walk up to the ranch house?"

She ignores me and keeps going. I hop into my squad and tail her there, admiring her ass the entire way.

Three

JESSE

"I SAY THIS WITH LOVE," Cash says, clapping me on the shoulder and squeezing, "but you're out of your fucking mind for even thinking about it."

Just the vote of confidence I need from my famous little brother.

"Gee, thanks." We're gathered near the fireplace in Cash's dining room with its log cabin vibe.

Savage runs his hand over his beard and considers me. "Why not? He's the funny guy. People love a funny guy."

Savage is my brother's best friend and has been for years. He's ex-military, and keeps to himself, running self-defense training camps on his ranch at the edge of town.

The kind of guy who has neck tats, rides motorcycles, and could probably murder you in your sleep without you waking up. Or anyone finding out.

"I'm not the funny guy," I say, with a shit-eating grin that fades fast. "I'm the reliable guy."

"Reliably funny," Cash says. "Come on, brother. The

folks in this town won't take you running for sheriff as a serious thing."

I don't let it show that my younger brother has eviscerated my ego.

"Why not?"

"Because you're *you*," Cash says. "Jesse."

"And that means?"

"I think what he's trying to say," Savage puts in, helpfully, glancing toward the dining room table where most of the women are sitting along with the leftovers of Jayjay's insanely good roast, "is… Well, shit, Jesse, you've been in and out of the beds of a lot of the town's women."

"And I've been honest about my intentions with all of them," I say, sweeping a hand through the air. "It's not like I'm a fuck boy. Besides, what the hell does that have to do with running for sheriff? I have a few relations with people, and I'm not fit to look after the town?"

"You've got a rep," Cash says, but he's distracted by his gorgeous fiancée at the table nearby. She catches him watching her and they exchange a smile. Those two are sickeningly in love, and while I'm happy for him, there are only so many PDAs I can stand witnessing. "And you let people get away with stuff."

"Huh?"

"Remember Dad? When he was drunk and disorderly?" Cash asks. "Before his healing journey? You should have arrested him multiple times instead of once."

"You pulled me over for speeding once and let me get away with it." Savage's gaze wanders away from me toward the fire crackling in the grate before drifting to the women.

Hannah, Marci, and June are hunched together, their heads over Hannah's phone. They look serious.

"Look, Jesse," Cash says, punching me lightly on the arm. "You're one hell of a good guy. And that practically means you can't be sheriff. Because you're too good to be in that position. The politics? The bullshit? You don't want that."

Marci tucks strands of that auburn hair behind her ear and glances up at me. Our eyes meet for the briefest moment, but she breaks the eye contact with an expression of disgust.

I open my mouth to argue the point, but my brother squeezes my shoulder again.

"If you're serious about running, if it's what you want, then we'll support you," Cash says. "Just, uh, yeah, I'm not sure it's the wisest thing for you to do."

Savage taps his fingers on the side of his bourbon glass, still distracted.

"So, you staying here the night?" Cash asks it loudly, over the gentle music playing from the stereo in the corner.

Marci's head snaps up. "Absolutely not."

An awkward silence fills the expansive dining area.

"See," I say, after a beat, "that makes me want to stay over even more. Not like Cash doesn't have any room. Last time I checked, he had like fifty fucking guest rooms in this place. Or are you afraid you're going to bump into me on a late-night bathroom trip, Angel?"

"You…" Marci scrapes her chair back.

I seldom call her Angel in front of my family. Just because they already razz me about having a thing for her. I don't have the patience for it.

"All right, kids," Jayjay says with a soft smile. "Let's bring it down a notch. There's a moody teenager in this house trying to grab some shut-eye."

"He can't stay here," Marci says. "If he stays here, I'm not staying here."

Cash pinches the bridge of his nose. Savage smooths his beard, hiding a bemused smile.

"Marce," Jayjay says. "What—"

"I'll tell you why later," she says. "Just trust me, I don't —I can't be under the same roof as him."

This is a new level of anger from her.

Because I saw her naked. Because I detained her. Because I spend my spare time teasing her. Because of her brother.

Another awkward quiet.

"Fine," I snap. "That's fine by me. You stay. I've got better shit to do anyway." I head for the door but pause on the way out. "Try not to steal any cars while I'm gone."

Her furious hiss has me laughing on the way out.

But my joy fades. I get into my squad and take the long drive away from Cash's log ranch house to my beach cottage on Boiler. Heatstroke is on the cusp of fall, and I leave my window down and breathe in the smells. A distant campfire, a soft whiff of mesquite, and the salt of sea air.

I don't love anyone except my family and this town. But Heatstroke doesn't love me back.

Inside my cottage, I head to the kitchen and root around in the cupboard for cat food before pouring some into a bowl and setting it out on the back porch for the stray cat I'm trying to convince to live with me. Then I switch on the TV and flick through to a music channel. One of Cash's songs is playing, and I grit my teeth.

It pisses me off that Cash doesn't think I can do it. Or that I shouldn't do it.

Fuck.

All of my siblings *have* something.

Cash is a fucking famous country music star. Hannah was a straight-A student and is a librarian. Leo plays rugby for the Eagles. Fuck, even Lily is doing what she wants. What she loves. She's a reality TV star, for fuck's sake.

And what am I? The brother nobody takes seriously.

Fuck it. I'm going to do it. I'm going to run for sheriff. I can't be the only Taylor in my family who doesn't do the family proud.

After a shower, I place my camera on its tripod, set up the timer, and then sit down on the edge of my bed, grasping the white sheets and staring dead-on. The camera clicks.

I go to bed alone.

Four

MARCI

"YOU'RE AN ANGEL, MARCI."

Todd blinks rheumy eyes at me over his plate of sunny side up eggs and the mug of black coffee at the counter in my diner.

I smile at him. "How's Cora doing?"

"Oh, she's having a blast working at the library. Always got her head in a book and a cup of coffee halfway to her mouth. Not that I can talk," he says, lifting the cup and taking a sip. "You make the best coffee in the country. I've got good news, though."

"Tell me about it."

"I started a job as Heatstroke's only taxi driver. So, you need a ride, you give me a call," he says.

"That's amazing news, Todd. Congrats!"

I sweep back to the open window that looks in on the kitchen. My chef, Grant, frowns at me from behind the grill, halfway through cooking another morning special.

"You going to keep letting him do that? He's going to

have to pay his tab at some point. Unless you're planning on turning this place into a soup kitchen."

"Have I ever been late on your salary, Grant?"

"No. But that don't matter," he says, flipping a sausage criss-crossed with grill marks. "I'm more concerned about the overall wellbeing of the restaurant."

"We're fine."

But it's a lie. We are most definitely *not* fine. The Heart-stopper, my father's legacy, is emptier than I'd like it to be. We might be popular with the locals, but not everyone can afford to eat out. And when the tourist season officially ends, we'll be plunged into another punishing fall.

I'm already starting to panic. And plan.

There's got to be a way to drum up more enthusiasm for the diner, and I'm determined that this season is going to be the difference-maker.

I grab my phone from inside my purse and set it on the countertop, casting my gaze around the place, the linoleum, the bright red booths, the retro-styling, and the pictures of my father on the walls, many of those images with customers who loved him.

Damn the lump in my throat. I unlock my phone and skim through my emails. My accountant has made things pretty clear. If we can't figure out a way to drum up money, the diner isn't going to last much longer.

I yawn, because last night wasn't exactly the best night. Skinny dipping was fun, Taylor seeing me naked wasn't, and then there is the stolen car issue to deal with. If he came in here and gave me stick about it, I—

"Marci."

My brother's voice lifts my gaze.

Billy's got a walnut brown tan and wrinkles creasing

his forehead. He's younger than me, but he looks older, and he flashes me a grin that lasts a millisecond. Blond hair like our mother.

"Billy."

He holds up his palms. "Woah. What did I do?"

"What did you do?" I pocket my phone. "Let's see, huh, what about the fact that you gave me a *stolen* car for starters? How about that?"

He pales, scratching the back of his neck. "Stolen?"

"Don't act the fool, Billy Walsh. You stole a car and gave it to me, and I nearly got arrested for it."

"You didn't tell them it was me, did you?"

I glare at my brother.

It's always been like this with us. Billy struggling and me trying to help him get his life together. He's the only blood family I have left, and I can't pretend we had a normal childhood.

But there are only so many excuses.

"Billy, you've got to get your shit together," I say. "Otherwise, you can't come around here anymore."

"What? To the diner?"

"That's right," I say.

Billy gnaws on his bottom lip. "I got… I need help."

"Huh?"

"I—Marci, I'm in trouble, I think."

"What was your first clue?" I ask. "The stolen car?"

That's only the start of the list. Billy keeps promising me that he's going to be better, try harder, but he winds up falling into old patterns, and it's frustrating. Especially because I'm partly to blame.

"Not like that. I borrowed money from a guy."

I groan, glancing sideways at Todd. My customer is

focused on his eggs, but the folks in Heatstroke are always hungry for gossip.

I round the counter and bring Billy to one side. "What are you talking about?" I brush my hands off on my apron. "What guy? How much money?"

"He's a guy who gives people money when they need it. You can call him Jonesy."

Another scratch at the back of his neck. Billy's green eyes flicker up to my face and away again, and I catch a tiny glimpse of my little brother in them.

"You're going to have to give me more than that."

"He gives good interest rates, but he doesn't like it when people don't give him the money back."

"A loan shark," I say flatly. "You borrowed money from a loan shark."

Billy shrugs.

"How much?"

He murmurs what sounds like an obscene amount of money.

"How much?"

"Fifty grand."

"Fifty!"

Billy hushes me, shifting around.

"What did you—" I palm my face. "The car? You bought a stolen car and gave it to me?"

Billy wets his lips. "Look, I—The guy's going to come for me, Marci. I need help."

I squeeze my eyes shut for a second, trying to find some semblance of inner peace.

This is bad. Real bad.

"I don't have that kind of money, Billy," I say at last. "You're going to have to work out a repayment plan with this guy and get a job, because I can't foot that kind of bill. It's not like the diner does great during the fall and winter."

"Yeah, but, I mean, if it's not doing well, then maybe you should sell it."

My jaw drops at the audacity, and Billy takes a shaky step backward, realizing that Mount Marci is about to blow.

Come for me, fine. Come for Dad's diner? Absolutely not.

The bell over the diner door tinkles, and two deputies in uniform enter.

The first one is Taylor.

The second is my ex-boyfriend, and general supreme asshole, Nate Davis.

Billy takes one look at them and opts for freedom. He makes a break for the bathroom. My money is on him climbing out of one of the windows.

A small part of me wants to follow him. Instead, I navigate to the counter and plant my hands atop it, tilting my head to the side.

"Morning, Marci," Nate says in his too-smooth tone.

He's under six feet with a soulless smile and a dimpled chin.

I nod to them, and there's already a sense of anticipation. Heat creeps up my throat.

The memory of last night and of the *incident* yesterday.

"Coffee as usual?"

Please do not be here to talk to me.

"Exactly."

Nate leans across the counter, resting his forearms on it, and smiling up at me.

"Marci, I've missed you."

"We're on duty." Jesse snaps the words out.

Nate straightens, arches an eyebrow at Taylor, who gives him a nothing stare in return.

The quiet is punctuated by Grant chopping tomatoes for the burger special. The door clangs, and another customer enters and heads over to one of the booths, newspaper tucked under his arm.

I nope out of the weird situation and fix them their coffees to go. I place the paper cups in a cardboard holder.

"Anything else?"

Nate opens his mouth, affecting another lean. "I was thinking—"

"Nate," I say, "kindly get off my counter. People gotta eat there."

Jesse smiles, but it's gone so quickly I'm sure I imagined it. "That your brother who just scuttled off?"

"Is that an official question?" I ask. "Because I believe you need to read me my rights for that. And I'll definitely need a lawyer."

"There's an open investigation involving that stolen car you were driving."

Todd chokes on his sip of coffee nearby, and I glare daggers at Jesse.

"We're going to need you to stop by the station to give your statement this afternoon," Taylor says. "Turns out your car was registered to your brother."

God damn it, Billy.

"Fine. I'll be there."

What choice do I have? Billy's made his bed yet again, but it's me that has to lie in it. It makes my blood boil, both at him, and because it's Jesse involved in our family business a second time.

Jesse grabs his coffee. Nate does the same. The pair make their way toward the exit, and I'm happy to see their backs. But Taylor stops, looking back at me once he reaches the doors, those blue eyes full of sharp intent.

"You gonna be there this weekend?"

"Where?"

"You know where."

To his credit, he hasn't called me his pet nickname yet.

"The potluck?"

"That's right. You remember what type of potluck it is, right?"

My breath catches. I'd forgotten. Every year, Ganny Taylor hosts the fall *wrestle and cook-off* at her house for family and friends. Every year, Jesse wins, but last year he had to sit it out because of a cop-out injury. I won instead.

"Yeah, I remember."

Jesse points at me aggressively, his lips pulled into a thin line.

"Your ass is mine this year."

"I'll see you in hell, Taylor."

Five

"FUCK," Deputy Davis says as he gets into the squad. "she's so fucking hot, man. I'd love to give it to her again, for old time's sake."

I force myself to exhale through my nose, staring into my coffee. I picture smashing it into the side of Davis' head. Unlike my brothers, I have *some* impulse control.

"Shut up."

"Huh?" Davis frowns at me. "What crawled up your pussy and died?"

What a piece of shit. But this piece of shit happens to be the sheriff's son.

"Keep your foul fucking opinions about women to yourself."

I set the coffee in the cupholder and glance at the diner. I have to get out of here. Much as I love fucking with Marci, hanging around her gives me unwelcome thoughts. It pisses me off.

"Oh, please," Nate says. "Like you're some fucking bastion of women's rights? You've boinked half the town."

"Consensually," I reply.

The women I've been with have known the deal. I've never lied to get anyone into bed, which is exactly what Nate does to get what he wants. I despise working with this guy, but I don't have a choice. Doesn't mean I'll accept his shitty views.

"Whatever, dude. You got a thing for her?" Davis asks, and guffaws like a psychopath. "Because you can have my sloppy seconds."

The coffee idea is becoming more appealing by the second.

"Not only is that my sister's best friend you're talking about," I say, "but a human fucking being. Not a thing. Not a meal. So shut the fuck up."

"She's not even worth the time. Fucking Walshes," Davis murmurs it under his breath.

I start the engine, roll down the window, and lean my arm on the car door. Inside the diner, Marci's smiling and laughing as she talks on the phone to someone. Must be Han or Jayjay. Her cheeks are pink, those green eyes alive with excitement.

She catches my eye and then flips me off.

I grin as I drive off, focusing on the road ahead and flipping my sunglasses down.

Heatstroke may be entering fall, but the heat isn't gone yet. We're patrolling today, looking for any signs of trouble, but with the tourists moving out of town, the calls we get are mundane. Drunk and disorderlies, one indecent exposure at the beach, and a suspicious guy hanging around the local bookstore. Turns out, he was a regular dude looking for a book to read.

I endure it with the sheriff's son, who walks through

the world like it owes him a favor. Makes me want to do the world a favor and give him what he's owed. Knocking out another deputy is, uh, frowned upon, unfortunately.

We grab a couple of donuts from the popular donut joint in town, Doughies, and eat them with a view of the beach. Normally, I wouldn't be caught dead fueling the donut-loving cop stereotype but I defy anyone to resist the crullers that Doughies turns out fresh daily.

"You ready?" Nate asks, casting me a sideways glance.

"You're going to have to give me more than that," I say, because I'm already thinking about Marci, and how ready I am to take her down at the potluck this weekend.

And how *not* ready I was to see her naked last night. The thought makes my dick twitch.

"For my father to retire," Nate says, between chews. "For me to take over the reins. You'll be working for me, soon enough."

My chewing slows.

"You're going to run?"

"Sure. It's not like I won't win. People in this town love me." He waves at a passerby, and they wave back. "The Davis family has run this place for years, and I'm going to carry on that legacy."

"I'm going to run too," I say. "Guess you'll have some competition."

Nate snorts. "You're going to run? You?"

"Yeah."

"You?"

"You need me to slap you in the back of the head to get you out of whatever record skip you're stuck in?" I ask.

"Come on, Taylor. Get real," he says, rolling his gray eyes upward. "Nobody takes you seriously."

"And they take *you* seriously?"

"Fuck yeah, they do. I'm married. People respect me. And I haven't fucked half the town," he says. "Besides, like I said, legacy."

"People don't care about that shit," I reply. "This isn't the Middle Ages."

"They care. They want a responsible guy to run the town." Nate squares his shoulders and thumbs himself in the chest. "I'm that guy. I don't let people get away with shit. Whereas you… you fucking let someone out of cuffs yesterday. Don't get me started on the times you've let your father off the hook." Nate reaches out and pats me on the shoulder then gives it a hard squeeze. "Sorry, dude. Just don't think it's happening for you."

I shrug him off, instantly reminded of Cash and Savage last night. Their doubt might have been well-meaning, but it was as shitty as Nate's.

"I'm running," I say, and finish the last of my donut.

Nate exhales a laugh. "It's your funeral, dude."

I have many reasons to hate this motherfucker, and he's added another one to the list.

I'm going to run for sheriff, and I'm going to win.

Six

MARCI

MARCI
How are you holding up, Han?

HANNAH
I've been better. I don't get why he had to be so mean about it. Like… This is the worst breakup I've ever had, and it's not even a conventional breakup.

BELLE
Men are assholes.

MARCI
I second that. Apart from Cash. June's one of the lucky ones.

JUNE
I'm sorry you're going through it, Han. <3 If there's anything we can do, say the word.

> **MARCI**
> Want to do one of those evil ex-bf rituals where we burn his shit and chant naked in the driveway?

> **HANNAH**
> I mean… I would, but I think my neighbors might complain. And he didn't give me that much stuff. So there's not much to burn.

> **BELLE**
> That makes me hate him more.

I SET my phone on the counter in the Heartstopper, shaking my head at the fuckery that is Hannah's love life. Mine is non-existent, and the last man who touched me put me off guys for years. I'm still dealing with the after-effects of that particular relationship.

My phone buzzes as more texts come through in our girlies group chat, and I smile. I love these women. They're my best friends, my sisters, and the only other people in the world, apart from my brother, who I would die for if it came down to it.

I place my fists on my hips and scan the interior of the diner. It's empty, the street outside dark except for the vignettes of light cast by the lampposts.

If I close my eyes, I imagine my father in the kitchen, cleaning up after a long day. Tears build up, and I let out a shaky breath.

Grief is an asshole. Just when I think I'm managing, it rears its ugly head.

I grab a broom and start sweeping to keep my hands busy while I think. I need to inject some interest and excitement into this business. I've failed at plenty of stuff in my life, but failing at running my father's diner isn't going to be one of them.

My phone rings on the counter, and I grab it, tucking the broomstick against my side.

I don't recognize the number.

"Hello, you've reached the Heatstroke Mortuary. How may I help you?"

I hate unknown numbers. If I wanted you to call me, I'd give you my number. Period.

"Marci." I don't recognize the caller's voice. "Marci Walsh."

"Who's this?"

I pin the phone to my ear using my shoulder and shift the broom out from under my arm.

"Miss Walsh, you and I need to talk about that diner of yours."

"I doubt it," I say. "Is this some weird new tactic insurance companies are employing?"

Or a hyper-realistic robot call?

"Your brother owes me money."

My stomach sinks.

Fuck balls.

"And you are?"

"That's not important," the guy says, his voice thick and raspy. "What matters is that you come up with the money. Fifty grand in two months. Got it?"

"You're out of your mind," I say. "How the hell do you expect anyone to come up with that kind of money on short notice?"

"You've got an asset, don't you?" he asks. "You'll come up with the money. And if you don't—"

The line goes dead, and I pull the phone away from my ear, my pulse ratcheting upward.

An ear-splitting crash sends me careening back into the counter. I drop my phone and the broom, spinning toward the front of the Heartstopper. The window bearing our logo, the hamburger dripping with fixings, and wearing a cute smile is broken. A half brick rests on a table near the front.

Tires squeal outside, and a black car with tinted windows zips past.

"Hey! Hey, you asshole!" I yell, but they're already gone, and I'm shaking like a leaf.

I can't believe that happened.

The diner. My father. The money.

I can't breathe. I try to suck in a breath, but the linoleum is speckled gray. I grab hold of a stool closest to me and sink down.

The diner door opens, and a man enters. I push myself backward, fear clawing at my throat, and—

"It's me. Angel, it's me."

Jesse Taylor drops down to his knees beside me. He swipes my hair back from my clammy forehead.

"Hey. Talk to me. What do you need?"

"What are you—?" I manage.

"Walking home," he says. "It doesn't matter. Stay here."

Jesse locks the diner door and then rounds the counter. He clatters around in the back before reappearing with a glass of soda.

"Drink this. Sugar will help. Are you injured? Do you need me to call medical?"

It's such a cop thing to say, and it brings me back to the present.

"No," I say. "No."

I take the water from him, mumble my thanks, and sip it. And god damn it, he's right. It helps. The sweetness and the coldness.

Jesse sits on the floor beside me, wearing jeans that hug well-defined thighs, and a white tee and a flannel shirt rolled up over muscular forearms.

"Are you sure?" he asks.

My gaze snaps up to his face, and my cheeks heat. Did he catch me checking him out? Why the fuck am I even looking at him? Must be a stress response. I scan the front of the diner.

"Marci, do you need me to call medical?"

It occurs to me that he's called me by my name, and that irritates me even more.

"I told you, Taylor, I'm fine."

"Fuck." He gets up and walks toward the front door. "Fuck. I wish I was in my squad tonight. I came around the corner as the fucking car sped off. I didn't get a chance to memorize the plates. I—"

"Memorize them?"

Why was he even in the area? It wasn't like Main Street was that close to Longhorn's, Jesse's usual hang-out spot.

"What are you even doing here?"

"I told you. Walking home. And what the fuck does that matter?" he asks.

It doesn't. I take another sip of the water, already feeling heaps better. The shock got to me, as much as I hate to admit it, but it's because of the diner. This place is sacred to me. It's not my home, it's an integral part of who I am, and somebody trashed it.

"Where's your phone?" Jesse spots it on the ground and reaches for it.

"What are you doing?"

"I'm calling this in, of course."

"What?"

I set the water aside and get up, rising to my knees in front of him first, then stopping.

Jesse looks down at me and swallows, his throat working.

"Give me my phone," I say, getting to my feet and extending my hand.

"I'm calling the cops. You need to sit down."

"No," I say. "I'm not going to sit down, and you are not going to call the cops."

"Did you bump your head when you fell?" he asks, narrowing those poisonous eyes. "Because you're not talking sense. I suppose that's a regular thing for you, Angel, but for me, not so much."

"Give. Me. My. Phone."

Jesse grinds his teeth, and we square up. He holds the phone toward me. I grab the end of it. He doesn't let go.

"You have to call the cops. Someone vandalized your fucking diner." His gaze flickers upward. "Which means your apartment is compromised too."

"Why the hell do you care?"

"It's my job to care."

"Spare me," I say. "I don't need your pity. You've already done enough."

"When are you going to stop blaming others for your brother's problems?" he asks.

I suck in air through my nostrils. "What did you say to me?"

"I arrested Billy because he had an outstanding warrant," Taylor replies.

"That's ancient history. Why bring it up, huh?"

And that doesn't matter. The sheriff and his star son, Nate, have it out for my family.

"You and I both know the reasons you hate me, Angel," he says.

"Stop calling me that."

"Then stop being a little Angel," he replies, breath hot against my face, sending shivers over my skin. "Goodie two shoes, Marci."

"I wasn't so good the other night when I was skinny dipping, was I? Huh? So what is it? Am I an angel or a wild child? A lawbreaker. Make up your mind, Taylor."

"I've already made up my mind about you, Angel. A long time ago. It's you who has the fucking issues."

"What's that supposed to mean?"

I tug on the phone, but his grip is iron.

"It means you'd better call the cops. I'm not leaving until you do."

"Then you can sleep on the floor like a dog," I say.

"As long as you feed me a treat before bedtime."

I let out a frustrated shriek, and he gives me that grin I despise.

"You can't stay here if it's not safe."

"It's kids," I say. "Kids acting the fool."

"Bullshit."

"Once again, I don't want or need your opinion or your presence, Taylor," I say. "When are you going to get tired of making my life difficult?"

"When are you going to get out of your own way?"

"Wow, I had no idea you could be *that* hypocritical. I mean, I expected it, but the way you confirmed it is … chef's kiss."

Jesse stares at me for a long moment, and the silence builds between us. His gaze flickers over my face, down to my lips, lower, and then back up again. My breath comes rapidly, rising and falling.

"Fine."

He releases the phone.

I slip it into the pocket of my cut-off shorts. The victory flares in my chest but shrinks fast, leaving emptiness.

"Don't call it in," he says, and leaves me standing there.

"Where are you going?" I ask.

"I thought you wanted me to leave."

"I do."

Taylor rubs his palm over his shaven jaw, pulling the skin and releasing it. He opens his mouth, shuts it, then slams the door behind him on the way out. He turns back and points at the lock on it, then leaves.

I sink onto the barstool, the sudden quiet so stark that my ears ring.

What the hell happened? One second, I'm cleaning, and the next…

I'm going to have to talk to Billy about this. Or find a way to come up with a lot of money fast. I shouldn't bail my brother out again, but the picture on the wall behind the counter is a constant reminder of what should be. What could have been.

My father stands in the middle, his arms around me at

age eighteen, and my little brother, eight years old. It was taken two months before Dad died.

Billy is my responsibility and has been since then.

I'm still sitting there, gathering myself, when the purr of a car engine intercepts my thoughts. A squad car, bearing the sheriff's department logo in black and white, pulls up outside the bar.

"Oh no," I mutter. "Oh, hell no. No, no. no."

I scoot off the barstool and exit onto the sidewalk.

Jesse ignores me. He switches off the engine and then reclines the driver's seat way back and tucks his hat over his eyes.

I rap on the window and he slides his hat up, over his forehead, and looks at me.

"What do you think you're doing? You can't do that."

He doesn't answer me but closes his eyes.

"Hey! Hey, you can't do that, Taylor. Get out of here."

But I can't tell him to leave. The street is public property.

I let out another undignified and incredibly immature shriek, and Jesse smiles, eyes still closed, which only makes things worse. I go back into the diner, shut the door, and lock it, hating the fact that the car outside provides me even a modicum of comfort.

Seven

JESSE

I **PULL** up outside Ganny's house at noon the next day and take a minute to collect myself before going in.

Because Marci's going to be there.

Last night isn't the first time I've slept in my patrol car, but I spent most of the night caught between arousal and concern for Marci. I spied on her while she cleaned up the mess, her body unreal under the fluorescent lights in the diner. Isn't that kind of lighting supposed to make you look bad?

Curvy around the hips, slender, bouncy tits, tall, her hair falling past her shoulders. Fuck.

The rest of the night was spent watching the street, making sure whoever threw a brick through the diner window didn't come back.

She's not telling me who it is. And she's going to have to file a police report if she wants insurance to cover it, but she's so fucking stubborn that she probably won't.

I grab the casserole from the passenger seat and head inside Ganny's house, stifling a yawn.

The minute I open the door, I'm surrounded by happy, familiar noises.

Alex, my niece, laughs as she speeds past, gangly now that she's in her teens. Fireball, my grandmother's Chihuahua is on her tail, barking like mad.

"Hey, Uncle Jesse!"

She spares me a quick kiss on the cheek before racing off again, her phone in hand.

I laugh at her antics. The rumble of voices penetrates the lower floor of my granny's old wooden house, and I walk past the pictures that line the hallway.

Most of them are of us as kids, playing, unwrapping Christmas gifts, or eating sundaes out back. There's even a picture of the first-ever Taylor family water wrestling event in action. I'm twelve years old, and I've got Cash in a headlock in a kiddie pool full of water while Hannah screams on the sidelines in diapers. She must be about two. Leo's beating on his chest like a silverback even though he's only eight. Lily's just a baby on my mother's hip. Mom is smiling like an angel.

My gaze moves away from the happy memory to a more somber picture.

My grandfather, his lips turned down at the corners, standing on his own. His bright blue eyes penetrate through time and fucking space, carrying unspoken judgment.

"You lost?" Cash asks, poking his head around the archway that leads into Ganny's living room.

I stroll into the living room and find Ganny on her favorite floral-print sofa, her knitting supplies in the basket beside her. She smiles up at me, and I plant a kiss on her delicate cheek. She pats me on the back and then pinches my cheek.

"'Bout time you got here. We're going to wrestle soon."

"First round is me and Ganny," Hannah says.

"Oh, you."

Ganny pats the air at my little sister. I sweep her into a hug as well and squeeze her tight. My sister always smells like flowers and books, which is hilarious because those are her two favorite things.

"Ready for another ass whooping?" Cash points at me.

I glance over both shoulders.

"Just looking for who the fuck you're talking to. I've beat you every single year, right?"

"Except for last year," Hannah says, rubbing one eye.

She looks tired, and I frown.

"Last year was a fluke. I was injured, and Cash didn't participate because he was touring," I say.

"Bless your heart." Hannah pats my shoulder. "You believe that, don't you? Marci's got freak strength. You'll see. She could beat you in an arm wrestling contest."

I snort.

But there's anticipation there. Marci and I might wind up wrestling today, depending on the bracket. Yeah, we take this shit way too seriously.

"Now that you mention tours," Cash says. "I'm leaving again in a couple of weeks."

"You're kidding," I say. "You? Mr. Celebrity Star, apple of our family's eye?"

And I don't mean it in a malicious way.

"I want to take Alex and June with me, but I can't. You'll keep an eye on them?"

I pat him on the shoulder. "Of course, brother."

The burble of a bike engine intercepts our conversation, and Savage pulls up on his Harley. He gets off, then opens his saddlebags and grabs a bouquet and a Tupperware from within. Hannah clears her throat and mentions going to the bathroom before dipping out of sight.

My little sister thinks we're blind to her crush on Savage, but he wouldn't touch her with a ten-foot pole. It's best if it stays that way. Savage is a lone wolf, and I don't see that changing.

Ganny starts trying to get up and we stop her.

"What do you need?" I ask. "Water? A drink?"

"Your daddy's in the kitchen, and I don't trust him with my potato bake for a second. I've got to check on him."

"I'll go," I say. "You stay here."

I head into the kitchen and place the casserole on the counter. Dad is nowhere to be seen, so I check on the potato bake in the oven. The cheese is bubbly, and it looks about done.

Footsteps tap on the tiles behind me, and I turn, expecting Han and finding Marci instead.

My chest squeezes, and my dick reacts to her instantly.

Marci smells like lavender and looks like torture. She's chosen a tight-fitting camisole and white skirt that I'd love to fuck off her body. The straps of her bikini top, a halter, sit against her pale skin, digging in.

"Taylor."

She's holding a casserole dish.

"Angel."

She rolls her eyes and brushes past me. I catch her wrist and squeeze.

"Did you call the cops?"

"No."

"That's fucking dumb."

"Eat my ass, Taylor," she says, and pulls free of my grip.

Don't tempt me.

Then she turns and places the casserole dish on the counter, right next to mine.

"Oh, you've got to be kidding me," she mutters. "Someone else made a King Ranch chicken casserole?"

"Me," I say.

Marci spins around and stares at me, her green gaze biting.

"Of course, you did, Taylor. Yet another attempt to harsh my vibe."

"Don't flatter yourself," I say.

"Huh?"

"You think I'd go out of my way to figure out what you're bringing to the potluck?" I ask. "And copy you?"

I take a step closer to her.

She places the heels of her palms on the counter behind her and glares up at me.

"I wouldn't put anything past you at this point. I bet you've been doing push-ups for the last month in preparation for the wrestling today."

"You're not wrong about the push-ups. But I don't need to prepare for you, Angel," I say. "I'm always packing heat."

Her eyes widen a little, her breath catches, and her jaw works. These micro-reactions drive my pulse through the roof. She's fucking stunned by my words, and I relish it. Bask in it. I've struck Marci speechless. Wiped the smart words right out of that even smarter mouth.

"You don't stand a chance," I say, leaning in closer. I turn my head and brush my nose against her cheek as I talk. "I'm going to make you beg today."

She makes the tiniest noise in her throat. I grab napkins off the counter behind her and take a step back, resisting the urge to readjust myself.

Marci's nipples are hard, puckering against her shirt, but her eyes flash, and her nostrils flare.

"You have no idea who you're messing with, Taylor."

I laugh.

"Can't wait to find out."

Then I stroll out of the kitchen and down the hall. I drop the napkins on a side table before entering my grandmother's downstairs bathroom, complete with a fake bouquet of peach roses, a matching sink, and a fluffy toilet seat cover.

I lock the bathroom door, unzip my pants and start stroking my cock like a man possessed. I finish in record time, thoughts of Marci's mouth on my dick, my fingers buried in her warm, wet pussy, getting me there. I clean up after myself and shake my head at myself in the mirror over the sink. I lost control.

It's not the first time I've thought about her. It's not going to be the last. I've got a feeling I won't be satisfied until I've tasted her at least once.

Neither of us will let that happen.

Eight

MARCI

I HANG BACK WITH JUNE, my arms folded.

"He thinks he's such hot shit," I mutter.

June laughs and loops her arm through mine.

"Oh, Marce."

"What?" I ask, narrowing my eyes at the wrestling pool.

It's a kiddie pool filled with water, and Cash and Jesse are currently in the middle of what feels like an endless battle for victory. Cash is trying to pin Jesse in the water, but the man is as slippery as an eel. He rises from the water, droplets running down his chest, finding the grooves in his abs, and I swallow and look at June instead.

"June?"

"I've been saying it for the past two years. You guys will, uh, work things out one way or another."

Her tone is suggestive.

"He arrested my brother, June," I say. "And detained me. And he's been an asshole to me for years. And he's a cop."

After everything with Dad, and with my ex, I struggle with the cops in this town. I get they're necessary, but I… can't with them.

June sighs. "I'm here for you. I'll jump on that hate train if you need me to, but Jesse's not a bad guy. He was doing his job."

"Yeah."

That makes sense, but it's not about the arrests or his job or any of that.

June gives me a one-armed squeeze. "I'm here for you. If I'm making you uncomfortable by talking about him, tell me, okay? I'll stop."

"Thanks, babe."

It's easier to distract myself with my anger at Jesse rather than focus on the incident at the diner. It's costing me money I don't have, to get the window fixed. And I've gotten two missed calls from the loan shark in the last couple of hours.

Going to the cops will land Billy in trouble. But not going risks the same thing. I want to make a rational, logical decision about my next steps. I also want to make my brother's problems go away because a part of me still feels like he's my responsibility. Like it's my fault.

Breathe.

Hannah exits onto the porch, phone in hand, tears in her eyes, and June and I move to block her from sight immediately. Ganny's on the porch swing nearby, her arm looped through her son's. Mr. Taylor clasps a can of Coke in one hand and smiles at the ongoing antics.

"What happened?" I ask.

"Han?" June reaches out and takes the phone from her, gently. She reads the text on the screen. "You can't be serious. He's still texting you? You have to talk to somebody about this."

"It's fine," Hannah says. "He's being a dick. Besides, it's not like he lives in Heatstroke. I'll block his number. I should never have given him a chance. I was…"

"You were lonely," I say. "And that's fine, Han. You didn't do anything wrong, and you don't deserve some asshole harassing you because things didn't work out."

A cheer goes up from Alex and Savage, who are manning the grill nearby, and we turn to find Cash tapping out.

June and Hannah join the applause, but I grind my teeth at the smug look on Jesse's face. His gaze finds mine, and he arches both eyebrows at me.

"Who dares challenge me?" Jesse calls out, spreading his muscular arms. "Who dares approach?"

"The ego on this guy."

Cash punches his brother on the arm, then jogs over and grabs June. She shrieks and kicks, giggling at how cold and wet he is. He lathers her with kisses.

Jesse sloshes around in the kiddie pool, imitating Connor McGregor's walk, and pursing his lips like a loon.

"Get real," I call out. "The only reason you ever win the family wrestling event is because Savage chooses not to participate."

A chorus of "oohs" rings out from the gathered Taylors and sundry.

"Big words for a woman who hasn't got the ovaries to challenge me." Jesse thumbs his chest.

I glare at him. And… *snap.* There goes my last reserve of patience.

"That's it," I say, pointing at him. "You're dead."

Jesse does a slow clap. "What a comeback."

Another round of "oohs."

I rip off my skirt but leave my shirt on. The last thing I need is my breasts making a bid for freedom during the wrestling match. I remove my earrings one by one, making eye contact with Taylor as I place them in June's outstretched hand.

"Let's go, pretty boy."

I vault down the stairs and streak toward him.

Jesse's eyes go wide at the last second, and he puts out his hands. I collide with him, looping my arms around his waist.

Our bodies slam into the water, and cheers go up from the audience.

I spider monkey onto him, wrapping my arms and legs around him and squeezing with all my might, trying to roll him so that he's face down in the water and pinned. I've got him dead to rights because he might be a big, strong guy, but I use his weight against him.

As a kid, my dad put me in martial arts classes. I have muscle memory from a life that feels like it wasn't mine.

"Looks like you're not such hot shit after all," I bite out, my body pressed against his muscular back.

Jesse chokes out a laugh against the water, then reaches down and tickles the underside of my foot.

"Just giving them a good show, Angel."

"You—"

And then he does a push-up in the water with me on his back.

"Dick," I hiss.

Jesse lets out a laugh and does a one-handed push-up, using the other hand to reach back and tickle my side.

I can't stand him using me as a tool to show off his strength, so I release my grip and slide off his back. The minute I do, he's on me, grappling with my arms. Jesse grabs my wrists and pins them over my head, and I kick out with my legs, rolling and twisting to the side.

He lets me go. I hate it.

Because he's *letting me go.* It's not like I'm fighting free or making him uncomfortable. It enrages me, and I turned toward him again.

Jesse's eyes flicker from my face to my chest and back up again, and I don't even care that my shirt is clinging to my body. I want to take him down. I want to make him pay in this small way. Just once.

Jesse's so smug. So unaffected.

He claps his hands and crooks the fingers on both hands.

I run at him. He catches me around the waist, easily, then falls to his knees and brings me onto my back in the water, almost gently.

"Fight me," I say. "Fight me."

"There's no contest." But his eyes flash at the challenge, and he pins me down, clamping my wrists above my head with one hand, the other resting on my waist. "Tap out. You're done."

"Never. Fuck you."

"Only in your wildest, wettest dreams, Angel."

The words are whispered into my ear.

I buck against him, but his hand presses against my midriff, holding me down, his fingers spread. Jesse laughs as the countdown starts up from the Taylors.

"Ten, nine, eight—"

"Come on, Marci!" June calls. "You can do it."

"Kick his ass!" Hannah puts in.

"Hey," Jesse says, turning his head, showing me his defined, cleanly shaven jaw. "Whose side are you on? I'm your brother!"

"Her side," Hannah yells back.

I grin, but the minute Jesse looks my way, I stop.

The countdown reaches zero, but he doesn't let go. "Guess I win," he says.

"Congratulations, Jesse. You're an asshole."

"Don't be a sore loser."

I resist the urge to stick out my tongue at him. I lie in the water, aware of how his hands feel on my body. He isn't hurting me, and the touch is... it sends my heart pattering like a traitor.

"Let me go."

Jesse releases me right away. He sits in the water rather than standing, and I get up and get out of the kiddie pool, rolling my eyes heavenward. "I'll get him next year," I say.

"That's the spirit, honey," Mr. Taylor says.

There's a round of golf claps as I head over to the girls. June hands me a towel and my skirt, and I go indoors to get changed in the downstairs bathroom. I lock the bathroom door and wrap the towel around my waist, stripping off my shirt and hanging it over the edge of the peach-colored sink.

My reflection stares back at me, and I don't like the flush at my throat, or the pinkness at my wrists, or the fact that the weight of Jesse's touch is indelibly etched on my stomach. I don't like that my nipples are puckered against my bikini top, sensitive against the moist fabric.

I back into the wall and lean against it, shut my eyes,

my pussy throbbing. I've got to be hormonal, because even I can't deny how hot that was.

My fingers chase over my stomach toward the hem of my bikini bottoms. My eyelids flicker open, and I meet my reflection in the mirror.

"You are *not* doing this," I whisper.

A knock rattles the bathroom door, and I'm saved from myself.

I tie the towel around my waist and open the door.

Jesse leans one arm against the doorjamb, bare-chested, a smattering of dark hair across his pecs. He scans me from head to toe, lingering on my breasts, finally focusing on my lips and then my eyes.

"You good?"

"Why wouldn't I be?" I ask. "You think I care about a wrestling match?"

"Just checking I didn't go too rough on you."

"I'm not afraid of rough," I say.

The corner of Jesse's lip lifts. "That so?"

"Don't make it weird."

But I'm aware that it's my nipples making this weird.

Jesse and I stand there, silently, our gazes locked, and there's tension building between us that's unfamiliar. My breaths come in ragged gasps. His hand balls into a fist and releases.

I lift my chin, defiant.

Jesse rests his hand on my throat and squeezes once lightly, then steps back and shakes his hand as if he's been burned. He turns and walks off.

What. The. Fuck?

I nearly fall over myself, shutting the door. My fingers

dip into my bikini bottoms again, seeking release from the torture of that moment, and—

My phone rings in the front hall. And it's my brother's ringtone. I have a specific one for him, so I'm prepared for anxiety.

"Fuck."

I turn around, lean on the door and bang the back of my head against it.

"Fuck. Fuck. Fuck."

It's for the better.

Wanting Taylor sexually is a line I don't want to cross. Have I thought about him before? Yes. Do I believe in hate-fucking? Sure. But there are too many difficult emotions involved when it comes to him, and most of them are negative. I don't need another negative experience with a guy. Especially after how things went with my ex. And he's a *Taylor*, for God's sake.

I open the bathroom door and run out to the entry hall to grab my phone as it goes silent.

A second later, a text blips through.

BILLY
I need your help. Please come get me at Jimmy's Range.

"What now?" I say, as I type out a reply that I'm on my way.

I don't want to leave, but if Billy needs my help, then it's necessary. I get dressed in my wet shirt and my skirt, then hurry out to the backyard to say goodbye to the family. Ganny gives me a kiss on the cheek, and I hurry out of there. I've got an old beater that I was using before Billy gave me the stolen Hyundai.

I get in, roll down the windows to let in fresh air, and start the engine. The front door of the Taylor house slams, and Jesse descends the wooden porch steps, pulling on a shirt.

"Where are you going?" he asks.

"Huh?"

"Is it Billy?"

I bristle. "None of your damn business."

"When are you going to realize that you don't have to run after him?" Jesse asks.

"That is so fucking hilarious, Taylor. You have no idea what you're talking about. Literally. It's easy for you to judge when you've got your perfect family who does potlucks, and brothers and sisters who love you, and a father—" I cut off. "You don't know. So how about you do us both a favor and stop acting like you do."

And then I drive off.

He stands there, watching me, and I force myself to focus on the road rather than the rearview mirror.

Nine

JESSE

I SIT AT THE LONG, worn wooden bar in Longhorn's with Cash and Savage on either side of me, my hand on a beer. I'm not driving my squad tonight, but I don't live too far from Longhorn's anyway, and I like the walk home along the beach.

All I can think about is walking home.

That's not true. All I can think about is Marci.

Her body underneath me. My hand resting on her throat. Her puckered nipples. The angry words she shouted at me before she drove off.

I squeeze the beer bottle and then drink a sip.

Longhorn's is alive tonight, with plenty of locals dancing on the wooden floor, music thumping through the speakers, and the back doors thrown open wide onto the beach sands. It's cooler than summer, but it's still pleasant at the start of fall, and there are folks sitting out at the tables, kidding around.

Couples with their arms around each other. I never got it. Committed relationships. Not because I can't care for somebody else, but because I don't see how or why they would care for me exclusively. That kind of shit is a gateway to hurt.

I take another swig of beer.

"You want me to get you a napkin, brother?" Cash asks. "You look like you're about to cry."

Savage thumps me on the back. "He's not wrong. What's up?"

He's infamously quiet, Savage. He's got a sense of humor, but he tends to keep to himself. He's more beast than man, especially after he came back from the military.

"Nothing," I say. "I'm good."

"Good?" Cash asks. "Usually, you've got a woman on either arm by this point in the evening."

I shrug.

Casual sex is fun, but it gets boring.

Savage stiffens incrementally next to me, and I glance up at his face and then follow his gaze. June, Hannah, and Marci have entered the bar together. Marci's red hair is tied up in a messy bun, and she's wearing a pair of skin-tight jeans that hug her shapely thighs. She's wearing a silky green top that's frilly at the bottom and ruched at the top.

Fuck. Oh my fucking God, I am in trouble.

The girls come over, and Cash sweeps June into a hug and plants a kiss on her lips. Hannah stands nearby with Marci, chatting amiably. Marci ignores me completely.

"I love this place," June says. "So many memories."

"Can you believe this place almost burnt down?" Marci asks.

"Not on Missy's watch," Cash says. "Wonder where she is? Haven't seen her in a while."

"She's getting old. It can't be easy being the owner of a bar at that age," Jayjay says, giving Cash a sickeningly sweet gaze.

"Would you two stop devouring each other?" I grumble.

June laughs. The girls order drinks, then leave together and go sit over at one of the tables ringing the dance floor. Marci catches my eye for a second and holds it before looking away.

Wanting her is pointless. She'll never stop hating me, because I can't be the sweet, friendly guy she wants. I can't be the guy who stands by while she lets people take advantage of her. I can't shut up about that, and I won't.

Cash and Savage chat idly, doing their best to involve me in their conversation but eventually leave me to my moody solitude. I sip my beer and watch Marci, but she doesn't look up.

The music changes pace to a slow song, and Marci rises from the table, laughing at something Jayjay says, and comes over. She crowds between the others at the bar and flags down Luke, the bartender.

Even watching her with a god damn bartender annoys me. I don't like Marci getting under my skin. It's supposed to be the other way around.

Luke takes her order, but I summon him over before he can fulfill it. Marci's distracted on her phone, so she doesn't notice.

"I'm paying for her round of drinks," I murmur. "But don't tell her it was me. Got it?"

Luke flicks his earring and arches an eyebrow at me.

"No offense, Jesse, but I don't think even you can pull this one off. She doesn't do one-night stands."

"I appreciate the input, buddy, but I'm paying for the drinks, not buying condoms."

Luke takes my money and gets the booze.

It's a pointless gesture. I don't care, because she's smiling and happy when she takes the beers. She glances around, trying to find the person who bought the round, and her gaze meets mine at the last second. She takes a step toward me, but a woman slides past her.

"A birdie told me that you were fixing to do something real stupid, Jesse darlin'."

The voice is both familiar and unwelcome.

My ex, or rather my ex-friend with benefits, Annaleigh Devan, leans across the bar in front of me. She twirls a long strand of blonde hair around her finger and releases it. She's wearing a crop top that shows off her body and enough cleavage to draw eyes, but I lean to one side, searching for Marci.

She's standing there with the beers in hand, lips pursed.

Annaleigh waves a hand in front of my face.

"Are you registering, Jesse? Like, do you see me standing in front of you?"

"What do you want?"

"Just checking in," Annaleigh says, and holds her nails out to examine them. "They recently promoted me to editor of the magazine."

"Congratulations. That's great news." When we broke up, Annaleigh threatened to write a piece about me in the gossip column. She never followed through, thankfully.

"Yeah, *great* news. I heard you want to run for sheriff, Jesse, and I wanted to encourage you *not* to do that," she says. "Because people don't want a player who only cares about getting his dick wet as their sheriff. They want a family man. Maybe you should have thought twice about breaking up with me." She's smug as hell. "Especially since I *run* the magazine."

"We were never dating. We were friends with benefits. I made that clear from the start."

This is a pointless conversation. It doesn't matter what I say to her, how nice I am. Annaleigh is sore about the fact that she couldn't turn me into husband material. She bragged to her friends that she could. Friends who then came to me and told me. It was part of the reason we broke up. That and the fact that Annaleigh wanted me as a trophy. A way to get under her father's skin.

"You should watch what you—"

Marci steps around Annaleigh toward me.

"Did you buy these for us, Taylor?"

She gestures with the beers.

Fuck. She's still here. She heard that.

"Nope," I say.

"Excuse me." Annaleigh whips around and narrows her eyes at Marci. "We're in the middle of a conversation here."

"And I'm in the middle of not giving a damn," Marci says.

"Jealous?" I ask, because it will drive Marci wild.

She blushes an attractive shade of pink. Petals on silk sheets.

"In your wildest, wettest dreams, Taylor."

"Be careful," Annaleigh says, dry as a cracker, "he might take you up on that offer, lead you on, and then leave you."

"If he treated you so bad, why are you so obsessed

with him?" Marci asks. The woman is *not* afraid of conflict. She doesn't care whose eyes are on her. "Seems like a great way to erode your dignity."

"'Erode your dignity?' What are you, an encyclopedia?"

"Dictionary," Marci says, "is the word you're looking for. And I'm here to tell you that you're making a dick of yourself in front of the entire bar."

Annaleigh laughs at Marci. "You have a crush on him? Get in line with the rest of the women who've been in his bed."

That's a lie. None of them have been in my bed.

"I'm not the type of person who queues," Marci says, "but if that's you, you do you. I'm saying, talking about how you got a promotion in lieu of trying to bring another person's aspirations down is a dick move. And you should be ashamed of yourself."

And then she turns to leave.

Annaleigh sticks out her foot and connects it with Marci's ankle. Marci tips forward, her eyes widening, and my hand snaps out and grabs hold of her wrist before she can fall. But I overcompensate and pull her backward a little too hard.

Marci tumbles into my lap, the beers crashing to the floor and shattering.

Heads turn, the noise loud even with the music pumping through the speakers. Annaleigh slinks off with a triumphant smile, and my chest rises and falls rapidly, my teeth set against each other. She tried to hurt her. She *fucking...*

Marci's palms touch my forearm, and I move my gaze down to her face.

"Bette Davis Eyes" by Kim Carnes thrums through the bar, taking up the tiny spaces between us.

My forearm loops around Marci's waist. Her hand resting against it. Her thighs across my lap. My throat dry. Her pink, wet lips. Green eyes, sparkling, wide. Soft breaths, hot against my chin. Her fingers bite into my forearm then relax.

She glances away, but I keep staring at her. At the top of her head, the side of her face, the wisp of auburn hair resting against her throat.

"I'm fine," she says, tapping on my arm with her fingertips.

I release her.

She slips off my lap, side-stepping the glass. She looks like she wants to clean it, but I hold out a hand to stop her. I bend and start picking up the pieces as one of Longhorn's servers comes over to help. Cash and Savage offer to help too, ask Marci if she's fine, try to make conversation that falls on deaf ears.

Marci bends to help, but, again, I put out an arm.

"I've got it."

"I'm fine."

But there's a strange look in her eyes.

Marci's not fine. She's so far from fucking fine. Carrying the weight of the world on her shoulders. It annoys me that I care, but I do, and I'm starting to think I don't have a fucking choice in the matter anymore.

After the glass is cleaned, Marci returns to Jayjay and Hannah. I say goodbye to Cash and Savage, then walk out of the back door of Longhorn's and along the beach toward my cottage.

At home, I fill the bowls of food and water for the stray

cat and place them on my back porch, then shut the sliding glass door.

I set up my camera, sit on my bed, and wait for another picture. When I'm done, I head out my door again and start the long walk toward the Heartstopper.

Ten

MARCI

I SHOULDER my purse and wave goodbye to Hannah and June, then head for the diner's front door. June's been drinking mostly water so that she could ferry us home, but Hannah is going to have a headache tomorrow for sure.

I'm going to have one too, but for different reasons.

Jesse. What the actual fuck happened tonight? Today? And why do I care?

It's so frustrating to be this confused about someone I despise, who's already caused enough damage in my life. Yet another sign that Taylor is *winning*.

I unlock the front door of the diner and enter. The window of the diner is fixed, thankfully—I managed to get a guy out to install another pane of glass this morning, but it cost me way too much, and it compounds the problems I have.

Billy is in need of money. My diner is under threat. And the fact that business is waning thanks to the fall months makes a bad situation worse. I need a minute to breathe and think about it.

Maybe some kind of joint venture with another business? But I've tried that before. Or a festival? There's already the chili pepper festival in summer, but what if I hosted a burger-eating contest? It feels like a good solution, but the fact is, I can't afford it.

You can do it. You'll figure this out.

The words are in my father's voice, and I take comfort from them. I shut the door behind me and start toward the door behind the counter that leads to my apartment. I'm halfway to it when a dark figure steps out of the kitchen.

My heart freezes in my chest, and so do I.

The guy rounds the counter and moves toward me. He's wearing black. Including a balaclava, but dark eyes peer out at me. He lifts a hand, and something glints in it.

I backpedal and scream, scrambling for the pepper spray in my purse.

The attacker advances toward me, moving fast as lightning, and I'm done.

"Help!" The word is strangled.

A crash sounds behind me, and Jesse streaks past me, heading straight toward the guy with the knife.

"Watch—" I start, but Jesse's almost on top of the guy.

The attacker's eyes go wide, and he scrambles away, vaulting over the countertop and running back through the kitchen. Jesse yells wordlessly, sliding over the counter and charging after him.

I tremble on the spot, my hand on the clasp of my purse. I bring out the pepper spray and take a step toward the kitchen. And then another. And then I'm running because that man had a *knife* and Jesse doesn't have a weapon.

I skid around the counter, holding out the pepper

spray, my thumb on the trigger, and crash into the kitchen. It's empty. But the door at the back is open. I run out and spot Jesse at the end of the alleyway.

"Wait!" I scream. "Wait! He's got a knife!"

Jesse stops and looks back at me, and then, instead of pursuing the guy, he jogs over to me.

He grabs hold of my arms, thumbs pressing into my flesh. "Are you good?"

I open my mouth, but the words won't come. *He's got a knife.* The thought repeats.

Jesse's brows are slashes above those deep blue eyes, and he guides me back through the kitchen, reaching for his phone.

"I'm calling it in."

"I—"

"I am calling this the fuck in."

His words are furious. He walks me into the diner and sits me down on a chair, and I let him.

I let him because I can't think straight. A man with a knife. First the window, now this?

Jesse talks on the phone nearby, pacing back and forth, his broad shoulders stiff. I've never seen him *angry.* Annoyed, yeah. Irritated, sure. But never downright angry. His body vibrates with tension, and he brushes his fingers through his short, dark hair, clenching his jaw so that it pops.

I stare at the kitchen door, holding the pepper spray like it's my anchor to reality.

Jesse comes over to me. "They're on the way."

"You shouldn't have—"

"Fuck." Jesse drops down in front of me. "Fuck that. Fuck. That. You could've been killed."

I glance at the front door and gasp. The glass is shattered.

"I kicked it in," Jesse says, following my line of sight. "I'll replace it for you."

I don't have words.

"Who did this? Who was that? Tell me who it was. Tell me, Marci. Who's responsible? I'll break his fucking legs. I'll break every finger on both his hands so he can never hold a fucking toothbrush again, let alone a knife."

My eyelashes flutter. "Taylor, I—"

"Who?"

I shrug.

Billy won't tell me his real name. He calls him Jonesy. I've never met anyone in Heatstroke with that name.

"But he's threatening you, yeah? Why?"

"Money. He wants money."

"Why?"

I hesitate.

"Tell me."

"Billy borrowed money from a guy. He keeps calling him Jonesy, but I don't think that's his real name. I'm the one on the hook," I say.

Jesse rears back. "That fucking brother—"

"Don't."

Jesse gets up and walks away from me. He stands on the other end of the room for a minute, swearing under his breath. He presses his fists to the top of a table, bowing his head, and then he comes back.

"I'm staying here tonight."

"What? I— There's no chance in fucking hell. No way."

"I'll sleep in the diner. You're not staying here on your own tonight, do you understand?"

Jesse's tone brooks no argument, and even though I despise this man, he laid his life on the line for me.

"What are you even doing here?" I ask.

He hesitates. "That's not important. What's important is that you're safe."

"Fine," I say. "Fine."

Because though I hate to admit it, I'm afraid of being alone after that. Even if he's down here, and I'm up in my apartment alone.

Sirens wail nearby, and I shut my eyes.

"Thanks," I whisper.

"Whatever you need, Angel."

The reply is soft, and his footsteps retreat to the front of the diner.

Eleven

JESSE

I'VE SPENT the night in the diner, alternating between pacing and hanging out in one of the diner booths. I want to keep her safe. I shouldn't want to, but I do. The fear in her eyes last night made me feel capable of cold-blooded murder. And the fact that her brother is connected to what's going on makes the situation worse. More complicated.

But I have a plan. One that could benefit us both.

The door that leads to Marci's apartment opens. She comes out tired but fucking gorgeous as always. Marci's always been beautiful, and she's always been full of shit. The combination is strangely irresistible.

"Good morning," I say.

"What's good about it?" She narrows her eyes at me and then heads toward the counter. "The usual?"

"Sure."

Marci fixes two cups of coffee, and I head over to join her. "How'd you sleep?"

She shrugs, taking a sip from her cup.

I leave mine untouched on the counter. Fuck. Am I really going to do this? Marci hates me with a passion that could light a thousand campfires, and the tension between us isn't helping.

"Nothing happened last night," Marci says. "So, guess you can scuttle off back to whatever hole you crawled out of."

There's a crass pun about holes I'd like to make, but that's a step too far, even for me.

"Speaking of things that scuttle," I say. "What are you going to do about Billy?"

"Don't start with me, Taylor."

"You started first, Angel."

"I do *not* want to discuss last night. Not with you, or anyone else. I'm still... Look, I didn't want to get the cops involved."

"Because you want to protect your brother?" I ask.

She takes a sip of her coffee, and I'm jealous of the mug. Those lips.

"You can't protect that man from himself," I say.

"Come on, Jesse, get real. Sheriff Davis will use this as an excuse to make my life more difficult. To make my family's life more difficult. He hates Billy, and he hates me. And so does his son. The minute they smell blood in the water, they'll be all over this," she says, sounding more tired than angry. "Just like when they tried to enforce some bogus town rule and shut down the diner a few years ago."

"Oh yeah?"

I remember, but the way her lips move when she talks makes me want to listen to the story again.

"Heat regulations," she says. "Can you believe that?

Deputy Dickhead Davis threatened to shut me down because my diner was 'too hot' during summer. He came in here with a thermometer. I had to get a new air conditioning unit installed. And then, after that, they tried to get me in trouble for how much hot air was venting toward the building next door. If it's not Billy, it's them, and they're going to find a way to weaponize this against me. And it's the last thing I need when we're approaching the off-season. It's not like the diner makes tons of money when there are no tourists around, and the menu… Ugh. Why the hell am I even telling *you* this? You're as bad as them."

"I take umbrage at that comparison. Davis has serious small dick energy," I say.

Marci snorts. "Yeah, you're not wrong." She realizes that she agreed with me and frowns. "I didn't need to get the cops involved."

"That guy had a knife," I say. "You had to report it."

"No, I didn't. I—"

"Then how are you going to deal with this?"

Marci glances past me at the street outside. The sun has started its ascent, and low light filters through the front windows. Cars drive by. The townsfolk will start opening for business soon, and Marci's staff will be here any minute.

"What does it matter?" Marci asks. "It's none of your business."

"You almost died last night. I'm the one who saved you. I'd say that makes it my business."

"It doesn't. Just forget about my problems, Taylor. I can handle them myself. You and I? We're never going to be friends. I can't stand the cops in this town, and you're basically the uber cop. The coppiest cop to walk the face of the earth. You're running for sheriff for God's sake."

I wish the rest of the town saw me as the "coppiest cop." They see me as a player with nepotistic tendencies.

"Hey!" Grant, Marci's chef, gestures from outside, through the empty door frame. She lets him in, and he's followed by two servers. I push up from the table, coffee untouched, and exit into the street. I stand there, watching Heatstroke come to life, my hands tucked in the pockets of my jeans.

Marci wants me to leave, but I can't bring myself to do it.

Mrs. Peddleson from the florists across the street waves at me, and I wave back, giving her a broad smile. Until David, the bookstore owner, brushes past me and goes over to her. I drop my hand to my neck, pulling a face.

Fuck. Fuck.

People know me because I'm a Taylor. Not because I'm Jesse, the responsible, dutiful deputy who helps the town. I do my best, but I'm not going to win any popularity contests. As much as I don't want to care what people think, I do.

The diner door slams behind me.

"Are you going to stand out here all day?" Marci asks. "You're loitering."

I turn to her.

"I have a proposition."

It's the exhaustion. I'll blame it on that.

"Huh?"

Marci blinks those pretty green eyes, blue flecks highlighted by the morning sunlight.

"You need help, and so do I."

She scrunches her freckled nose. It's adorable. I hate it. Fuck this.

"Are you running a fever?" she asks.

"Only when I'm around you."

Marci rolls her eyes. "Whatever the fuck that's supposed to mean."

"Marry me."

Marci's jaw drops so fast, I nearly laugh.

I tap the bottom of her chin. She closes her mouth, and her teeth click together.

"Fake marry me," I say.

She babbles incoherently. "Taylor, you... I—What? You—?"

"You need protection from this guy, right? This loan shark dude who's after your money. I bet he's not going to come around here too often if you've got me hanging around. Especially after I chased that motherfucker out of here. You won't have to call the cops because I'll be around."

"I—"

"Hold on, let me finish," I say. "You won't have to call the cops, I'll protect you and your diner while you figure out your financial problems, and I'll have a wife."

"Why would you—?" Her eyes widen. "Oh. Oh, because of what that asshole ex of yours said at the bar last night? Are you serious? You're worried about what the town thinks of your sexual history? What in the *Footloose*, Taylor? This isn't the 80s."

"Say what you want, Angel, but it matters. The people in this town don't take me seriously," I say, hating that I have to admit it. "They want a family man. So I'll give them a family man. It'll be a mutually beneficial arrangement. We can fake 'break up' once we've both gotten what we want out of the deal."

Marci taps her chin and considers me. "I read in a book once that when your fever gets too high, your proteins kind of cook themselves and pop apart and you cease to function properly. Your enzymes go poof."

"What's—?"

"I'm saying you should go see a doctor," she says. "You might be on your way out. This is the most hare-brained scheme I've ever heard."

"It's crazy enough to work."

I arch an eyebrow at her, putting on my most charming smile.

"See?" Marci points at my face. "You get people to fall for that. You don't need my help. Besides, I'm a liability for you, Taylor. The current sheriff hates me, and, unlike you, I'm not afraid of what people think of me."

"Ouch."

"That one wasn't a jab at your character," she says. "I'm being honest. I'm not afraid. Which means I'm not going to be the right woman for the job."

"None of that shit will matter," I say. "They'll see that I'm getting married, and it will be enough."

"And how long would this agreement last?" she asks.

"Until our problems go away."

"That could take a year. More. You realize that, right?" she asks. "We'll have to pretend to like each other."

"The alternative is you getting stabbed by some lowlife because you're too stubborn to go to the cops. And what do you think will happen if I do become sheriff? It will beat having Davis in charge. Or his son. He's running too."

"Nate's running?"

Marci pales.

"That's right." What happened between them? I don't like that look on her face. I've heard rumors, but I want it from the source, and the only source I trust is Marci.

She gnaws on her bottom lip.

"It's—"

"It will work."

There's a glimmer of hope in her eyes, but it wanes.

"I can't do it. You're… you. And I'm me."

And then she turns to the diner.

"Please." The word whips out. "Please, Marci."

She stops, turns to face me, and folds her arms.

"What did you call me?"

"Marci."

She glances up and down the street. There are more people around. It's Main Street, for fuck's sake. Maybe discussing this *inside* would've been a better option.

I wait for her verdict, jaw clenching and releasing.

"Get on your knees."

"What?" I ask.

"I want you to get on your knees. Here. Right now," she says, her lush lips turning upward at the corners.

"You've got to be fucking kidding me."

"Fine. Then in the immortal words of Simon Cowell, 'it's a no from me.'"

I drop to my knees in front of her, and the back of my neck heats. I sense Mrs. Peddleson staring from across the street, and there are others. So many others.

My gaze fixes on Marci's face. Her lips part on an inhale.

"Please, Marci," I say. "Fake marry me."

Twelve

MARCI

I HATE that my heart skips a beat whenever the bell above the door tinkles.

And I hate that I agreed to Jesse's stupid plan. Or not so stupid plan. Utterly deranged plan. But I have to admit, the thought of him coming by more often, while odious, gives me a sense of comfort, simply because it will keep my attacker away.

"Can I get a burger to go?"

The question comes from a dude I don't recognize. He's got ginger hair, is short, and his smile is more of a snarl.

"Sure," I say. "You want fries with that?"

"No."

Polite.

"Grant, can I get a burger to go?"

"Yeah."

The reply is a grunt—Grant was about to clock out for the night, but the kitchen isn't technically closed yet.

The guy taps his manicured nails on the countertop and

stares at me like he can see through my soul. His eyes, mouth, and nose are collected together in the center of his broad face, and he licks his teeth continuously while he waits.

"Marci, right?"

"Do I know you?"

"Nah. Just heard your name around town. Nice place you got here."

"Thanks."

An awkward silence.

"Order up."

I collect the burger and hand it over to the guy then accept the payment from him. Except the guy doesn't let go of the money.

"What are—?"

"You should be careful with that attitude," the guy says. "Pretty girls should be seen, not heard."

The bell tinkles over the door a second time, and Jesse enters. The customer releases the money, grabs the burger, and walks out.

What the fuck?

My skin goes cold, and I swallow.

"What?" Jesse asks. "What's wrong?"

"Just that guy gave me a weird vibe," I say.

Jesse spins around on the spot and goes to the diner door, but the guy is long gone.

"What did he look like?"

I tell him, then stop.

"Doesn't matter," I say, releasing a breath. "I'm paranoid after last night."

"As you should be," Jesse says. "Paranoia keeps you alive."

"It also drives you crazy, as evidenced by the fact that you asked me to—"

I cut myself off and gesture over my shoulder toward the kitchen. Grant's still here.

Jesse takes a seat at the counter, his stool swiveled to one side so he can simultaneously watch the front of the diner and talk to me. Not that I have much to say. One day of being moderately irritated with him rather than outright despising him doesn't make me want to hang out with him.

Nor does it stop me from admiring his jawline, the set of his shoulders, those blue eyes. Ocean blue. Blue enough to drown in.

I hate him for how good he looks, even with dark circles under his eyes from last night. He rests his hand on the counter, occasionally tapping, and I watch the muscles flex in his forearm.

What would it be like to be Jesse Taylor for a day? To be strong, fearless, arrogant. To think I could take on the world.

My mind instantly goes to an image of him fisting his cock.

Thankfully, Grant exits the kitchen and says goodnight before I embarrass myself. He grins at Jesse, and I sigh. Even my grumpy chef likes Jesse. I don't see why he needs my help.

"Ready to go?" Jesse asks.

"Go? Go where?"

"Out?"

"Out where?"

"You know, out," Jesse says. "Like out there. Into the

wilderness. I was thinking maybe we go fucking glamping under the stars."

"That's—"

"I'm kidding. You should see your face, though," Jesse says.

"I hate you."

His grin falters for a millisecond. "We've got to talk brass tacks. If we're doing this, there's a lot we need to arrange. Let's do it over dinner."

I narrow my eyes.

"Dinner."

"Yeah. The thing people eat. With knives and forks. Or their hands." He opens and closes his mouth, pointing toward it. "Ingestion. Digestion. That kind of thing."

"The only thing I'm digesting is my doubts about this agreement."

Jesse clicks his fingers.

"Ah! That's what we should discuss. A contract."

"A contract."

"You're going to have to stop repeating everything I say. I get you're like my biggest fan, but you're starting to sound like a parrot."

"I'm merely repeating the sheer stupidity so you can hear it from a fresh perspective."

"Touche."

Jesse scoots off his chair and beckons for me to follow him.

It occurs to me that Jesse *likes* our verbal jousts, but I dismiss the thought.

"I need to get dressed. Can't go out there looking like this," I say, slipping off my apron. "If I'm going to be a deputy's fake fiancée."

"Wife," Jesse says, and my skin prickles. "And no, you don't… you look…" His Adam's apple bobs up and down. "Fine."

"Such a charmer."

I glance down at my strappy top covered in flowers and my jeans.

He holds out a hand.

I walk past him.

Out in the street, I lock up the diner, my heart pounding at the thought of running into that guy again. I double-checked that the kitchen door was locked today. The police said there was no sign of forced entry, so I've given Grant strict instructions to keep it locked.

Jesse opens the passenger side door of his squad, and I want to run for the fucking hills. Nausea washes over me.

"Hey," he says. "We can go in your car if—"

"No. It's fine."

I get in, and he shuts me inside.

The drive over to Longhorn's is quiet. Jesse and I grab a table on the beach, even though the weather is cool, and we order a round of Cokes and a pizza to share. I don't care what I eat tonight. I want this to be over.

Already, the locals at the bar are staring at us.

"This is never going to work," I say. "We hate each other."

"There's a fine line between love and hate," Jesse says.

"Where'd you read that? The inside of a Valentine's Day card?"

"I've never given anyone a Valentine's Day card."

"No? I find that difficult to believe," I say. "Come on, Jesse, it's no secret that you're pretty popular around town."

"Exactly the reason we're doing this," Jesse says. "And no, I've never given a woman a card like that because I've never been in love. And I don't lead people on."

My insides squirm.

It's the least romantic thing I've ever heard, so why is my heart beating faster? Jesse isn't noble for being honest. But being honest is sexy.

The soft wash of waves punctuates the music playing from inside the bar. It's a weeknight, so the noise level is pretty low. I kick off my sandals and dig my toes into the sand underneath the bench.

Our waitress delivers the Cokes. Jesse pops the tab on mine and pours it into my glass, ice clinking.

"Thanks," I say.

"We should discuss terms."

"All right."

"I'm going to need you to make public appearances with me," he says. "The first one is the department picnic next weekend."

"Great. More cops."

"Yeah," he says. "You're going to have to get used to that. There's going to be a lot of cops, a lot of being seen together in public. We're going to need to get to know each other. What do you want from this?"

Jesse sounds businesslike, and I prefer it that way.

"I… yeah, I guess I'd need you to make appearances at the diner," I say. "To keep the guy away. And we'd need to spread the information around town that we're engaged."

Jesse nods. "I'll sleep at your diner."

"What? No. That's not necessary. Engaged couples don't have to sleep under the same roof."

"Sure, but you're not safe without me there. The only

way I'll let you sleep on your own is if you get an alarm installed."

"I can't afford—"

"I'll pay for it."

My eyes nearly bug out of my head.

"No, that's way too much. I can't accept that."

"Then I'll sleep on your couch if you have one."

"I hate that," I say. "But fine."

I'm not taking handouts from Jesse friggin' Taylor. I've got to have *some* boundaries.

God, what is Billy going to think? Jesse arrested him.

Billy also deserved to be arrested.

"Good. I'll take care of the proposal. We'll make it public so the town hears about it. We're going to the museum tomorrow evening with Alex. Jayjay and Cash invited me," he says.

"I'll do my best to smile when I see you," I say.

"I don't care how you look at me," he replies. "Just as long as you're looking. Once we're fake married, you're mine for however long it takes. Could be a year. No actual paper's signed, but we'll look like the perfect couple."

"Ditto, fuck boy," I say. "That means no touching other women. Can you do that?"

"Yes."

The reply is immediate. Firm.

"Rule number one," I say, drawing a line in the condensation on the side of my glass. "No sex."

Jesse chokes on his drink.

I bite back a smile.

His nostrils flare. "Rule number two. You call me your husband. I call you my wife."

My core heats.

I glare at him. "Rule number three. You don't tell me what to do."

"Rule number four. You don't fall for me." A smirk.

"So arrogant," I say.

"I'm serious, Angel. I don't do love. I'll only let you down."

The pizza arrives before we can continue down that avenue of broken glass, and I'm grateful. Pepperoni is my favorite, and I take a bite and moan.

Jesse stares at my mouth.

I hold up a finger.

"Rule number one."

His jaw clenches and pops, and I love that, for once, I'm the one getting to him. Maybe this fake marriage agreement won't be that painful. Jesse crams pizza into his mouth, and I do the same, both of us eating like pigs over a damn trough. We both slow and stare at each other at the same time.

"Are you mocking me?" he asks.

"No. Are you mocking me?"

"No."

We continue eating.

I wipe my fingers off on a napkin, then drag it over my mouth.

"Can I ask you a question?"

Jesse takes a bite of his pizza and shrugs.

"Why do you want to do this?" I ask. "Why do you care about being sheriff? And don't tell me it's because you want to protect the town. You already do that as a deputy."

He finishes his bite.

"You remember my grandfather?"

"Vaguely. I think he died when Hannah and I were pretty young."

Jesse grabs a napkin too, wipes his mouth, tears off a strip, and crumples it between his fingers.

"He was important around town."

"He was the sheriff," Jesse says. "Died the sheriff."

"Oh."

"When I was fourteen years old, he called me into his office during one of our visits to my grandparents. We were there for Sunday lunch. I remember it like... I remember the smell of his cologne and cigarettes in his study. And how big he looked." Jesse shakes his head. "He told me I needed to be more like Leo."

"Wait, what?"

"Yeah. He told me that Leo was going somewhere. That playing rugby was a valuable thing to do. Told me I was pissing my life away and that I wouldn't amount to anything and that I could learn from my little brother."

"Well, fuck that guy."

Jesse's gaze snaps to mine.

"Yeah, I can still feel him watching me sometimes. Judging."

"What an awful thing to say to a kid. Like, that is heinous. What the hell?"

"What about you?" Jesse asks. "You got any fucked up memories?"

"Just my dad passing," I say.

"Shit, sorry. I shouldn't have—"

"No, it's okay. He's a good memory. The best I have. The diner was his, and he left it to me when I was like, eighteen. It's like I can keep him alive if I keep the diner running. Family is important to me. It's all I've got."

"And your friends?"

"They're family too," I say.

Jesse balls up the napkin and drops it on his plate.

"I lost my mother too, but we had time, at least, to deal with it. Your dad was sudden."

I swallow, but the lump of emotion in my throat doesn't budge. Jesse Taylor *should* be the last person I want to talk to about this, but it's surprisingly easy to tell him about Dad.

"Yeah. He was my hero. Billy's too. He was at my soccer games, at parent-teacher meetings. My mom left after Billy was born, but my dad made up for it. He was two parents in one."

Tears well up.

Jesse grabs a napkin and hands it to me. I dab under my eyes.

"The diner and my family are the two most important things in my life."

"I'll help you keep them safe."

And I believe him. Even though he's still my enemy. Even though he drives me crazy. I believe him.

Thirteen

JESSE

I CAN'T SAY I thought I would propose. To anyone. Let alone Marci Walsh.

But now that it's about to happen, I'm nervous. My palms are clammy, for fuck's sake, and it feels like I'm about to step off a cliff into nothingness. I pull up outside the diner and find Marci behind the counter, smiling and laughing with one of her customers, and the feeling leaves.

That smile wipes it away.

I get out of the squad and go inside, stopping short of the counter.

"Ready to go, Angel?"

Marci's gaze snaps to my face. There's a heartbeat where I'm sure she's going to hit me with one of her infamous *Taylor* one-liners in front of her customers.

"Angel?" Todd, who's practically a fixture in the diner, scratches the lines on his weathered forehead. "When did that happen?"

Marci takes a deep breath, forces a tight smile, and strips off her apron.

"I was born ready, Taylor."

She circles the counter.

I grasp her hand and spin her into my arms, pressing a kiss to her forehead.

"Taylor? Is that what you call your boyfriend?"

Marci trembles in my arms and then stills.

"What else would I call you?"

"Baby? Honey? Sweet cheeks?"

"Sweet cheeks?"

She pulls back, her lips falling into a bemused smile.

"I mean, have you seen this ass? It won't quit."

Marci pinches my arm, and I release her, grinning to myself. She's hot under the collar, and I love it. She calls out to her server, Rebecca, who gives her a thumbs up. We head out, and I open the door to my squad.

Again, she freezes. Pales. Swallows.

"We can take your car," I say.

"No. I'm good." She gets in, and I shut the door and circle to the driver's side. "Does my car smell?" I scratch my brow. "I pride myself on being pine-fresh."

"You don't smell like pine," she says.

"Oh? What do I smell like?"

"The devil. Spice and cinnamon."

"You left out the sulfur."

"Uh huh."

"So, what's with the reaction to the squad?"

"Just don't like these cars," she says and folds her arms.

I'm not going to push her for information she doesn't want to offer up.

I start the squad and drive us toward the Heatstroke Museum. It was one of my favorite places to go as a kid, because of the melted stuff. It's got some natural history displays, but most of the museum is dedicated to interesting things that have melted in the extreme summer heat in town.

June, Cash, and Alex meet us outside. Alex is thirteen and too cool for school, but not for melted items or for running at me full speed.

"Uncle Jesse!"

"Little devil!" I catch Alex and squeeze her tight before setting her down and pressing a hand to her head. "Why are you so tall? This can't be right. You're going to wind up taller than me."

Alex pulls herself up straight, goes onto her tiptoes, and measures from her head to mine.

"Looks like I'll get there pretty soon."

"No shot. I'm six-foot-one, dude."

"Watch me," Alex says, then grins at Marci and gives her a hug. "Hey, Auntie Marci."

"You look gorgeous, Ally," Marci says.

"We weren't expecting two of you," Cash says, his gaze gliding toward Marci. "But the more the merrier."

Jayjay comes over, hugs me, and then drags Marci off to one side. The pair chat, and I'm curious whether Marci will let her in on the truth, or whether she'll stay true to our deal. We're not going to tell a soul that this is fake. Not our families or our friends. It's less complicated that way.

Jayjay gasps and shouts, "No way!"

Marci shushes her.

"What's that about?" Cash asks.

"Dunno. So, we going to see some melted shit or not?" I ask.

"Swear jar," Alex calls.

"You must have your entire college fund saved up at this point," I say, and clap my little brother on the back. "Especially living with this guy."

The women rejoin us, and we head inside, Jayjay casting wide-eyed looks back my way.

"What did you tell her?" I murmur out of the corner of my mouth.

"That we're dating."

"What did she say?" I ask.

"That she saw it coming."

"That's… interesting."

"Right?"

Marci starts moving ahead, but I catch her hand and hold it. And I fucking like it too. I like the softness of her skin, the way she looks up at me out of the corner of her eye, sly and sweet. Fiery.

The Heatstroke Museum has high ceilings and polished floors, with a gift shop off to one side and a tractor as the centerpiece, its tires melted over the sides of the display. Three separate paths lead off in different directions, yellow vinyl footprints leading down the different routes.

"Where are we going to go?" Cash asks. "Down Melted Mayhem, Heatstroke History, or Nature vs Nurture?"

"Melted— Auntie Marci?"

Alex gasps, eyes widening at the sight of us holding hands.

"Melted Auntie Marci?" Cash thumbs his bearded chin. "I'm afraid that's not on the list. I—" He sees us holding hands and smirks. "Ah. Finally. Auntie Marci has melted."

"You're an asshole," Marci says.

"Swear jar," I say in unison with Alex.

Alex laughs hysterically, and it's infectious. We head

down the Melted Mayhem pathway together, Cash occasionally giving me knowing looks.

My brother has always been convinced that I'm into Marci, and he'll never let me live this down. I don't want to think about how much shit he's going to give me when we get fake divorced for the town to see.

Alex, Jayjay, and Marci wander off ahead, drawn to a display of a melted set of plastic gnomes, and Cash falls into step beside me.

"What are you doing?" he asks.

"Putting one foot in front of the other," I reply.

"She's not the kind of woman you mess around with, Jesse."

I arch an eyebrow at him. "Little brother, you're not seriously giving me a 'don't hurt her' talk, are you? What do you think I am?"

"It's not what you are. It's who you are. And you're not the type of guy who settles down," Cash says. "Marci doesn't need a man who's going to flit in and out of her life. She's already got enough shit with her brother, and if you piss Marci off, you piss June off. You fuck with those women, you fuck with me."

"That's noble of you, Cash," I say, "but I'm not fucking with anybody. Marci and I are consenting fucking adults, and I'm not planning on breaking her heart." She won't even give it to me to break, and I'm not planning on giving her mine either. "So, how 'bout you fucking chill?"

"I'm looking out for both of you." Cash scratches under his beard. "Y'all are acting the fool. Neither of you are ready for a relationship."

I grit my teeth. "Not ready for a relationship. Not ready to run for sheriff. Is there anything else you think I can't do that you want to tell me about? Tie my shoelaces? Drive a car?"

"Jesse, that's not what I'm saying," Cash says.

"Yeah, well, that's how it's coming across to me. You don't have faith in me. I get it."

"That's a crock of shit. I'm—"

But I walk off before I get into a brawl with my brother. There's too much ego between us. Cash is a natural star, a leader, and I'm his older brother, standing in his shadow. I'm done being in the shadows. And I'm drawn to Marci like she's a flame, and I'm a fluttering fucking moth. I don't care if my wings get burned to a crisp. I want her anyway.

"Marci," I say.

She turns, and I drop down on one knee in front of her, retrieving the velvet black ring box from my pocket.

Alex and June grab each other and gasp. Cash stands there, gaping. Around us, people turn and stare. Familiar faces from Heatstroke, eyes widening, and whispers start up.

Marci's hand flutters to her chest.

"We've had our ups and downs," I say, meeting her gaze. "Things haven't always been easy, but I can't picture my life without you. I want to spend the rest of it, devoted to showing you that you were made to be loved, and that I'm the one who was made to love you. Marci Walsh, will you do me the honor of being my wife?"

Marci's mouth opens. The sides of her lips curl, and I'm left hanging for what feels like a fucking eternity.

She's enjoying this. She's enjoying me on my knees in front of her.

"Yes," she says, then clears her throat and puts up an ecstatic smile. "Yes, of course, I'll marry you, Jesse."

She puts out her left hand, and I slide the ring onto her finger. Her eyes go wide at the size of the pear-cut stone in its platinum band.

I rise and sweep her off her feet, spinning her on the spot while she laughs. I squeeze her to my chest, then cup her cheeks in both hands and plant a quick kiss on her lips.

A quick kiss that's so fucking electric, I jolt back from it.

Marci's eyes widen, and she glances away from me.

I press her into another hug and whisper in her ear.

"You're pretty good at this. You should've been an actress."

"This is the fanciest dollar store ring I've ever seen," she murmurs, her words soft against my throat.

Fuck. Fuck, she is delicious.

Her smell, the way she feels, those soft lips. It's fucking dangerous being this close to her, but there's a thrill to it. How long can we get away with this? How long can I resist her physically? My resolve is already starting to crumble, and we have *rules* we agreed to.

Marci raises on tiptoe and brushes her lips to my cheek.

"Don't worry, Taylor, I was a drama nerd in school. I've got you covered."

Her soft voice, the touch of her skin against mine, sends a wave of desire straight to my cock.

She pulls back and gives me a bright, vicious smile. She's enjoying her power over me, as I've always enjoyed my power over her. Marci's getting her revenge for the jabs or jokes with touches that drive me wild.

And there's nothing I can do about it. I hate it. And I am so totally fucked.

Fourteen

MARCI

BY THE TIME we get back to the diner, it's closed and locked up, courtesy of Rebecca. I unlock it, but Jesse puts out a hand to stop me from entering. He goes in ahead of me, scans the interior, and moves to the kitchen.

"Coast is clear," he calls back.

I enter my diner on a tide of mixed emotions.

The ring fits perfectly on my finger, and it's pretty, even though it's fake. If I could've picked a ring, this is the type I would've gone for. Pear-cut rimmed with red stones. It's fiery and cute, and fake!

Fake. It doesn't matter. It's not real.

I hate that I like it.

Why did I agree to do this again?

"I need to check upstairs."

Jesse's voice interrupts my frantic thoughts. He leans against the wall beside the doorway that leads to my apartment. He raps his knuckles against it. It's locked.

"Fine."

I lock the diner door and then walk past him. I'm

keenly aware of his presence, his cologne, and the way my body reacts to him.

Jesse's hot, that's why he's never struggled with women, but he's still the enemy. I have to be careful around him. Maintain control. I remove my keys from my purse and miss the keyhole entirely.

"You good?" Jesse asks. "You need help *unlocking a door?*"

"Fuck you."

"We've already discussed this," he says. "Your dreams. Wet and wild? Remember? I pinned you and won that wrestling match. You threw a temper tantrum."

I remember afterward too. Him grasping my throat. How close I'd come to snapping and touching myself in a literal bathroom.

"Here." Jesse takes my hand and helps me insert the key into the lock, his grip firm. "Got it?"

"You're such an asshole."

"Just trying to help my fiancée."

"Fake fiancée," I say, smiling at him. "Don't get it twisted, Taylor."

"As if you'd let me." Jesse puts out a palm, gesturing for me to wait, then goes upstairs to look around. He comes back down a minute later. "It's clear. Lock that door behind you, though."

I roll my eyes at the instruction but do it anyway. My apartment feels too small with him in it. Granted, it's small without him in it too. The living room and kitchenette are open-plan, and I've got a single bathroom and my bedroom down the hall. A lot of my stuff is worn. I've poured my money into the diner, not my home, and my old leather sofa is a relic from my dad.

Jesse moves through my living room with his typical swagger, stopping beside my bookcase. He removes a romance novel from it and flips it over, reading the back, his eyebrows climbing.

"Don't you have better places to be?" I ask. "If the coast is clear, you can leave me here, right?"

"Nope," he says, setting the book down carefully. "We have a deal, and protecting you is part of that. Besides, I've already fed Mr. Skitters."

"I'm sorry, what?"

Jesse unbuttons the top of his shirt, exposing a sliver of chest and dark hair.

"Mr. Skitters. My cat."

"You. You have a cat?"

"Do you think I'm actually the devil?" he asks. "Why the surprise?"

"You don't strike me as a cat lover. I thought you'd keep snakes. Or white rabbits. Like an evil mastermind."

He chuckles. "Nah. I like cats. But Mr. Skitters isn't technically my cat. He's a stray cat that I'm trying to make into my cat. It's been a journey." He lifts his hand and shows off a scratch. "But we're getting closer. I'm hoping he adopts me soon."

Damn you for being nice to a stray cat.

"That's…"

"Do you like cats?"

"Yeah."

Jesse sweeps his gaze over me from head to toe.

"We're going to have to get to know each other if we want to make this look real," he says. "Likes, dislikes, goals, dreams, that kind of shit."

I clasp my hands together, the ring an ever-present reminder of what we've done.

"How romantic."

He gives me one of those panty-melting grins that's probably worked on every woman in this town. I try to resist his natural charm, but it's difficult. And that frustrates me.

Jesse strolls to the sofa and drops onto it, smiling up at me.

"The picnic this weekend is going to be interesting if you can't stop hating me."

"I played the part today, didn't I?"

Even though he jerked away from me when we kissed.

"Hmm."

He glances at my lips.

"Want a drink? I have beer, water, tea, coffee."

"Coffee at this time of night?"

"It's seven. And I struggle to sleep most nights anyway, so—"

I shrug.

"Why? A beer would be good."

I grab two bottles and bring them over. Jesse unscrews the caps off on both of them and tilts the neck of his bottle toward mine.

"To getting what we want," he says.

The way he's staring at me sends shivers racing over my skin.

"To getting what we want."

I take a sip of beer with him, then sit down on my old, squeaky armchair across from him.

Jesse smirks.

"You're not going to sit next to me?"

"I don't trust you to control yourself," I say.

His gaze darkens.

"You're not wrong."

Fuck, fuck, fuck. Walked right into that one.

"So, why do you struggle to sleep at night?" Jesse asks.

"It's the falling asleep part that's tough. I've got a lot to think about," I say. "The diner does badly during the off-season months, and I'm honestly struggling to make ends meet. A part of me wishes I could redo the diner, the menu. But I can't afford that. And it would feel wrong to change things."

"Like letting go of a part of your dad?"

"Yeah."

I take another sip of beer, tucking my legs underneath myself and resting my nails against the glass.

Jesse tilts his head to one side, exposing more of his muscular neck, but it's his eyes that are the real challenge. There's a softness in them I don't like or want to like.

"Maybe he would've wanted you to make the place your own," Jesse says. "Since you're his daughter. If he's as good as you say he was, then he would want you to be happy and do what's best for you, right?"

I lift my shoulders.

"Doesn't matter. I can't afford it anyway. And a menu change…"

"Why a menu change?"

"Before the accident," I say, "I wanted to be a chef. I applied to a couple of schools, and I got in. My dad was so proud, and then he—"

It's hard to finish the sentence. The way my father passed has left an indelible mark on my soul.

"You don't have to talk about this. When I said get to

know each other, I meant like favorite colors and which side of the bed you sleep on."

"It's okay."

It isn't. Why would I trust Jesse with this information? He's not only a cop, but he's also the one who arrested Billy, who made it his mission to make sure my brother always got into shit. I've lost count of how many times Billy's called me to tell me that Jesse was hassling him.

"Angel," he says, softly. "None of what happened to your father is your fault. Neither is what's going on at the diner. You're doing your best. On your own. It can't have been easy, trying to raise a kid like Billy as a fucking teen."

I stand up. "I should go to bed."

"Marci."

"I'm tired."

"Marci."

I take my bottle of beer with me, heading for my bedroom.

"There are extra blankets and a pillow in the hall closet."

"Marci."

My name comes out rough.

I spin around and stare at him.

"What? What do you want me to say? Thank you for being nice to me for once in your fucking life?"

"Once?"

"You don't think I've forgotten, have you?" I ask. "I haven't forgotten the bullshit you put me through in high school."

"I was an idiot," he says.

"Stringing my underwear from the flagpole, telling people to stay away from me, leaving me mocking notes, showing up when I acted in *Romeo and Juliet*, and smirking at me from the audience. You don't think I didn't see it? And then Billy? Fucking arresting him, following him around, and—"

"I do *not* follow your brother around. I've arrested him once, Marci, because he stole a fucking car."

"Whatever. This isn't about him. You've spent my entire life trying to make me uncomfortable, and I won't let you. I won't let you do it anymore. So don't pretend you care about me. I don't believe you."

He stands there, his shoulders tense.

The silence rings in my ears. I enter my room and slam the door behind me.

"Marci." My name is muffled. "Marci, I'm sorry."

I press my back to the door and sink down until my butt hits the ground. It's not Jesse. It's everything. The diner, my family, even Hannah's going through a tough time. Having *him* here when I'm at my lowest point is not easy.

"Marci, I—Fuck." He mumbles.

"What?"

"I was an asshole."

"Still are."

"Still am," he calls back. "I was an asshole to you because I didn't like how much attention you got when we were kids. My family loved you."

I take a sip of the beer.

"And I was a dumb kid who hated you for that. Then, when we got older and you started... You became... Fuck. Fuck. I'm sorry. I'm sorry for being an asshole to you and making you feel that way."

I don't know whether to believe him or not. How can I trust him?

I didn't have to. This is a temporary agreement. Soon enough, it will be over, and Jesse can go back to being my friend's annoying brother.

There's a dull thump against the door.

"Marci?"

I get up and open it, and he nearly falls inside my room. He catches himself on the doorjamb in time, and it's almost comical enough to make me smile. Almost.

"I'm sorry," he says.

"I heard you. And that's fine. The high school stuff is… Yeah. That's fine," I say. "And the kid stuff."

"I was wrong."

"Okay, Taylor, you don't have to go that far. I shouldn't have lost my temper."

I put up a hand, but I misjudge the distance between us and slap it onto his chest.

We both look down at it, then up at each other.

My breaths grow quicker.

Jesse's chest rises and falls in time with mine.

"The blankets are in the—"

"Closet, yeah," he says.

He takes a step back and breaks the tension between us.

"Thanks, Angel."

And strangely, I like it this time. It's easier to hate Jesse than to think of him as a nice guy. Because if I do, I'm going to cave and get what's left of my heart trampled again.

Fifteen

JESSE

THE SHERIFF'S Department annual picnic always takes place at the start of fall, when the weather's cool but the sun's still out. I usually attend alone, apart from a stacked picnic basket, and feel like an asshole for it.

I grab the picnic basket out of the back of the car, the checked blanket laid over the top. Marci stands beside me, wearing a pair of sunglasses, her hair loose, wearing a pair of cut-off jean shorts that expose her thighs.

I want to bury my head between them. I'm also tired of making myself come every five fucking minutes. Marci's got me twisted into knots.

"Oh, my tote," she says, reaching for the bag that she's stacked with extra snacks and sunscreen.

I grab it for her.

"Got it."

"I can take it."

"You're good."

I loop the picnic basket and the tote over one arm, shut the trunk, and then take Marci's hand.

To her credit, she doesn't flinch.

"Shit," she whispers. "This is it. The first real test."

"We've got this. My favorite color?"

"Green. Mine?"

"Purple. Favorite animal?"

"Cat. Same for me," Marci whispers as we approach the entrance to Heatstroke Park. "You like beers, but you're partial to a mojito."

"Margaritas. You want to visit Rome one day because you love pasta. Your favorite flavor of ice cream is mint because you're a heathen who likes eating toothpaste."

"At least it's not vanilla," she says, giving me a helping of her most bombastic side-eye.

"Trust me, Angel, that's the only thing about me that's vanilla."

"Not that I'll ever find out," she says. "Because of rule number one."

"We should write those down."

And tear them up. Burn them. She's so fucking gorgeous.

Marci swallows.

"I'm nervous."

"Look," I say, "just smile and say nice stuff about me. Dig deep."

She laughs, that whispery, breathy laugh that makes my dick twitch and roll in my jeans.

"You like animals."

"Exactly."

"And you care about your family."

Wait, is she serious? She finds that attractive about my personality?

"You're funny too, in your own way. Even if you are a dick."

"Sounds like you're warming up to me, Angel," I say.

"Just trying to come up with ways *not* to despise you, Taylor."

We approach the group of gathered off-duty deputies, Davis among them, laid out on blankets or sitting on park benches. The sheriff looks up from where he's grilling meat and tips his aviator sunglasses down his nose to get a better look at us. He's a future version of Nate, thicker around the middle, with the same asshole frat boy swagger.

"Well, I'll be," he says, breaking the sudden quiet.

"This has got to be a joke," Deputy Dickface says.

"Only joke around here is you willingly buying that shirt."

I gesture to the flame decals besmirching the fabric.

Marci snorts a laugh. I lift her hand to my lips and brush a kiss over her soft skin. She lets out the tiniest of sighs.

I can't tell if it's fake. I don't want it to be.

I loop my arm around Marci and draw her to my side as we walk toward one of the nearby trees. I lay out our blanket in the shade and then make sure Marci gets on it comfortably before joining her.

Davis glares at us.

I've packed some of Marci's favorites in the picnic basket—orange juice, a packet of barbecue chips, donuts from Doughies, dusted with confectioner's sugar.

"This looks great, Tay—baby," she says.

"Baby."

The word comes out snarled by desire. Fuck. I like that. I like her calling me that *too much*.

"Sorry," she says. "I meant Sweet Cheeks."

I laugh, and that draws more stares. People are talking, and it's a good thing. They slowly return to their conversations as we settle in.

"Did you hear about that woman who's running for sheriff?" Davis says nearby, chest puffed out, arm around his wife. "Some lady named Francis. Old. As if she stands a chance."

"I don't know," Deputy Josefs says. "Might be nice to hear what she says, right?"

Davis glares at him, and I'm reminded that I like Josefs.

Josefs breaks the tension by starting up a game of touch football, and my competitive side is already hyped to go play, but staying with Marci will be more fun.

"You going to join them?" Marci asks, picking up a donut. "I'm sure it will go a long way toward you shmoozing. And I should probably get to know the wives and girlfriends, right?"

She keeps her voice low.

"You don't want me to hang out?"

"Is that a trick question? The sooner you leave, the sooner I can eat most of these donuts," she says. "Without shame."

She loves food as much as I do, and that makes me real fucking happy. "Save, like… two for me."

"One."

Her lips are coated in sugar. I want to lick it off.

"Three."

"Two."

"Sold," I say, and then push myself up and run over to join the guys.

All through the game, I can't help glancing over to check on her. She's surrounded by women, chatting and laughing, likely asking her questions about us. I'm not arrogant enough to see myself as a desirable bachelor but the women in this town know I don't want to settle down. They'll be curious why I chose to do it.

I crouch over, ball in my hands, my gaze drifting to Marci again.

"Down, set…"

She flicks auburn hair over one shoulder, the column of her throat working as she talks. So delicate. So fucking—

"Hike! I said, hike. Taylor, are you alive over there?" Hamill, our quarterback, shouts.

Another of the guys sniggers, and I straighten.

"Fuck, sorry."

"Bro, are you going to play the game or stand there with a hard-on?" he asks. "We're losing."

"Yeah, I'm out."

I toss him the ball, and he catches it.

Because he's right. I can't concentrate on the game when she's sitting there, fucking distracting and pretty. It's annoying as hell. I head over to the bathrooms, freshen up, then wind my way back to the cluster of cops and their wives. I approach the tree from behind, admiring Marci's hair, the way it rests against her back, a river of red, and—

"…saying, you need to be careful."

The voice comes from Hamill's wife, I think. She's older than Marci, her dark hair piled into a messy bun, and her thin lips pursed. She gives Hamill a hard time, but he's one of the few guys who's faithful to his wife. It's the reason I like him better than a lot of the other deputies. Fuck bro code. If you can't keep your dick in your pants when you're married, you don't deserve my respect.

Marci takes a bite of her donut, eating daintily in front of the girls, and it irritates me.

"What do you mean by that, Sheryll?" Marci asks, after a beat.

An awkward silence follows.

"What I mean," Sheryll says, "is that he's… Marci, honey, he's a player. He's not the type who settles down. That's a pretty rock on your finger, but *be careful.*"

"Sheryll," Marci says, and then sighs. "Oh, Sheryll. That's sweet and all, but don't talk about Jesse like that. Just because he didn't date anyone long-term, doesn't mean he's not trustworthy. In fact, I'd say that makes him more trustworthy because he didn't offer women false hope or settle for less than he wanted or deserved. He's a better man than any—"

"Better man?" Deputy Dick approaches. "I wouldn't finish that sentence if I were you."

"Or what?" I stride over.

Davis, whose lips are peeled over his teeth like a wolf before it attacks, straightens instantly. He sniffs and folds his arms like I didn't catch him talking to Marci disrespectfully.

I put my hand out to Marci and lift her into my arms.

"What are you going to do, Nate? Huh? What are you going to do if she finishes her sentence?" I ask, my vision tunneling on him.

Marci presses a palm to my chest and strokes her fingers beneath my shirt.

"Relax, Taylor," she murmurs.

"Talk to my wife like that again, and I'll—"

Marci presses a finger to my mouth, and distracts me. I meet her gaze, my anger cooling.

"Don't," she mouths. And then, "Sheriff."

She's right. I'm going to run for sheriff. It's a popularity contest. And Nate wants a rise out of me because it'll prove I'm not fit to take care of this town.

The fact that Marci cares about that in the face of being confronted by her shitty ex, the one I'm pretty sure is responsible for her avoiding relationships for years, evaporates my last reserve of control.

I remove her finger from my lips, slide my hand into the hair at the base of her neck, and take her mouth.

Marci stiffens and then melts into me, releasing a tiny gasp against my lips. I take her hungrily, greedy for her tongue, her taste, her fucking soul. The kiss spirals, breathless, heated, nearly pornographic, and I break it before I take things too far. I could make this woman my religion after that kiss.

"Get it together, Taylor," Nate says. "Do you need a fucking knife and fork?"

"What can I say? We're in our newlywed phase."

Nate blows out a breath. "When did you get married?"

"Yesterday," Marci puts in, quickly, raising her left hand to show off the engagement ring. "We couldn't wait." We haven't discussed when we're going to go from fake engaged to fake married, but god damn if the phrase "my wife" didn't slip out without trying.

"I don't see no wedding ring," Nate says.

"Like I said, we couldn't wait," Marci replies.

I hold her closer, my hand cupping her waist. The other women excuse themselves and head back to join the husbands who've finished their game. The kids are over playing ball on the other side of the park together, but they're heading back too.

Nate's wife, Helen, draws near, bearing a bright smile, and his bravado drops. He takes her hand and walks off, glancing back at us, shaking his head. Nate doesn't buy it, but I don't care. There's nothing he can do to prove it, so fuck him, and fuck this entire picnic.

I want to take Marci home.

Sixteen

JESSE

"THAT WENT WELL," Marci says, hesitating before she gets into the front of my squad. I want to know what that's about, but I can't ask her. She won't answer me, and I'm mind-fucked.

The kiss.

I'm the kind of guy who prides himself on how he uses his mouth in the bedroom. Kissing is one of the many types of foreplay I enjoy, but that was something else. I've never lost track of time kissing a woman before, but with Marci, the world faded away.

I load our stuff into the back. Inside, I put on my seatbelt, start the engine, and sit back, leaning one arm over the back of the seat.

Marci pulls a face. "That was, uh— Yeah, I think you're going to have an uphill battle trying to get people in this town to trust you, but you'll get through it."

"I heard what you said about me."

"I'm playing the part of your wife, apparently, so I

have to be nice. Color me weird, but I don't want to be with a man I don't like," she says.

Fuck.

"Yeah, well, I appreciated it."

"Sure. Of course. About the wife thing, though?"

"We'll tell people we had a shotgun wedding in Austin," I say. "Nobody's going to ask too many questions, except maybe your dumbass fuckhead of an ex, so—"

"Whoa," Marci laughs. "You really don't like him."

"Do you?"

"No," she says. "He makes my skin crawl."

I drive down the road, heading back toward her diner. I don't want to drop her off and leave, but it's early afternoon. If she was mine, for real, I'd take her home and lay her down, strip her clothes from her body, and worship her for the way she talked about me. I'd also install an alarm in her diner. Hunting down the guy who harmed her? Already working on that.

It's quiet in the car. "Next time I kiss you in public, moan less," I say.

"Next time you kiss me in public," Marci says, "try not to grope me."

"I didn't grope you."

"You were close," she says, a smile lifting the corners of those fucking lips.

I want them wrapped around my cock while I eat her pussy. I want it so bad it's a problem.

"Close, huh? If you think that's close, I've got a couple of things to show you, Angel."

"Rule number one."

I'm inches from saying fuck the rules, because Marci's cheeks are pink, and the way we responded to each other was pure fire. But I'm not going to break those rules unless she wants me to. And she hasn't said she wants that outright.

Besides, it's meant to be fake, and that kiss was too real. Marci doesn't want me, and she never will.

"How are you feeling now that I'm sleeping over?" I ask, turning the corner into Main Street. "Did you feel safer the past couple of nights?"

Marci wets her lips.

"What?"

"The kitchen door was open this morning," she says.

My foot eases down on the brakes, and I pull over, bumping my tires onto the curb.

"What?"

"The kitchen door was unlocked and open a little," she says. "But I've been double-checking it each night. Grant has the keys, so it might be him, but I don't see why he would come by on a Sunday when we're closed for—"

I start the engine again and take off down the street.

"Taylor," she says. "What are you doing?"

"Taking you home." I speed past her diner.

"That—" Marci turns in her seat. "That was my home."

"Not there. Your home. My home. The cottage. You're staying with me from now on."

"What the fuck? You've lost it, Taylor. I am *not* staying with you."

Heat spreads down the back of my neck, and I clutch the wheel so hard, my hands shake with red hot rage I am not accustomed to. I'm supposed to be the calm guy, the funny guy, but I want to find the motherfucker who threatened her and tear him limb from limb.

"We're already staying under the same roof," I say, through gritted teeth. "Doesn't make a difference if we stay at your place or mine."

"It does! The diner—"

"I'll drive you to work each morning, or we can get your car, and you can drive yourself," I say. "Marci, it is not safe there. I wouldn't suggest this unless I seriously thought you were in danger. The kitchen door being unlocked is *fucked*. You're not going to call the cops, and we have a deal that I would protect you, which makes this my responsibility."

"Taylor."

"No."

I pull up outside my cottage on Boiler. It's ensconced between shrubs with a view of the ocean, and it's a place that usually brings me peace, particularly since it's at the end of the street with my closest neighbor twenty feet away.

"Taylor."

"No," I repeat. "You are my wife, and I have a responsibility to uphold my side of the deal. I can't protect you properly when there are people who have the keys to your diner coming and going as they please, and when you refuse to install an alarm."

"I can't afford an alarm!"

"Then let me install one for you."

"No!"

"Fine."

I get out of the car and march over to her side. I open the door, reach in, and unclip her seatbelt.

"What are you—?"

I grab her around the waist and lift her out of the car.

Marci lets out a shriek as I put her over my shoulder and carry her toward the front door. The distant sound of waves crashing on the beach doesn't mute her complaints, unfortunately.

"What do you think you're doing," she says and smacks me on the back. "You put me down right away, or I'll—I'll scream!"

"You're already screaming."

I unlock the front door and bring her inside, then let her down, my hands on her waist again. That blouse she's wearing does nothing to hide her curves or how good her body feels.

"There. I've carried you over the threshold, wife."

"I think we're about to have our first fight as a fake married couple."

"First?"

"Fucking fiftieth, whatever," she says. "You can't manhandle me like that and make me do what *you* think is right."

"I can if you're not thinking sensibly."

I walk over to the fridge and grab two Cokes. I try to hand Marci one, but she folds her arms.

I sigh and leave a can on the rustic dark wood coffee table.

"I can't uphold my part of the deal under these circumstances. Face it, Angel, you need me and I need you, so let's cut the shit."

"I need you like I need to have explosive diarrhea!"

"That's so fucking hot." I tip my can toward her and wink. "You know what to say to get me going."

Marci's gaze darts through my cottage, past the living room with its flatscreen TV and plush recliner, and comes to rest on the entrance to my bedroom door. The king-sized bed, with its white sheets, looks particularly inviting.

"How many beds do you have?" she asks.

"One. Same as you."

"And you expect me to, what, sleep on that?"

She points at my recliner.

"Excuse me, lady, but that is a fucking state-of-the-art recliner." I walk over to it, sit down, and pop my legs up, taking a leisurely sip of my drink. "This puppy cost me a thousand dollars."

"You spent a thousand dollars on a chair?"

"You should see my toilet," I say.

"You're insane!" She throws up her hands.

"You'll sleep in the bed. I'll sleep on the masterpiece. Got it?"

But Marci's eyes flash with a challenge. She got it. She just doesn't like it.

Seventeen

MARCI

"I AM NOT GOING to sleep in your bed."

I don't care if Taylor is speaking sense. I'm in my stubborn era, and I'm not going to do what he wants me to, especially not when it scares the crap out of me. That kiss shook me to the core today, and it was *fake*.

What would the real thing be like? I hate the confused feelings and the way he smiles at me from where he's reclining, so I walk over and bring my foot down on the base of the chair, popping him upright.

"I'm talking to you," I say. "You're going to take me home."

"Then the deal's off."

"You can't blackmail me into staying here with you."

"Blackmail you?" Jesse arches an eyebrow. "Me? I wouldn't do that. I'm not your brother."

I back up several steps until I'm right by his front door. I grab it and slam it because it feels good to take out my aggression, even though it's so god damn toxic.

"He's never…"

But I can't even finish the sentence because I can't say that Billy wouldn't do that.

Jesse pushes up from his chair, places his can on the coffee table, and walks over, putting his hands up.

"Look, we agreed to this. I get you're angry because you're in this position, but I'm not the one who put you here."

I hate how calm he is. Why can't he lose control? Why am I the one who's angry, and he's so damn calm?

"Billy didn't put me here either."

"Oh? No? He didn't put you here? Your brother, who is indebted to loan sharks, who gave you a *stolen car* and almost got you arrested for it? He didn't put you in this position? If you weren't so fucking stubborn, you'd see what a user your brother is."

"Don't you dare talk about him like that."

"Or what? What are you going to do, Marci? Leave? Oh wait, you can't because you're my wife, and we *need each other*. Because your brother can't stop causing god damn problems for you and this town."

My skin flushes hot. Memories flood in. Of the anger and pain and fear, of Billy in cuffs, of Jesse arresting him.

"You want to slap me, don't you?" he asks.

"What?" I snap.

"Slap me."

"No."

"Come on," he says, and pats his cheek. "I want you to. Either you're going to slap me, or we're going to fuck."

"Excuse me?" I gasp.

"Tell me you didn't want me when you kissed me earlier. Tell me. Look me in the fucking eyes and tell me."

I can't.

"That's what I thought. We've got to get rid of the tension somehow, so go on, Angel." His voice deepens. "Slap me."

"You're losing it."

"I want you to. Do it."

I lift my hand and swing.

Jesse catches it and then pushes it down.

"Too slow."

I swing again, letting out a shriek.

This time, he grabs my wrist and drives me backward until we hit the wall. He pins my arm above my head and brings his mouth down on mine. I moan against him, bite his lip hard, suck on it. He palms my breast.

"Lost your chance."

He rips down the front of my top and groans at the sight of my pink lace bra.

"Taylor," I whine it out like a curse.

He slips his fingers beneath the lace of my bra and pinches my nipple, then kisses me again, his free hand moving to my thigh and hiking it up. He grinds into me, and I'm losing it. Losing my mind. Losing my soul to him when I shouldn't.

"Don't." He sucks my tongue into his mouth. "Do." He slips his hand over the front of my shorts, cupping my pussy. "That." Taylor grasps my throat and squeezes lightly. "Again." He kisses me and owns my entire mouth.

"Or what?" I hiss.

"I'll make you come so hard, you won't remember why you started hating me in the first place."

Oh my God.

It's hot and heavy, and I tug on him, kissing him back with a ferocity that's bubbling over. His fingers move to the buttons on my shorts, and I rip at his shirt, wanting it off that muscular body.

I'm already halfway there. The tension between us is exquisite and—

Jesse steps back, breaking the kiss, the outline of his cock pressing against the front of his jeans, his lips glistening. He grabs the back of his neck and exhales.

"Rule number one."

He's toying with me. The man is toying with me, and I fell for it.

But the way his gaze travels over my body, from head to toe, is—

"I'm not going to touch you again unless you want me to," Jesse says.

I tilt my head.

"What?"

"Something happened with your ex," he says. "I'm not going to be another guy who fucks with you. I find it difficult to control myself around you. You're... Fuck, you are so fucking annoying and so hot. But it's no excuse."

"You're giving me whiplash. One second we're going to fight or we're going to fuck. The next you're pulling back. Am I a game to you?"

"No," he says. "Not a game." He draws closer, presses his hand to my waist, and pins me against the wall, his forehead pressed against mine. "I'm not going to touch you again until you tell me you want to break the rules. That's all you have to say, Angel, and I will strip you down and wring every last bit of pleasure out of your body."

I shiver and fall into those eyes. Blue as a broken heart.

Jesse smirks.

"You're my wife," he says, "fake or not, and I'm going to protect you, worship you, and treat you with the respect that is your right. I don't have love to give you, but orgasms won't be a problem."

I blink up at him, slow deliberate blinks as I process what he's saying.

What happened to Taylor? First, he apologizes for what he's done, and then he says this? It's so at odds with the mental image I've had of him for years, that I'm struggling to piece it together.

Our breaths mingle.

Jesse releases me and walks over to the recliner. He sits down, pops his legs up, and grabs his drink, watching me. He takes a sip, his throat working as he swallows.

I'm frozen.

I open my mouth and then close it again. Heat lingers on my lips, between my legs, but if we cross this line, I'm not sure where it will lead. Jesse wants to be the sheriff, he wants Heatstroke to love him, and I couldn't give a crap what people think about me, and I'm not going to play pretend forever. Jesse and I aren't compatible.

I push off the wall and walk into the bedroom, then open the sliding door that leads out of it onto his back porch. I fold my arms and stare at the rolling waves as they crash onto the soft, golden sand.

I'll do what it takes to save my diner, but how long can I resist the tension between us?

Eighteen

JESSE

I OPEN the sliding door that leads onto the back porch, a glass of water in hand.

Marci's been out here most of the afternoon, only popping into the apartment to use the bathroom. She's tucked her legs underneath herself on the porch swing, her gaze fixed on the waves, crashing on the beach.

"Careful," she says. "Don't."

"I brought you water," I say. "And I made you dinner."

She stiffens. "The cat's here. I've been trying to get it to eat and drink while I'm sitting here."

Mr. Skitters is a tiny ginger cat, an adolescent by my guess, and he's crouched underneath a bush beside the low steps that lead onto the sand. He watches both of us with wary yellow eyes, but this is the closest he's come to the house while someone is outside. Usually, he waits until I've put out his food, and then I stand inside, staring at him through the glass sliding door like Hannibal Lecter. Minus the cannibalism.

"He doesn't usually hang out like this," I say. "He must like you."

She hums softly.

"Hungry?"

"It's not food I can't stomach," she says, and rises from the swing.

She follows me through my bedroom, casting an accusatory glance at the bed, and into the living room, kitchen combo.

Marci stops after a few steps, her nose wrinkling.

Adorable.

Fuck.

"What?" I ask, turning the plate of pasta toward her.

"It smells great. You cook?"

"On occasion," I say. "I don't usually have anyone to cook for unless it's for the potluck."

I gesture for her to sit down at the kitchen counter on the stool beside mine. She does, setting down her glass of water, the ice clinking.

"It's a lemony, creamy pasta. I watch this one chef on YouTube who makes these incredible videos. He's got a kickass recipe for beef stew I want to try," I say.

"Thank you."

Marci picks up her fork and studies the tagliatelle like I've poisoned it.

"Parmesan?"

"Sure."

I grate some over her plate.

Marci takes a bite and lets out a moan that sends arousal shooting through my body. She presses a hand over her mouth.

"Sorry."

"Don't be. I enjoyed that more than you enjoyed the food."

She chews slowly, then turns to me.

"Taylor," she says.

"We don't have to figure it out," I reply. "We don't have to fuck either. We can stick to the rules and that shit, but if I want to cook for you, I'm going to cook for you."

"I don't have a problem with you cooking for me," she says. "I love food, and this is good, so thank you for that. I'm trying to be civil with you, but I find that exceedingly difficult after everything that's happened between us."

"The kissing or the way you hate me?"

"Both," she says.

"Complicated."

"Exactly." She twirls the pasta around her fork and lifts it. "I don't want to complicate what's already a complicated situation."

"I hear you."

I take a sip of water to mask my disappointment.

"So it's better that we don't hate-fuck each other."

I nearly do a spit-take and choke on the water.

Marci bursts out laughing but thwacks me on the back.

"Are you good?"

"Just—Uh." I hold up a finger. "Did *not* expect you to use that turn of phrase."

"What else would you call it?" she says. "We're not love-fucking each other."

That cools my mirth fast.

"No," I say, "we aren't. We're going to have to stick to the ground rules if we want to—"

Marci's hand comes down on my arm and squeezes.

"We should probably keep physical contact to a

minimum if you don't want me to bend you over the counter and fuck your pussy with my tongue," I say.

"Look."

She squeezes my forearm, her thumb stroking it.

Is she messing with me?

It's working.

I follow her line of sight.

"Well, shit," I whisper. "No fucking way."

Mr. Skitters creeps through the open doorway into the living room. He stops, a white-tipped ginger paw raised as he scans the kitchen and the living room.

"Looooook at that," Marci hisses. "That, my friend, is the magic of the Marci touch."

"Are you… Did you just talk about yourself in third person? I thought I was the cringey one."

Marci lets out a muted squeak of excitement. "He's inside. He's actually inside."

"This is some bullshit," I say. "I've been trying to get him to warm up to me for weeks. You sit on the porch for a couple of hours and suddenly he's mellow? What kind of Disney princess shit is that?"

"Anything you can do—"

"Don't push your luck," I say.

She sticks out the tip of her pink tongue at me, and I grin at her, loving it. She's so fucking cute.

Mr. Skitters watches us with mistrust but takes a couple more steps into the living room. And then a couple more. And then he leaps up onto my recliner, turns in a circle, and lies his furry ginger ass down on my sleeping spot for the night.

"Ha!" Marci grins. "That *is* some Disney princess shit. I should start wearing flowing dresses and singing songs."

"Hmm." She's good without any of that.

"What?"

"Just that you seem remarkably happy with the fact that the cat sentenced us to sharing a bed tonight."

Marci's full lips part, and she tucks those fiery red locks behind her ear. She tugs on her earlobe.

"Shit."

"Yeah. Unless you want to be the one to disturb the cat, wife."

Is it wrong that I'm happy this has happened? Not because I'll finally have a cat, but because I'll finally have Marci Walsh in my bed?

I shouldn't be happy because we've agreed that we won't do anything about it. Sharing a bed with Marci without touching her will be torture.

"Huh."

She eats a bite of food and mulls it over. She licks her lips and takes a sip of water. I fixate on the way she moves, her fingers grasping the glass, those French-manicured nails, short but neat. So sexy.

"I'm fine with it, Taylor, because I have self-control. Can you say the same?"

"We'll see how much control you have," I reply.

She arches an eyebrow at me and takes another bite of food, then pulls a face.

"Ugh. I can't even be pissed at you when the food is this good."

"You mentioned you wanted to be a chef," I say. "Life got in the way, right? But what's stopping you from taking more control?"

Marci rests her fork on the side of her dish. "Money," she says. "Mainly money and time. I can't exactly go study to be a chef, and even if I could, I can't leave anyone else in charge of the diner because I can't afford it. And Grant…"

"What about him?"

"He's been the chef forever. He doesn't trust my menu suggestions," Marci says.

I grit my teeth. "I'll talk to him."

"What? No," she says. "I can handle my own shit, Taylor. Besides, it's not the right time."

"It's never the right time. The only difference between the right and wrong time is you."

"Ooh, deep, Taylor. Did you read that in one of those teenage self-help books?"

I narrow my eyes at her.

"Maybe."

Marci laughs again, and it occurs to me that I want to hear more of that noise. Her joy. I've never wanted that before. Sure, I want people to be happy in a general sense, but I've never been addicted to a sound.

"The problems I have aren't going to disappear overnight. I have to focus on fixing what's broken first."

"What do you think is broken?" I ask.

"The diner doesn't get business over the off-peak months like it does during the summer, even though our overheads are the same," she says. "And then there's the debt to pay off from Billy."

I try not to get irritated at the mention of that lowlife asshole. I want to respect her "family is important" rule, but he doesn't give a shit about her. If he did, he wouldn't constantly put her in this position.

"Maybe I can help you with that," I say.

"Help me?"

"Yeah. Let me think about it," I reply. "No wife of mine is going to struggle."

Marci and I finish the rest of our meal in companionable silence, while Mr. Skitters eyes us from his new sleeping spot.

Nineteen

MARCI

I PEEK out at the cat sleeping on the recliner.

Would it make me a bad person if I accidentally made a loud noise that scared it off? Yes.

Am I going to do that? No.

But I can't help thinking about it because it's getting late, and Jesse's in his en suite bathroom, showering.

I try not to fixate on that part. On water running down his naked body. On how good he probably looks.

I've already changed into my PJs—silk shorts and a matching strappy silk top—that Jesse fetched from my apartment, along with my toothbrush and a change of clothes. I pace back and forth in his bedroom, trying to ignore how cute the room is.

He has a leather armchair in the corner, his bed is huge and comfy looking, and the furniture is done in dark woods, with cream walls, and floaty white curtains over the windows and a view of the ocean. I'm a sucker for a guy who gives a shit about how his house looks, and it's clear that Jesse's put in real effort.

There are interesting trinkets scattered throughout his cottage—the type of curios you'd find in a museum, each one different but intentional somehow. A perfectly smooth stone, a carved wooden flute, a shield hanging on the wall in the living room next to the TV.

For a guy who loves Heatstroke, he's sure collected a lot of stuff that's not from around here.

He's also got books—psychological thrillers and romances, and a few non-fiction—stacked on his bedside table.

The shower shuts off, and I freeze, mid-stride.

Fuck. Just take a breath. It's going to be fine. It's an agreement.

I fiddle with the ring on my finger.

Fine. Nothing's going to happen. We're good.

The door opens, and Jesse steps out of the bathroom, shirtless. It's nothing I haven't seen before, but it still makes my insides curl in on themselves. Jesse's chest is broad and muscular, a few dark hairs spread across his pecs, and he has a tattoo underneath his heart on his rib cage. The date his mother passed. His hair is wet and curls at his temples, and he eats me up with a look.

"Ready for bed?"

My voice is way too squeaky for my liking.

"I've got to do one thing first," he says.

Jesse removes a tripod from the closet and then sets it up in front of the bed.

"Whoa, there, buckaroo. What exactly do you think this is?"

Jesse chuckles.

"I, uh, I like to take photos in my spare time. I'm working on a project at the moment."

"What is it?"

Taylor is into photography? Color me fascinated. I've never seen him with a camera before. I plop down on the end of the bed and watch him take out a camera and set it up.

He messes with the settings and takes off the lens cap.

"Kind of like a self-portrait project. I take a picture of myself before bed. I've been doing it for years. I've got a damn folder on my computer. I want to make one of those progression videos over time, one for each year, and then a large one that shows off my life."

"That's—"

"What?"

"Nothing."

"Since when have you cared about holding your tongue around me, Angel?" Jesse asks, straightening.

"It seems a little sad," I say. "You sitting on your bed, alone, taking a picture of yourself."

"Yeah," he says. "That's what I want the cat for. You want to be in it? You don't have to be."

I hesitate.

"I'll be in it. I'm your fake wife, and that's part of your life, right? So, you can document me."

Jesse gives me such a genuinely bright smile, I can't help but smile back.

No, no, no.

But the denial is muted. Jesse and I might fight like cats and dogs, but I'm starting to see a side of him that's kind. That's not bravado and mockery.

"Timer for ten seconds."

He clicks a button and hurries over, then sits down beside me.

We sit stiffly, side-by-side, staring at the camera.

The shutter clicks.

"Great," Jesse says. "Another night."

"Can I see it?"

Jesse grabs the camera and holds it, then shows me the exceptionally awkward photo of us. He gets up and packs the camera and tripod away. I like how purposeful he is about it. I imagined Taylor would be messy, chaotic, but his house is neat, and he likes things in their place. We're similar in that regard. Which is weird.

"Bed time?" I ask.

"Bed time."

Oh God. Oh God, help me. How am I going to make it through this night next to him?

I get under the covers fast, drawing them up to my chin.

Jesse laughs and gets into bed beside me. He switches off the lamp on his bedside table.

"Goodnight," he says.

"Goodnight."

I lay stiff as a board beside him, the day's events panning through my mind like a slideshow. How he defended me, the first kiss, the second kiss, the way we argued. Just thinking about it has me wet, and I turn over onto my side, my back to him.

I have to get over this. It's Taylor.

Taylor who arrested my brother. Taylor who made it his life's mission to tease me and mess with me. Taylor who is running for sheriff, for fuck's sake. We're a match made in hell. It could never work. Complete opposites. He cares what people think about him, I don't.

I try to keep my breathing even, but the scent of his

cologne, that spicy smokey goodness, is delicious. And he's right there. Right next to me. In bed.

Oh God.

Jesse moves, and my eyes widen. I fixate on the wall, the curtains against it, the sliver of moonlight that pierces the gap in them.

Say something, Taylor.

But he doesn't say a word. His breathing evens out, and I relax a little. Okay, so he's asleep. The crazy thoughts can calm the hell down because there's no shot that anything can happen.

I turn onto my back and stare at the ceiling. My heart rate refuses to slow.

His hands on my body, my breasts, him between my legs, pressing into me, grinding. Biting his lip.

I slide my hands over my breasts, sure that he's finally asleep, and ashamed of myself for wanting him this bad. Am I going to resort to this? I'm all about women being the sexual goddesses they are meant to be, but this is crossing a boundary.

I dip my hand below the waistband of my panties, my fingers brushing over sensitive skin, and I inhale sharply.

"Keep doing that," Jesse says, voice rasping with restrained desire, "and I'm going to consummate this fake marriage right now. Wife."

I snap my arms to my sides, my cheeks hot as hell.

I turn my head and find Jesse on his side, his eyes open, reflecting the moonlight, and focused on me.

"What do you think you're doing?" he asks. "The only person who's going to make you come while you're in this bed is me."

My skin prickles.

"We have rules, remember?"

"Rules that we won't break," he murmurs. "Like I said, the only person who's going to make you come in this bed is me, so if you're in need, you should go sit in that armchair in the corner like a good girl."

My breath hitches.

Is he serious?

"You need to come, Angel," he murmurs. "If I'm not allowed to do it, then you're going to do it yourself." He sits up in bed. "I won't fucking touch you unless you beg me for it. Take off your shorts and go sit in the armchair."

The command is throaty and filled with lust.

I get out of bed and slip off my shorts. Part of me wants to punish him too. If I have to be this horny for him, then he's going to feel the same way about me.

On the way over to the armchair, I open the curtains so that moonlight slices through the room. So that he'll see enough.

I sit down in the armchair.

"Open your legs. Show me that pretty pussy, Angel."

"Taylor."

"Call me Jesse. Or call me your husband."

"Baby," I say.

His head drops back against the headboard, and he swallows audibly. "Open your fucking legs."

I do it, hooking them over either arm of the chair so that I'm angled upward.

"Fuck."

Jesse's pitching a tent in his striped PJ pants.

"You're not allowed to touch yourself," I say. "You can watch."

He drops his head against the headboard a second time. "Fuck."

"Those are my rules," I say. "Do you want to watch me or not?"

"Don't tease me, Angel."

"Do you want to watch me or not?"

"Yes."

"Then keep your hands where I can see them," I whisper.

My body thrums with anticipation. It's like I'm a tuning fork, and Jesse is the instrument.

"Angel."

I slide my palm over my pussy and dip my fingers toward my slick entrance. I gasp and squirm in front of him, arching my back. It's exquisite, and it's been so long since I've done anything. I've been too busy, too tense.

I want that tension gone.

"Put a finger inside," he says.

I do it, arching again.

"Another one."

I slip a second finger inside, using my other hand to rub circles over my clit.

"That's it. Fuck that pussy for me, Angel. I want to hear the noises you make."

I pump my fingers in and out, whining and hot, picturing his hands on my body, shivering with need. This is so wrong, and it pushes me toward my climax with a frantic speed.

"Look at me, Angel. Look at me when you come."

I meet his gaze.

Jesse's got the sheets wrangled in his hands, his knuckles white.

"Come for me, Angel."

The orgasm erupts, and I cry out, the pulse taking me over the edge.

"Jesse, oh my God. Yes. Yes, baby."

"Fuck."

I descend from the high and slump in the armchair, exhausted but giddy from the release. Jesse gets up and comes over. He scoops me into his arms and then carries me to the bed. He lays me down, then grabs my shorts and pulls them up and over my body, lifting me where he needs to. Finally, he tucks me in, takes my fingers, and raises them to his lips.

"Rule number one," I manage.

"I'm helping you clean up, Angel," he says. "Give me this one small fucking pleasure."

"Take it," I murmur.

He sucks my fingers, placing a fist on the wall above his bed, his body shuddering. Finally, he goes to the bathroom and comes back with a wet towel. Then he leaves me alone, the click of the bathroom door is followed by the sounds of him groaning, saying my name, and then a grunt as he releases.

"Oh my God," I whisper.

Because we didn't even touch each other, and Jesse Taylor rocked my world to its foundations.

Twenty

MARCI

I WAKE up to the sounds of waves crashing on the shore and the scent of Jesse's cologne on the sheets. Last night, I fell asleep moments after he got back into bed. We didn't cuddle, we didn't talk, we slept, but at one point during the night, my foot touched his leg, and I left it there.

I left it there.

This fake marriage stuff is getting out of hand.

I crack an eyelid and scan Jesse's bedroom.

He's not in bed with me, which is a blessing since I'm already hot at the thought of last night. Flashes of it come back to me, and it feels like a dream. A *great* dream.

In the quiet, I make the bed and get ready for the day. It doesn't matter, I have a diner to save and debt to pay off, and a brother who might get in trouble for stealing a car.

The kitchen is as quiet as the bedroom. Mr. Skitters is gone, but he's left some fur on the recliner. Jesse's left a bowl, empty glass, and a note beside a flower in a vase on the kitchen counter. I walk over to it, my pulse skyrocketing.

Angel,

We don't have to talk about it. Pretend it's a dream if you want. Hate me all you like.

There's freshly brewed green tea in a pitcher in the fridge, as well as yogurt and cut fruit for breakfast. I left the granola on the counter.

If anything happens today, call me imme-diately.

Your husband.

I gnaw on the inside of my cheek. Not Taylor being sweet. Just because we're husband and wife in public, doesn't mean we need to act intimate in private, so why is he putting in this much effort? I don't want the answer.

The tea is delicious. The fresh-cut fruit is mango and kiwi, and the granola is crunchy and home fucking made. Is he kidding me with this? I'm not used to men who fend for themselves, and, honestly, this makes him sexier.

I clean up after myself then head out. Yesterday, Jesse and I went back to the diner to grab my car and some clothes. I get into my old beater and drive down to the diner, the salty sea air tangling my hair.

Focus. You have to focus.

It doesn't matter that Jesse and I crossed a line last night. It doesn't matter that I want him. If I focus on what's important, I can ignore that.

"Good morning," I sing as I enter the diner.

Grant waves at me from the kitchen. One of my servers, Riley, gives me a small smile. She's from Prickly Poppy Bay, the town over, and she keeps to herself most of the time. When she rolled into town looking for work, it was serendipity—one of my longtime servers had married and moved away the week before.

Riley's got long, curly blonde hair and is in her early twenties, but she hardly ever talks. She grabs some menus and sets to work cleaning them.

"You good, Riley?" I ask.

"Yeah," she says, her voice soft. "And you?"

"Let's say, it's complicated."

"Seems like *life* is complicated," she sighs.

"Do you want to talk about it?"

Riley's deep brown eyes fill with emotion, and she glances out at the street, with another smile.

"Maybe sometime."

The rest of the morning passes at a glacial pace. Todd comes in, and I give him his regular order on the house, much to Grant's chagrin. There are other locals who stop by to grab coffee and food, and it's getting close to the time when my ex and Jesse usually come by for coffee. My nerves build at the thought of seeing him after last night. It's a nice reprieve from being tense about seeing Nate.

I grab my phone to distract myself and drop in on the group chat.

LILY
Hi, ladies. Not sure how long I'm going to be able to participate in the group chat. <3 Something biiiiiig is coming!

HANNAH
Ugh. Who added my gorgeous sister to the chat?

LILY
That would be... you, Han.

HANNAH
Well, we hardly ever get to see you or hear from you soooo... Also, spill. What's the big news?

LILY
I can't talk about it. But it's exciting. And you might be seeing me sooner than you think. Just not in person.

JUNE
I love riddles!

BELLE
What am I, Bilbo Baggins?

MARCI
Can't wait to find out what you're up to.

LILY
What I'm up to? What about you, Walsh? What's this I hear about you getting engaged to my brother?

"Shit."

Lily is younger than the other girls. We didn't connect when we were younger, because while I was in high school, she was starting middle school. But from the few times we've chatted, she seems awesome.

MARCI
Yeah, Kind of sudden and unexpected, but we're happy.

HANNAH
Kind of sus if you ask me. You haaaaate
Jesse.

BELLE
Makes for great sexual tension. We love
that for you.

HANNAH
My eyes!!

I start typing out a private text to Han to check that she's okay after what she's gone through with that freak in Austin, but I'm interrupted by a call from a number I don't recognize.

"Hello?"

The line crackles.

"Hello? Who's there?"

"Marci?"

Billy's voice comes down the line.

My pulse hops up a notch. It's never good news with my brother, unfortunately, and I haven't even told him about my "marriage" to Jesse. He hates him more than I do. Did. God.

"Marci, are you there?"

"Yeah, I'm here."

I don't bother asking him what he wants because he'll tell me anyway.

"I need you to bail me out. Bail is $5,000."

"What?" I say it so loud that Todd turns. "What? Billy, are you—?"

"Yeah, that asshole ex of yours arrested me this morning," he says. "For stealing that car. They're talking about a third-degree felony. So yeah, the judge set my bail for $5,000, and I'm going to need you to help me. It's $500 for my bond."

"Billy, I'm kind of in the middle of trying to help you work off the debt from the last problem you presented me with," I say.

"I don't have much time to talk, Marce." His voice goes soft. "I've been causing trouble for you lately, but I… Look, ever since Dad died, things have been tough for me."

We've had this conversation so many times, I could mouth the words as he says them. Billy's using our trauma as an excuse, but I'm not in a place where I can switch off my emotions around my brother.

"Marce, please help me."

"I don't have the money. For this or for your debt. I'm trying to figure this out, Billy, but the diner isn't exactly making a lot and I have a loan to pay off."

"So, take out a loan," Billy says.

"A loan. To pay off your debt?"

"Yeah. Or, shit, you could sell the diner."

I nearly hang up on him.

"We had this discussion. It's not happening."

"It was a suggestion, damn."

I let out a rough breath.

"I love you, Billy, but I can't afford to pay your bail. I suggest you get in touch with a bondsman."

"Can you find one for me?" he asks. "Marce, my time is up, but can you get hold of a—"

The call goes quiet, and I pull the phone away from my ear.

I ball my hand into a fist. How am I supposed to save the diner like this?

Twenty-One

JESSE

I WALK BACK to the squad, my jaw clenched because I've got nothing. I've spoken to every unsavory asshole in Heatstroke and none of them know who "Jonesy" is or what he looks like.

Either it's a fake name, or they're too scared to tell me the truth. Both options piss me off. And then there's the fact that I'm on duty with Davis today, and being around him makes me want to break things.

My phone rings, and I answer it as I'm getting into the squad.

"This is Taylor."

"Hello, Jesse, darling."

Ganny's shaky voice comes down the line. She's getting older, and I hate the thought of missing any of her calls because of that.

"Hey, Ganny," I say, ignoring Davis' gum-chewing beside me.

"Marjorie told me that you went and got married

without so much as an engagement party or a wedding reception. Is that true?"

Shit. Of course.

Ganny's always the first in our family to know things. I didn't have the chance to break the news to her yesterday because I was too fucked up over having Marci in my cottage.

"I always knew you and Marci would wind up together," she says. "Y'all compliment each other so well, but I won't abide by you having a shotgun wedding without your family, honey."

"It was a spur-of-the-moment type thing," I say. "I'm sorry you missed it."

"Don't be," she says. "I want you two to come over after work. We'll start arranging a real wedding party with family and friends. Is that understood?"

Ganny doesn't get serious often. This means a lot to her.

"We'll be there."

"Good. Love you, honey pie."

"Love you, too."

I hang up and stow my phone in my pocket.

"Huh."

Davis continues chawing on his gum. The man needs a fucking spittoon.

I ignore the off-hand grunt and start the squad's engine. We're patrolling along the beachfront at the moment, but my thoughts are with Marci. How can I help her? Who's this Jonesy motherfucker? Is she safe at the diner? How can I make her come like that again? The way she tasted was enough to make me blow.

"You hear me, Taylor?"

Davis grates on me with that question.

"I'd prefer not to," I say, "but here we are. What do you want?"

He sniffs.

"You must be some type of stupid to hitch yourself to Marci Walsh."

I elect to ignore the comment. If I reach over, grab the back of his head, and ram his nose into the dashboard, he'll get blood everywhere. And I'll get fired. And the reason Marci and I struck up the rules in the first place will cease to exist, because no way will I make sheriff after emulsifying Deputy Dickhead's face.

"She's always going to cause trouble for you."

I'm circling toward the diner without even realizing it, and I force myself to put on the indicator and take a different road.

Davis leans forward a little.

"Just because you got married doesn't make you sheriff material, especially since you chose her. She's a piece of trash with a piece of trash family, and the rest of Heatstroke knows it. They—"

I hit the brakes hard.

Davis' face hits the dashboard with a satisfying thwack. Not enough to break bones, but enough to leave a nasty mark on his nose.

"Ow, what the fuck?"

"Cat in the road," I say, and continue driving. "What dumb shit were you talking about? I wasn't paying attention."

"Fuck you, asshole."

I smile.

"I can't describe how much I don't give a fuck about

your opinion of my wife," I say. "Other than to say that if you disrespect her again, you'll find out how strong that seatbelt is."

"Your wife," he scoffs. "Come on, dude, do you think I was born yesterday? We both know she's not your wife."

"Live in your dreamworld," I say. "She's mine. Ain't a damn thing you can do about it."

"I arrested her lowlife brother this morning."

Fuck. That's not good.

I slow the car, my thoughts turning that over. That's bound to happen because there's enough evidence to prove that Billy stole that car. And now that Marci's my wife, I'm connected to him.

Dickhead is right, Billy is a liability to our plans. And when Marci finds out, she's going to be furious.

"I'm telling you," Davis says, "she's bad news. That family is bad news. Nobody's going to support a man with a wife like that. They won't want you in as sheriff while you're bound to that family."

"Then why do you give a fuck about me marrying her?" I ask. "Doesn't that work out in your favor?"

"I don't give a fuck. I'm warning you as a friend."

"We're not friends," I say. "I choose my friends carefully."

Davis opens his mouth to say something that will likely lead to an altercation, but my phone rings again before he can. I pull over and park the squad, then remove my phone from my pocket.

"Seriously, Taylor? More personal calls during work hours?"

"It's my wife," I say, and then I get out of the squad and walk over to the sidewalk. "Angel? What's wrong?

Has something happened? Do you need me down there?"

"No," she says. "I—This is dumb. I shouldn't have called you at work."

"What's going on?"

"Nothing. Billy was arrested. He needs bail money. I didn't know who to call. Shit, I don't even know why I'm calling you."

I grit my teeth.

"You're calling me because you want and need help, and that's fine. That's normal, Angel."

"Not for me, it's not," she says. "Jesse, forget about it. I'll see you after work. I shouldn't have called. I didn't know who else to talk to. I don't even know what I want to talk about or say."

"I'll be there as soon as I can," I say.

"Taylor."

"Angel."

"You don't have to do anything. This is not an emergency."

But her needing to talk to somebody is a code red in my mind.

"I'll see you soon."

And then I hang up and stride toward the squad.

Twenty~Two

MARCI

I'M PANICKING, which is weird because I'm not usually a panicky person. I prefer to attack my problems head-on unless they've got a knife.

I spend as much time as possible in conversation with people in the diner, then switch my attention to my phone. I shoot off texts to Hannah who's living her librarian fantasy while I'm in a waking nightmare of my own creation.

Everyone's fine.

I am not.

And I can't bring myself to tell the girls about this because they've got their own shit going on, and frankly, it's embarrassing. There's pity in June's eyes when I bring up Billy's name. And Hannah, she gets so mad when I talk about Billy, because she's of the same opinion as Jesse. That I don't owe him anything.

But I do. I'm the only mother figure he's ever had. And that is all colors of fucked up, but it's the truth.

Around lunch time, the bell tinkles over the glass front door, and Jesse enters the diner, alone.

It's a sign of the times that I'm relieved to see him, rather than annoyed.

"Angel," he says.

"Coffee?" I ask.

He sweeps me into a hug. Jesse cups the back of my head in his hand and presses me to his chest, curling me into him like he can protect me from the world. Too bad he can't protect me from my poor choices.

I hug him back, melting into him even though I should despise this, and pretend that I'm doing it for show.

"I missed you," he says. "What's going on? I'm sorry I couldn't come sooner."

"It's not your fault," I reply. "It's—I didn't know who else to call."

"You did the right thing," he says. "I'm your husband. You can rely on me." He tucks my hair behind my ear, tracing a finger over the shell. "I'll always be here when you need me."

I reject the thought.

Fake. It's fake, and as strong as the sexual attraction is, that doesn't mean any of his words are real. The fact is, Jesse and I are telling lies to get what we want, and it doesn't sit right with me.

"You want to talk about it?" Jesse asks.

I lead him upstairs to my tiny apartment. He sits down on my worn sofa, larger than life in his uniform. A uniform that I've despised for years, but that looks good on him.

"What's going on?"

"I don't like any of this," I say, tucking my hands into

the front pocket of my Heartstopper apron. "I don't like that we're lying to people. I don't like that my brother has been arrested, and I'm the one who's married to a cop, and I don't like that my business is failing."

And then, because I've got nothing else to do with my hands other than fumble in my apron, I walk to the kitchenette and start preparing a pot of coffee.

Taylor doesn't say anything at first.

"Ganny wants us to come by after work today," he says. "She wants to put on a wedding ceremony. I think she'll want to arrange it with you."

"See? That's another candle on top of the cake of lies we've baked."

"That was… A cake of lies?"

"Don't start with me, Taylor," I say.

He smirks at me while I pack the coffee grinds. The coffee machine in my apartment is the one thing I splurged on. Good coffee is the difference between a good day and a bad one. The world can go to shit, but as long as I have my coffee, I'm good.

"The lying thing, I can't do anything about," Jesse says. "Trust me, I'm with you on that one. It sucks. It sucks to have to play dirty to get what we want, but fuck it. Can you say you want Deputy Dickfuck to wind up as sheriff one day?"

"No, I don't."

"Exactly. And you're safe with me," he says.

We wait for the coffee to brew in silence.

I bring him over a cup of coffee and he thanks me. He's been taking it black, no sugar, for years. He takes a sip, pulls a face, and swallows.

"What's wrong?"

"Nothing. Just my first sip of coffee for the day." He sets it down on my coffee table. "As for your brother being arrested, I can't say I didn't see that coming." Jesse raises a palm. "I'm not going to talk smack about him, Angel, but there's nothing we can do about that. He made his bed."

"He needs bail money."

"He needs a fucking CT scan, the way he acts," Jesse mumbles, then shakes his head. "I assume you're not going to give him the money."

"I told him he needs to speak to a bail bondsman," I say.

"Good. Because I'm not giving him shit. He's your brother, but he's also his own fucking person, Marci."

I suck in a few deep breaths and glance over at the pictures on the walls. Pictures of Dad, me, Billy, over the years. I don't have any from the time after it happened.

"Angel, it's okay," Jesse says. "Now, let's talk about the diner."

"What about it?"

"What kind of plans do you have in place to drum up excitement during the off-season?"

I tell him what I've got so far—a new special, a burger eating contest, a joint venture with the specialty smoothie place at the boardwalk. Ideas I hope will bring in more customers.

"Then, when they buy a burger from the Heartstopper, they get a stamp on their card. Five stamps equals a smoothie at Frank's, and vice versa."

Taylor scratches his chin.

"Those are great ideas," he says. "But some of them are way more expensive than others."

I bristle.

"Unless you've suddenly gone from cop to businessman in the last five—"

"Easy," he says and gets up.

I'm so stressed I've spent this conversation pacing back and forth, wringing the end of my apron. Jesse grabs my arms and captures me with a gaze.

"Easy," he says. "Your ideas are good. And as for me being a businessman, I'm not going to pretend I'm a professional, but I dabble in investments. I've got money saved up. If I didn't, going on the campaign trail for sheriff would be difficult."

"What are you saying?"

"That I think there's another way we can excite the locals," he says. "So, hear me out. The problem is that you don't get as many tourists in the diner during the slow periods, right?"

"Right."

I'm stubborn, and I've still got my doubts about Jesse, but I want to hear what he has to say.

He sweeps his hand over the back of his neck, then adjusts his neat uniform shirt. For a second, I picture stripping it off him.

"So, that means we need to get more locals interested, and not just Heatstrokers. I'm talking about people from Prickle Poppy Bay, Yonder, Santa Elena, the whole damn county. You could still do the burger eating contest, but what about outreach to those towns?"

I tap my chin.

"I like that. I feel like it would cost a lot of money, though."

"I'll help you."

"Taylor."

He draws up straight, his blue eyes narrowing.

"You're my wife, fake or not, and I'm going to make sure I hold up my end of the bargain. That means making sure the guy who's responsible for threatening you pays, and that your diner flourishes. I'm not going to take no for an answer when it comes to helping you with this. It's not charity. It's what we do for each other."

I'm not used to leaning on anyone else, so the relief of what he's said is foreign to me.

"Thank you," I manage.

"Anything you need, Angel. I've got your back."

And then he squeezes me into a hug that lights me up from the inside out.

Nothing has changed between us. He's still the asshole who arrested Billy and who made my life hell growing up, but at the same time, it's different.

And it scares me.

Twenty-Three

JESSE

I'M OBSESSED with the way she smells. She's got this gentle coconut thing going on this evening, and she comes out of the en suite bathroom with her hair wet, but fully clothed. We're due at Ganny's soon, and we haven't discussed last night.

Probably better that way.

I'm convinced that if we talk about it, I'm going to lose it, push her up against the wall, and fuck her until she screams my name over and over and over—

"Taylor?"

I blink up at her.

"Yeah."

"You going to sit there, staring into space? Or are we going to get this show on the road?" She pulls a face. "I can't *wait* to lie to your grandmother, who's literally the only motherly figure I've ever had. Fun."

I get up and brush off the black tee I've chosen for tonight. Mr. Skitters hasn't been around, but there's fur on it somehow.

We lock up the cottage and get in my squad. Marci hesitates less this time and gets in with more ease. The drive over is leisurely, and I roll down the windows to let in fresh air.

"Can I ask you something?"

"Depends on what it is," she says.

"What happened to your mom? You never talk about it."

Marci swallows and looks away.

"Fuck, forget it. Shouldn't have asked."

"It's fine," she says. "There are only a couple of people who know the real story. My mom left when we were little."

I nod. That rumor's gone around town plenty.

"But she left after she had Billy, a year after. She had… She had bad postpartum depression, that evolved into chronic depression, and she couldn't do it. With Billy or with me. My Dad tried to get her help, but eventually, it was too much for her to take. She believed that she was bringing us down, that we would be better off without her, and she left."

"I'm sorry, Marci," I say.

"It's in the past, and honestly, I don't blame her. She felt like she couldn't do a good job, and I remember how tough things were before she left. My parents were fighting a lot, and she barely spent time with me or even with Billy. She used to disappear for hours at a time. I was about ten when she left. And it hurt like hell, but I remember feeling weirdly… relieved. Like finally, we could be at peace. Of course, I felt super guilty about that, but my Dad was always there to listen. Always. He was the best."

"I'm happy you had him," I say. "That he could be there for you in ways that your mother couldn't."

"Yeah. It's weird to open up about this."

"Thanks for telling me about it."

"Yeah. I trust you not to spread that information around. You might stick to the letter of the law and care what people think, and you annoy the crap out of me, and act high and mighty—"

"I hope there's an end to this sentence that's positive."

"But you're loyal. And you're committed to this fake thing we've got going on."

"There it is," I say.

"Besides, this is kind of my comfort zone. Weirdly enough."

"What do you mean?"

"Apart from my dad and the girls," I say, "my relationships have been transactional."

"Uh..."

"Not like that, Taylor," she snaps. "I'm saying that people always want something from me. My relationships are conditional. Exactly like this one."

That pisses me off. I don't want to think about why it pisses me off, but it does.

We fall into an easy silence for the rest of the drive over. I place my hand on her thigh because I can't resist doing it. I want to feel her skin underneath my palm, and those shorts she's always wearing drive me wild. If Marci wore a skirt, I might lose it completely.

She smiles and looks out the window.

"Still haven't gotten your fill, huh, Taylor?"

"I'm starving for you, Angel," I say.

We pull up outside Ganny's house with its shiplap

walls and memories and head inside together. My father smiles at us from the living room. He's an older version of Cash, with gray hair and eyes that used to be kind but have hardened since Mom died.

"There you are, my boy. Your grandmother's waiting for you in the kitchen."

"We've been summoned," I say.

"Pretty much." Dad laughs. "Marci, darling, you're looking radiant today." He draws her into a hug. "How are you feeling? You two have gotten hitched so quick, you've made our heads spin. Haven't even gotten the chance to congratulate you on your engagement, let alone your marriage."

Fuck.

I don't want to disappoint my family, but that's all I ever do.

"It happened so fast," Marci says, reaching out and taking my hand.

She squeezes it, and I appreciate the gesture.

"Jesse's a man who goes after what he wants. I hope you're not upset that you weren't included."

"I understand how it is," Dad says. "Let's see what Ganny's got to say about it."

"What I've got to say about it is that you two owe us a party."

Ganny stands in the doorway to the living room, her hands on her hips. She's tiny, her hair puffy and tinged blue, and she always smells like roses and, strangely, old paper.

I hug her and she pecks my cheek.

She puts out her arms to Marci, who walks into the embrace with a smile that's laden with guilt.

"I don't know what you two were thinking, running off like that without telling a darn soul about it," Ganny says. "I expected more from you, Jesse. It's almost like you were rushing to get married before Cash and June."

"Why would he need to do that?" Marci asks. "Jesse doesn't need to compete with anyone. He's his own person."

Ganny's hand flutters to her throat.

"Oh, of course not. I didn't mean anything like that, dear. I'm sad we didn't get to partake in the celebration."

"We can remedy that." I draw Marci to my side and slide my hand over the curve of her waist. "We'd be happy to have a wedding party with family and friends."

"More than happy," Marci puts in, and I like the set of her jaw.

I like that she stood up for me.

"Wonderful," Ganny says. "Now, come into the kitchen and have some lemonade. I made it fresh."

She beckons for us to follow her.

Dad touches my shoulder, and I hang back while Marci follows her.

"You sure about this, son?"

Thomas Taylor always gets straight to the point. I like that about my father, but I don't need this from him.

"Of course."

I frown.

"Wipe that look off your face," he says. "I'm not trying to offend you. I'm curious if you realize what you're getting yourself into here. This is not a one-night stand, Jesse. This is the rest of your life. Don't rush into this. Marriage is a commitment."

"I'm aware, Dad," I say. "And I'm not rushing into anything. Marci is the one for me."

He scratches his chin, the gray stubble rasping.

"If you think this will make people take you more seriously, Jesse—"

"Where did that come from?"

"Come on, son. People aren't stupid. Rushing into a marriage with any woman for reasons other than love, is a bad idea. And rushing into it with Marci is worse. She's practically a part of our family at this point. You fuck this up, it'll fuck up more than just your life."

"Even if we were rushing, it's too late to go back," I say.

Dad lifts his shoulders and lets them drop.

"Sure. Just telling you I care. If you say you got this figured out, I'll trust you."

And he enters the hall where that picture of my grandfather sits high on the wall, glaring down at those who pass underneath it. Dad turns back.

"Let's get some lemonade."

There isn't any amount of lemonade that could clear my head.

Twenty~Four

MARCI

JESSE'S BEEN ACTING DIFFERENTLY since we got back from Ganny's house. I don't blame him. Pretending to be married is hard enough without a caring family who wants what's best for you. That's not even sarcasm. He's so connected to the Taylors that their opinion is everything to him. I get it. I *like* that.

Words I never thought I would think regarding Jesse Taylor: *I like that.*

Jesse's in the kitchen again, preparing dinner. He insisted I settle in on the reclining chair with a good book and a glass of chilled water. He squeezed a dash of lemon into it and then tucked a blanket over my legs.

The smell of garlic and white wine drifts through his cottage. I shouldn't be enjoying this. I should be fuming that I'm here. But I don't have any fight left in me tonight.

It has been a long day of Jesse treating me right, and my God, I can't be a bitch about it.

"What's on the menu tonight?" I ask, marking my place in the book with a finger.

"Chicken with a white wine sauce, potato wedges, and braised green beans," he says. "Simple."

"Sure, simple."

He doesn't look up from the stove where he's tending to the sauce. Jesse's gorgeous in side profile too, a strong nose, his clean shaven broad jaw. He's put on an apron over his black tee, and the way his forearm muscles tense as he stirs the sauce is borderline pornographic.

But he's not talking to me tonight.

"You good?" I ask. "Usually, I can't get you to shut up."

"Hmm."

"All right, Taylor, what's up?"

"Just thinking about things," he says. "Our agreement. What it means for the future."

Ah. So Ganny and his father freaked him out. My hunch is that it's got to do with the private conversation he had with his dad in the living room.

"Do you want to back out?"

"No. I don't want to back out," he says, and scoops up some sauce in a teaspoon.

He blows on it gently and brings it over, then feeds it to me.

"Oh my God, that's delicious."

"Thyme," he says. "It's the thyme. I watched this Michelin star chef make this sauce on YouTube. Amazing how much you can learn if you look in the right places."

He returns to the stove.

"So you don't want to back out of the deal?"

"No. Just as long as we stick to the rules. If we get physically or emotionally involved," he says, "this is going to turn sour fast."

I place a bookmark in the book and set it aside.

"How so? We already hated each other before. What difference does it make if we hate each other afterward?"

"I never hated you," he says.

I forget to breathe.

"But I get you hated me," he continues, removing the sauce from the heat. "I want us to keep this professional because it's more than us at stake here. I can't afford to lose the people I love, and neither can you. We don't need a rift in our family."

"You're assuming that if we got emotionally involved, which is not going to happen, that we would eventually break up?"

"Yeah," he says. "I've never felt love. And you wouldn't trust me with your heart."

He's not wrong about the second part. I wouldn't trust anyone with it after Nate.

"Good thing we haven't broken any rules then," I say.

He spears me with that Taylor gaze.

"Dinner's ready."

We eat in silence. Mr. Skitters wanders in halfway through dinner and takes up on the recliner. Outside, thunder rolls in the night, and the thick, wet patter of rain on the windows makes the cottage homier.

After dinner, Jesse waits for me to freshen up in the bathroom and get dressed. I sit on the edge of the bed when it's his turn. He comes out of the bathroom wearing nothing but his cotton PJ pants. They leave nothing to the imagination.

Jesse sets up the camera on the tripod, and we sit together on the edge of the bed. This time, I loop my arm around his shoulders and rest my head against his.

The shutter clicks. The moment is over.

We get in bed while lightning cracks outside the windows and the rain rattles on the roof.

"Goodnight," I whisper.

"Goodnight, Angel."

And then we lay there in the quiet. Jesse's breathing slows, mine does too, but I can't sleep. Regardless, I keep my eyes closed, going over today. From Billy's call to me turning to Jesse instead of my friends.

Minutes pass, maybe an hour, and I'm on the brink of getting up to get a glass of water when Jesse shifts beside me.

He brushes the hair back from my forehead, then bends over and kisses me on it. So light, it's barely there.

I keep breathing evenly, curious about what he's going to do. Because that soft kiss doesn't match his actions from earlier, or the words we've shared over the years. Where's the sexual tension, the hatred, the determination to not get involved?

Last night was an experience for both of us, and it's blurred a line.

"Angel," he whispers. "Marci."

I want to respond, but I'm terrified of where it will lead.

Jesse's weight shifts on the bed, and the headboard clicks against the wall.

"If you want the truth, Marci, about why we can't break the rules," he whispers. "I'm starting to regret pretending to be married to you because all I can think about is having you for real. Touching you. Making you come. Making you smile. Even though you would never let me. Who am I to you? Just the guy who broke your family apart. Just the guy you could never love."

My heart squeezes in my chest.

What the hell?

"And I'm the guy who will never be worthy of that love. The attention-seeker, the cop, the guy you can't trust. Fuck. If things were different, if we were different people, or we didn't have the history we had, I can't help wondering if you would see me as more than Taylor."

I'm stunned.

He legitimately thinks I'm asleep, so this isn't a ploy to soften me up. He's not like Nate. He doesn't need to lie to get what he wants. He got what he wanted last night without having to lie.

Jesse doesn't annoy me because he's a bad person. He annoys me because he challenges me, and it is so dang hard to deal with that along with the diner, Billy, and life.

And I always figured he hated our family like the other deputies and cops in town.

Am I wrong about him?

The rain keeps pouring down, and Jesse settles onto the bed at last. His breathing evens out slowly. I risk a peek at him. He's got one arm thrown above his head, those curls brushing his forehead, eyes closed.

I sneak my foot across the space between us and rest it against his calf.

Twenty-Five

JESSE

SUNDAY ARRIVES, and I'm grateful for the reprieve from work. I'm struggling to make headway on finding this "Jonesy" asshole, but, thankfully, Marci's kitchen door at the diner hasn't been found open this week.

I lie in bed on my side, watching her sleep. She's got the day off, too, and I want her to get as much rest as possible.

This shit with her brother is stressing her out, and while we have a plan for the diner, she doesn't have the capital to invest in it. And she won't take handouts, as she calls them.

Marci's cute upturned nose is begging for a kiss, but after I confessed my feelings to her while she was asleep, I haven't dared touch her again.

I want her so bad it physically pains me.

But my father is right. If this goes bad, and it will if we go a step further, we'll fuck up more than our short-lived friendship. I have a feeling that the peace that exists between us can snap back into hatred quickly.

Going to bed each night and not touching her has been a trial, and I'm growing weaker by the day.

I slip out of bed and leave her to rest, her red hair strewn across the white pillow, and get breakfast ready. Tea and waffles with clotted cream, fresh fruit, and syrup. I'm halfway through breakfast prep when my phone buzzes on the table.

Cash's name flashes on the screen.

"Hey, brother," I say, "what's up?"

"You haven't heard?"

"Heard what?" I ask, keeping my voice down.

"*The Heatstroke Hit Piece* published an article about you. A tell-all, claiming that you faked your marriage to Marci to curry favor with the locals," Cash says.

"Fuck."

I haven't even formally announced that I'm running for sheriff yet.

"Guess that ex of yours wasn't kidding the other night, huh?" Cash asks. "I'm not going to ask you if it's true or not. Frankly, I don't care because I trust you to do the right thing. Just thought you should know."

"Thanks."

I say goodbye, my gut burning with humiliation.

I can't stop myself from bringing up the website and reading what they've written about me. There's not much for them to go on other than the fact that we got married fast. But a quote from none other than Deputy Dick himself catches my attention near the bottom of the article.

"Thing is, there's a public record of every legal marriage that's taken place in the state of Texas. It takes one quick search, and you can find out who's got a marriage license."

I press the heel of my palm to my forehead.

I'm an idiot. I *knew* that, but I didn't consider that he'd be suspicious enough to look it up. I underestimated how much Nate hates Marci. And me.

"Me and my big fucking mouth."

If I'd kept it together at the department picnic, this wouldn't be a problem. We could've stayed engaged for a while until Davis was thrown off my scent. Then again, he was running for sheriff, and I should have counted on him using this against me.

Which leaves one option.

A fucking crazy one.

Even crazier than getting fake married.

"Fuck."

I finish making the rest of the breakfast while I turn the idea over in my mind again and again. A half an hour later, Marci appears in the door to my bedroom, still in her cute silk PJs, her hair tousled. She's fucking adorable.

"Hi," I say.

"Is that… Did you make waffles?"

"And tea." I set down a cup in front of her and then bring her plate over. "Syrup if you want it."

"Thank you," she says, and starts eating at a ferocious pace that matches mine.

Another thing I like about her.

I eat too, but my appetite isn't great after what I've read, and what we're going to need to talk about. I want her to finish her meal first because the last thing a woman needs first thing in the morning is a healthy dose of bad news.

We finish the meal, and a meow from the bedroom draws my attention. Mr. Skitters is on the back porch, waiting for food, but he darts into the bushes to wait when I go out there to fill his bowl. It's major progress. Him sleeping on the recliner felt like a fluke, but he keeps doing it.

Inside, Marci sits at the kitchen counter, mug clasped between her hands, her gaze on the kitchen window. The ocean waves are choppy today, and the wind tousles the shrubbery along the path that leads down to the beach.

"We need to talk," I say as I return to the kitchen.

She purses those pretty lips.

"About the marriage," I say. "The deal."

"Is this a good talk or…?"

"It depends on how you view it," I say.

"Uh oh. Spit it out, Taylor. What's going on?"

"So, you remember my ex, Annaleigh?"

"Tits McGee? How could I forget?" Marci asks drily.

"Wow. That was… Wow, Angel."

"She's well-endowed," Marci says. "Not that it's a bad thing. I—"

"Your breasts are amazing," I say. "I haven't even seen them, and they've already made me come."

"What?"

Okay, maybe not the best approach to that particular topic.

"Fuck. Anyway, so Annaleigh is the editor of *The Heatstroke Hit Piece*, and she doesn't like me."

"I think that's the opposite, but go on."

"They published this."

I unlock my phone and slide it over to her.

Marci starts reading, and her eyebrows lift. "This is… Is she serious? Are *they* serious? How is this news?"

"Apparently, Davis took what I said at the picnic and

ran with it. He doesn't want to compete. He wants to win."

"You have to fight back," Marci says. "You have to."

The screen goes black from inactivity, and she taps it to wake it up, but it's got a passcode.

"0120," I say.

"What?"

"My passcode. 0120. Don't tell anybody else."

"You're giving me the passcode to your phone?"

"Yeah. I trust you," I say.

She types it in and keeps reading, casting nervous glances my way.

"What do you want to do about this, Taylor? We can't let them keep— Oh. Oh no. Oh, no, no, no."

"Yeah."

"No."

"I'm afraid so."

"There's no way," Marci says. "I mean, this is interesting, but I don't want to *actually* marry you. Like for real, marry you."

"I get that."

"I don't see myself marrying anyone," she says. "I don't even believe in marriage."

"Me neither," I say.

Marci falls silent and stares down at the screen, reading and re-reading.

"So, the problem is that we don't have a legitimate marriage license and that anyone with a brain stem and two fingers can pull up that website and find out if we're legit or not. And when they see we aren't, then the protection I offer you falls away, and my 'good image' does too."

"Yeah, but we can't get married for real."

"We can," I say. "People get married and divorced daily."

"I—This is a big deal."

"Yeah. And to sweeten the deal, I'll give you a honeymoon gift."

Marci gives me a withering look.

"Now is *not* the time to talk dirty to me, Taylor."

"Not what I meant, but I like where your mind's at. If you marry me, like legitimately marry me, I'll invest in your diner."

She pushes back from the counter, and spins to face me on her stool.

"Taylor. No."

"It won't count as a handout then because I'll be your fucking husband, and you will be sharing the money that I have."

"Where are you going to get this alleged money from? I don't want to be a burden to you or anyone else."

"But you're happy taking responsibility for everyone else's problems?" I ask. "Like Billy. Your friends. Grant's issue with the menu?"

"Hey, that's not fair. Don't use that against me."

"I'm not using it against you, Angel. I'm telling you that I'm on your fucking side, and if we do this," I say.

I circle toward her, placing my hands either side of her on the kitchen counter so that she's caged in my arms.

"If we do this, I'm going to be team Marci and team Heartstopper until the day we decide to call it quits. We can keep the same rules for the fake marriage. We don't have to change any of that, and we probably shouldn't."

"Because you don't want it to ruin our friendships and family relationships."

"Exactly," I say.

"But I have nothing to offer you," she replies. "I don't have money to invest in your goals. It's not an equivalent exchange." She hesitates. "Jesse, I… I don't want this to escalate. I'm scared."

I hate that she thinks that's what this has to be, but I don't blame her for it. It's a deal. She has no feelings for me other than annoyance and occasional arousal.

"You don't have to be scared when I'm with you."

"I'm scared of you." Her eyelashes flutter. "I'm scared that we'll break the rules."

Fuckkkk me.

"Me too. But we're adults. We can do this."

Marci places a hand on my chest, and I catch it in mine.

"Will you marry me, Angel?"

"Yes."

This feels more intense than the museum or anything else that's happened between us so far. More intense than watching her come on the armchair in my bedroom.

"Then we'll have to arrange it," I say, and take a step back so I don't kiss her and fuck this up. "You've been arranging that wedding party with Ganny for next weekend, right?"

"Right."

"So, we'll get the marriage license and do the damn thing then," I say. "And we can claim that there was an error on our certificate and that we have to redo the whole thing. That we had an appointment with them."

"That's the official party line?"

"Correct," I say. "Marci, are you sure?"

"Yeah. It's going to help us both, but I'm still not sure how I feel about you investing money into the Heartstopper. I don't want to be—"

"Don't say burden, Angel. You're anything but that. You're a blessing," I say. "And trust me, I have more than enough money to help you."

"How?" Marci asks. "No offense, but how will you afford any of this on a deputy's salary?"

"My grandfather left me some money when he passed," I say. "I invested it wisely. That row of commercial buildings across the street from the Heartstopper?"

"Yeah?"

"I own them."

"What the fuck?" Marci's jaw drops. "Jeez, Taylor. Good for you, man."

Her cheeks color.

"I'm privileged enough to have had the money to invest. And I know a good investment when I see one."

"You think the Heartstopper is a good investment?"

Not what I meant.

"Yeah. So get excited. You might not want to be married to my annoying ass, but you won't have to stay that way. And we can draw up a contract so that we're both covered when we split."

"This is insane," Marci says, but there's a hint of excitement in her tone. "You'll invest in the Heartstopper?"

"Yeah," I say, "but I won't pay off Billy's debt. Not until I've found out who's threatening you in the first place."

It's a hard line I won't cross. Marci's endeavors, I'm all for, and I will protect her, but Billy is not going to get a fucking dime. Not when he treats my wife like a piggybank.

"We're doing this?" Marci asks, her hands tucked underneath her thighs, her head tilted so her hair cascades past her right shoulder.

MARCI

WE ARE FUCKING DOING THIS.

I stand in front of the mirror in Ganny's bedroom, turning this way and that as I examine my dress. It's one I found on short notice, a lacy cream dress that stops short of my knees. June moves around me, putting the finishing touches on my hair, her eyes glistening with tears.

"Oh my gosh, Marci, you're perfect," she says. "I hope I look half as good on my wedding day."

"You look stunning," Hannah adds, tucking her dark hair back from her face.

She's got that classic, model beauty, and both of my besties are pictures in green. Their outfits aren't matching, but it's the best they could do on short notice, and I appreciate them so much in this moment.

"I think I'm having a panic attack," I say, fanning my face. "I can't believe I'm doing this."

"Don't sweat too much," Hannah says, ever the practical one. "You'll ruin your makeup."

"Jesse adores you, Marce." June grasps my shoulders

and places her face next to mine, her blonde hair a stark contrast to my red. "You two are meant to be."

Except it's not real. The wedding might be, but we're not in love.

I repeat it again and again, because the only people who have loved me for me are my friends and my father. No man has ever accepted me. I'm not even sure I'm worth accepting.

The panicked thoughts stream through my mind.

My phone rings, and I jump.

"It's Belle and Lily," June says, showing me the video call that's coming through. "We organized a conference call with the girlies."

"Thanks," I manage.

June props the phone up against the mirror and hits the button to answer.

"Girllll, you are so fabulous, look at you," Belle says. "Oh my God, I wish I was there. Life is so unfair."

Belle tosses her silky black locks.

"It's okay," I say, gulping. "It was short notice."

"Short notice," Lily says, laughing.

Unlike the other Taylor siblings, Lily has green, hazel-flecked eyes and platinum-blonde hair. She looks a lot like Mrs. Taylor, whereas the rest of her siblings look like their father.

"Marci, the last time I visited, Jesse pantsed you at a potluck dinner."

"That goes to show how long it's been," Hannah calls out. "Sissy's too busy being a TV star."

Lily presses a finger to her lips and winks.

"Can't tell you what I'm up to, but I can't wait for you to see it. Anyway, enough about me! Marci, honey, I was a pain in the ass when I was a kid, and you were in high school, but I am so dang proud you're going to be a member of my family."

"Stop," Belle says, fanning herself from her office that has a view of the city skyline. "I'm going to cry. Crying is a weakness in my industry. If Mr. Wiggs sees me crying, he'll assign someone else to the next asshole sports star who dicks down a married woman."

"I thought you hated the asshole sports stars," I say.

"I do, but it pays the bills."

"Are you ready for this?" Belle asks. "You realize this is one dick for the rest of your life."

Hannah pulls a face. "Gross, dude, that's my brother."

"You didn't have a bachelorette party," Lily says. "No strippers. Boo."

"It doesn't make a difference to me," I say. "The 'one guy for the rest of my life' thing. I've only been with one other guy, so I—"

"Wait, what?"

Lily's eyes widen.

Belle makes a choking noise.

"You're kidding."

"Is that a big deal?" I ask. "Who cares?"

"It's not a big deal in like the old-fashioned way," Lily says. "I think they're shocked because you're so vocal about women taking care of themselves sexually."

"I believe the phrase she used last summer was 'you gotta get that pussy tapped, girl'," Belle says, helpfully.

"And I stand by that," I reply. "Sexual health is important."

I prefer to take care of my own sexual health rather than let a man do it for me.

June claps her hands.

"Ladies, it's almost time."

And I love her for it, because I would rather *not* discuss my ex with anyone, especially not on my fake-but-real wedding day.

"Say your goodbyes to Marci Walsh. Next time you see her, she'll be Marci Taylor."

Oh God.

I say goodbye to Belle and Lily, blowing them kisses, and then turn to Han and June. We clasp hands.

"Thank you for being here for me," I whisper.

"You'll always have us," Hannah says, picking up a bouquet.

"Always."

I hug them both, and we descend the stairs. Music plays in the backyard, and June opens the door and starts down the makeshift aisle. Chairs have been set up either side of it, and the only people invited are the Taylors, Savage, and the staff from the Heartstopper, including Grant and Riley. Billy's still in jail.

Don't think about it. Don't think about it.

He doesn't need to be here. It's not real.

I wait until it's my turn, then descend the stairs on my own, my throat aching when Mr. Taylor steps up and takes my arm. But I forget the pain when I find Jesse, standing underneath an arch covered in flowers. He's wearing a neat black suit that fits him perfectly.

His gaze fixes on mine, and the look of intensity he's wearing melts me.

The music plays and the backyard disappears. Mr. Taylor kisses my cheek and hands me over to Jesse.

"You're beautiful," he says. "Perfect."

"Thank you. It's a short-notice dress."

"Perfect," he repeats.

Cash and Savage are lined up as his groomsmen, dapper in suits. And the officiant, the local reverend, stands waiting for us.

We clasp hands as he talks, and I can't concentrate on anything he's saying because this is it. I'm marrying a man who I swore I hated for the wrong reasons with a plan to divorce him, and the people here, the people who love us, have no idea.

But I don't let go of his hands. I say "I do." And Jesse does too. We exchange wedding bands he got for us.

And then, he sweeps me into his arms and presses a kiss to my lips that's full of the unspoken desire that's been drifting between us for the past two weeks, since that first night we nearly broke the rules. I wrap my arms around his neck and kiss him back, arching into him.

The crowd cheers and—

"What the fuck?"

The shout comes from the back yard, near the fence.

Jesse holds me close as we break the kiss.

Billy is halfway over the fence, wearing a scowl, his dirty blond hair shaved at the sides. He's grasping a bottle of vodka as he tumbles into the Taylors' backyard.

No.

Jesse stiffens, but I place my hand on his arm.

"Please," I say. "Let me handle this."

Murmurs spread through the crowd. Grant and Riley pull faces at each other and rise from their seats like they want to help. We're a family at the Heartstopper, and they don't like Billy either. Nobody likes Billy except for me.

I walk over to my brother.

"You're drunk, Billy."

"Yeah, and? I got out of fucking jail, no thanks to you," he says. "I deserve to have a party. What the fuck is this even? You're getting married? To a cop. That cop?"

He spits on the grass.

Ganny gasps.

"You need to leave," I say. "This is not your property. You're trespassing."

"You even sound like a cop," Billy gives a wry laugh. "I can't believe it, Marci. After what they did to Dad?"

I clasp the sides of my dress.

"Billy, I've done my best to help you. I'm still trying, but I didn't have the money to bail you out again."

I've been trying. I want to scream it at him, but I'm not going to make a scene here.

"Done your best?" Billy takes a swig of vodka. "Done your best to do what's good for you and nobody else."

"That's not true, Billy," I say, and my voice raises a little. "Don't you think that's unfair? I fucking raised you when Dad died. You don't think it's painful for me to watch you piss your life away and get in trouble and try, and try, and fucking *try* to help you? I look like an idiot because I keep trying to make things better for you, but how can I do that when you won't make things better for yourself?"

Billy recoils. His bottom lip quivers.

"I try to," he whispers. "I try to. It's hard."

My heart. I can't do this in front of the Taylors.

"Billy, you need to get your act cleaned up. I want to help you, but you need to help yourself too. I need to know that you'll take this seriously. That you'll look for a job. That you'll try to do the *right* thing."

"It's easy for you," Billy says, swinging the vodka bottle. "Don't judge me when it's easy for you. You had a dad for longer than I did! You had more than me."

This conversation is going nowhere fast. And my temper has flared too hot.

"You need to leave. Call me when you're ready to take responsibility for yourself."

I walk past him and into the house, letting the screen door slam behind me.

Twenty-Seven

I **KNOCK** on the upstairs bathroom door in Ganny's house.

"Angel?" I murmur. "Angel, are you in there?"

No answer.

"If you want to leave, we can leave. We did what we came to do."

"Is he gone?"

"Yeah."

The door opens, and Marci's standing there in that lacy dress, her eyes red from crying. She dabs a tissue under her eyes and checks her makeup isn't ruined, sniffing.

"Sorry," she says. "This is not… This was not how it was meant to go today."

"We can leave," I say.

"They'll be disappointed."

"Who cares? Not me. If you're unhappy and you don't want to hang around and celebrate, we leave. Simple."

Marci bites down on her bottom lip, and I want to punch Billy for making her sad, but it won't achieve anything except to upset her even more. And that's exactly why I haven't done anything yet. Because she doesn't want me to.

"What do you want to do, Angel?" I ask.

"We can stay for a bit."

I hold out a hand to her, and she takes it. I sweep her into a hug and press a kiss to her temple because I can't resist her, and I get the feeling that she needs affection.

"None of that is your fault," I whisper. "You get that, right?"

"He's struggling, and it's because of me." She hugs me back, tight, burying her face in my shirt. "I don't want to be weak and cry. I don't—"

"You're not weak," I say. "And he's not struggling because of you, Marci. You did your best. You continue to do more than you have to for your grown brother. I know you feel guilty because he didn't get the childhood you did and that you feel like he's your responsibility, but by blaming yourself, you're only hurting yourself more."

Her shoulders shake, and I stroke her hair, breathing in the scent of her perfume, enjoying the warmth of her pressed against me too much.

Once she's collected herself, we go downstairs to join the others. The wedding reception is a meal with my family at the dining room table. We celebrate. We sign our marriage license, and we eat a couple of bites of a cake that Ganny prepared for today.

It takes forever.

I want to celebrate, but Marci's not in the right frame of mind, and I want to get her home, away from Ganny's house. And that's exactly what I do. I drive us home in the silence, with her staring out of the window, and bring her inside.

She sits down on the edge of the bed in her wedding dress.

"What can I get you?" I ask. "What do you need me to do?"

Marci shakes her head.

"What can I do to make you happy?"

I've never said those words before. There are a lot of things I've never said before today.

"Let's take the photo," she whispers.

"All right."

It's not close to bedtime yet. The sun is setting, and a salty breeze drifts through the open window. I set up the tripod and camera anyway, put on the timer, and then sit down next to her.

"Smile, Angel. You're my wife."

She sucks in a breath and the shutter clicks. "Your wife."

"That's right," I say, turning toward her. I take her hand in mine and lift it to my lips. "My wife."

Marci's gaze traces my movements, my face, and comes to a rest on my lips.

"Jesse."

"I love it when you say my name."

She licks her lips. Her hair rests against the hollow of her throat, and her breasts rise and fall rapidly. Those deep emerald eyes are filled with the promise of more.

"Baby," she says.

And I'm transported back to the night she came for me, my name on her lips, her fingers in her pussy, and those eyes locked onto me, daring me to break.

"Be careful, Angel. You're playing with fire."

"What are you going to do about it?" Marci asks. "Break the rules?"

"I told you I'm not going to do anything unless you beg me to break them."

"Beg you?" Marci asks.

"Yeah."

Marci gets up and walks to the other side of the room. She sits down on that fucking armchair and crosses her legs, flashing me the white lace underwear she's got on underneath her dress.

I groan.

"I'm not the begging kind, baby," she says and slips off one of the straps of her dress. Her finger hooks underneath the second strap. "But I know what *you* can do to make me happy."

"What's that?"

My restraint is close to snapping.

"Break the rules," she says.

I'm off the bed before the words are fully out of her mouth. I stride toward the armchair, and her gaze blazes with a challenge. I loop my arm around her waist, grasp the back of her head, and lift her out of the chair.

Marci lets out a squeak that I swallow with a kiss, furious and hot. She kisses me back with as much ferocity, her legs around my waist, her pussy grinding against me. Her hands rip at my shirt like she can get it off me by sheer force of will.

"Jesse," she moans. "Jesse, Jesse."

"I'm going to fuck you until you can't touch yourself without saying my name," I say against her lips, my hands grasping handfuls of her ass.

I slip my finger over that wet lace underwear. Then I walk Marci over to the bed and sit her down on the edge of it, pushing her down so that she's flat on her back, legs open.

"Jesse."

"There's one thing I will beg for, Angel," I say, and lift her skirt to reveal her soaked, lace panties. "And that's this pussy. Do you know how many times I've dreamed of eating you until you come?"

Marci rises onto her elbows to watch me, eyes wide.

I suck on her clit through the fabric, messy and desperate to taste her again.

"Please," I say.

"Oh my God."

"Please let me eat this pussy every night," I say, and then I wrap the sides of those lace panties around my fingers and pull. The satisfying rip of the material makes her gasp and moan. And then I feast on her.

I suck her clit into my mouth and pump two fingers inside her, finding her g-spot and teasing her relentlessly. She screams and arches into me.

"Yes, scream for me, wife."

"Jesse," She keens. "Jesse, I can't take it."

"We've only just started. I'm going to give you so much pleasure you're going to plead for more," I say, between luscious sucks of her clit. I remove my fingers and fuck her with my tongue. I return to her clit and pump three fingers inside her.

"This is going to be my cock soon, Angel."

"Jesse, I can't. I'm going to come. I can't."

"Yes, that's it. Come with my ring on your finger."

And then I circle her clit, nibble, and circle again, working to a rhythm, testing for what makes her wild.

She cries out wordlessly, coming so hard, her entire body shakes, and her pussy clenches around my fingers. Once she's well and truly done, I remove my fingers and stand over her, one hand stroking my dick through the fabric of my suit pants.

Marci's gaze is hazy, sated, but desire flashes through her eyes again.

"I want more," she says, adorably petulant.

She's fantastic in that wedding dress with those rings on her finger.

Mine.

All fucking mine.

Finally.

MARCI

THIS IS HAPPENING.

It's actually happening.

Jesse Taylor made me lose my mind, my body, my soul, my every-damn-thing. I never understood the infatuation with guys who liked to eat pussy. Because nobody has ever touched me the way Jesse did.

"Jesse," I say, cupping one of my breasts through the lace of my wedding dress.

He's ruined my panties. Torn them apart in his haste to get to me. I kind of want him to do the same to the rest of my outfit.

"Wife."

I shiver, moving my fingers down to the remnants of my underwear.

"Don't touch yourself," he says.

"What?" My temper flares hot. "I want it."

"I'm the only one who gives it to you. Next time you even *think* about making yourself come, you call me."

"But what if you're not in the mood?"

"I don't foresee that being a problem," he says. "But if it is, Angel, I will drop everything to make you come."

The rational part of my brain knows he probably won't be able to do that, but it turns me on anyway.

"I want more," I say again, aware of how I sound.

Demanding.

Needy.

"I love it when you talk like that. You're spoiled."

I raise my chin, defiant.

Jesse unzips his pants and strokes his cock, showing me the full length, the girth.

"Do you think you can take it?" he asks.

My jaw drops. Jesse reaches over and taps the bottom of my chin so that my teeth click together.

"I think you need to come again before it will fit," he says.

I squirm beneath him.

This is sex? The other times I've had sex have been disappointing. And sure, I've heard what it can be like, read about it, seen it on naughty sites, used toys to get myself there, but this is something else entirely.

It's overwhelmingly good.

My body is tense again, ready for him.

"Are you on birth control?" he asks.

"No. I—I don't do anything with *anyone.*"

His head drops back as he strokes his cock again.

"That's so fucking sexy."

He stops touching himself and goes to the bathroom, then comes back with a condom.

I bite on my bottom lip, tracing his movements, but he places the condom on the bedside table instead of slipping it onto his impressive dick.

"This," he says, tapping it, "is for when you're good and ready. Tell me what you want."

"What I want?"

Jesse smirks.

"Tell me your deepest, darkest desires about me, Angel. I want to hear them from that fuckable mouth."

Another wave of arousal.

"Tell me."

"I want you to rip this dress off like you can't stand not seeing my body," I whisper. "And I want… I want you to lose control. I want your hand on my throat while you do things to me."

Jesse reaches up and rips his shirt open, buttons pinging away, and then he places a knee either side of my body. His jaw clenches and works.

"I want you so fucking bad, Marci, I'm ready to blow all over that pretty face."

And then he grabs the top of my dress, the muscles in his chest flexing and rippling, and tears the fabric down the middle like a beast, my body rocking along with the vicious movements.

Jesse sucks one of my nipples into his mouth and bites it gently, sliding his hand up to my throat. He clasps it in his hand and squeezes.

"Say when."

He increases the pressure.

"Like that. Like that."

I squirm beneath him again.

Jesse uses his other hand and slides it down my body. He presses a finger inside me, then two.

"See? This is why you need to come again. It will never fit."

I whine.

Jesse uses his thumb to play with my clit, and I clench around his fingers, my eyes rolling.

With his hand still on my throat, Jesse lowers his mouth to my pussy again.

"I can't get enough of this cunt. You taste so fucking good."

His tongue lavishes me with attention. He worships me with his mouth. And I come so fast, it's almost embarrassing.

"Yes. Fuck," he says. "What else do you want, Angel? What fantasies have you had about me?"

Jesse's face glistens from the pleasure he's given me.

I can't say it, can I? Because it's ridiculous. I've thought about it ever since the day he arrested me, even though it shouldn't turn me on.

"Tell me," he says. "Nothing is off the table."

"You handcuffing me to the bed and having your way with me."

"Wow." Jesse brushes his hand over the back of his head. "Fucking hell, Angel."

"It's weird."

"It is *not* weird."

And then he gets his handcuffs from his bedside table. Jesse turns me on the bed so that my head rests on the pillow. He takes my arms, lifting them above my head and then slips the cuffs onto my wrists. "Are the cuffs too tight?"

"No. I think I could slip out of them."

Jesse laughs. "Of course you could."

He takes a step back and tilts his head.

"What?"

"Just memorizing how you look."

"I want you," I say, because I've lost patience waiting.

I'm wet and swollen and ready for him, and he still hasn't given it to me.

"That so?"

"Yeah."

Jesse doesn't bother taking off his pants entirely. He tears the condom wrapper open with his teeth then slides the condom over his length, his cock pulsing. Finally, he gets onto the bed and places one hand on my stomach to hold me in place. He places his tip at my entrance and presses into me.

My eyes roll back in my head.

"Oh my God. Jesse, baby, please. Oh God."

"I'm going to go slow at first," he says, holding me still, because god damn, I am squirming underneath him, bucking because I want more, but it's already *so much.* "Nice and slow, so you can take it."

He presses into me, another inch, and I'm already pulsing and rising toward him.

"I want it," I say, rattling the cuff beside my head, using my other hand to grasp the back of his neck. "I want it!"

"You'll get it."

He laughs and sucks my tongue into his mouth. He kisses me like a starving man, sheathing himself at such a slow pace that I whine and nip at his lips, angry that he's making me wait.

He presses the last few inches inside, grazing my clit with his abdomen, and I am full. Our movements are electric. I'm so intimately connected with him, I can't think straight.

Jesse takes my legs and places them over either of his shoulders. He kneels, grabs me by the hips and fucks me hard.

"Please," I choke it out. "It's so good. Jesse, please."

He's a fucking beast. His shirt hangs open, his muscles tensing as he thrusts, his defined abs rippling as he pounds into me again and again.

"My. Fucking. Wife," he says, in between thrusts. "Nobody's going to touch this pussy again."

My eyes shut, senses overwhelmed.

"Look at me, Angel. Look at me."

I find him.

"I'm going to leave this pussy gaping, begging for more," he says, and shifts so that I'm nearly folded in half. He captures my throat with a strong hand, the other finding my clit. Jesse's strokes are long and hard, and I struggle to stay with him, because my third orgasm has arrived, and I scream his name through it.

Jesse grunts his way through his climax, his cock impossibly hard.

After, he lays me down and presses a kiss to my forehead then one to my lips. He releases me from the cuffs, goes to the bathroom and cleans up, then brings back a moist towel. Carefully, he washes me, parting my legs, taking care of me while I watch him through sleepy eyes.

And then, finally, he gets into bed and curls my body toward his, whispering sweetness in my ear.

Twenty-Nine

JESSE

I WAKE up in the dark with Marci's body wrapped around mine. One of her legs lies across my abdomen, her arm is draped over my chest, and her hair is a mess. I ache to roll her over and bring her to the brink again.

The memory of her moaning for me has me hard, but there are things we've got to do before we go down that road again.

I get out of bed and head to the bathroom, then slip out into the living room. Mr. Skitters peers at me from the recliner, those little yellow eyes curious. He gives the tiniest of meows.

"Oh yeah?" I whisper. "Now you want to talk?" I grin at him. "You want a bite to eat? I'm feeling pancakes, personally, but I might have a poached chicken breast in the refrigerator with your name on it."

Another meow.

I haven't touched Mr. Skitters yet, but I'm willing to be patient. Good things take time, and relationships are a lot of work. I'm not expecting Mr. Skitters to come running over to me, purring and affectionate. I'm willing to take the scratches.

The wooden clock ticks high on the cream kitchen wall —it's past four in the morning. There's no way I'm going back to bed.

I busy myself preparing Mr. Skitters' breakfast and the pancakes for us. *Us.*

There's no us. We're married, but it's a sham, and fuck me, but I don't want it to be any more. I don't like to think of Marci leaving, but it's selfish of me to want that because she doesn't want to be loved, and I don't know how to love or be loved.

I think about it as I shred the chicken and place it in a bowl.

"What do you think love is, Mr. Skitters?" I ask.

He gives me a "cattish" look. Namely, one that says I'm insane for asking him.

"Are you good?" Marci appears in the doorway, one eye squidged closed.

She's changed out of her ruined dress and underwear into a pair of panties and a tank top. No bra.

I swallow.

"Now, I am."

"You're talking to Mr. Skitters about love?"

Fuck.

"Uh… I made him chicken. I was making pancakes for when you woke up. Did I—?"

"No," she says. "I got cold, and then I couldn't sleep because of reasons."

"I think I might know a few those," I say.

She shifts her eyebrows and rolls her lips together. "Uh, yeah."

"Tea?"

"You never have coffee," she says. "Are you out?"

"Yeah, something like that."

"Tea would be great."

I make her some and set it on the counter. Marci sandwiches the cup between her hands and watches me fill a bowl covered in paw prints with water. She laughs under her breath.

"You really want a cat," she says. "I like that."

"Cats were worshiped in Ancient Egypt. They used to mummify them so they'd join the pharaohs in the afterlife."

"Yeah."

"But I always wondered if they got to the other side and discovered that the cats were the ones in charge."

I take the bowls and set them on the floor in the kitchen.

Mr. Skitters eyes me with suspicion and pads out of the living room and into the bedroom. I've left the bedroom window open a crack so he can get in and out.

"He's not ready."

Marci sounds disappointed.

"All in good time."

I take the bowls out to the back porch. The air is crisp and salty, and I take a minute because I'm about to go back in there, make Marci pancakes, and talk to her about last night.

I want more of her. I want as much as she'll give me. Fuck the rules.

If I can't have Marci's heart, I'll have her body, her mind, and whatever she'll offer me, for as long as she'll give it. Even if it's scraps.

I enter the kitchen and find her whisking the pancake batter.

"Hey," I say. "I was making that for you."

"You've done enough for me over the past twenty-four hours. And before that," she says. "How about you take a seat, and I make *you* pancakes?"

"Angel."

"I want to," she says, smiling. "It will keep my hands busy."

If that's what she wants, I'm not going to take it away from her. I sit down on the stool and watch her move around the kitchen. She's beautiful, even when she's groggy.

"Why were you asking Mr. Skitters about love?" Marci asks, as she ladles batter into a pan on the stovetop.

"Hmm."

"Don't tell me you're thinking about us, Taylor," she says. "Because you and I both know that we're—"

"Incompatible. You don't want love," I say. "I don't have love to give."

Marci dishes the first pancake onto my plate. It's weirdly shaped and a little burned on one end.

"First ones are always a flop."

"That's what my grandfather thought about me," I laugh.

Marci freezes.

"Jesse. You're not a flop. You're not even as much of an asshole as I thought you were."

"Don't judge too soon. I might let you down." I clear my throat. "Anyway, fuck it. I want you, Marci. Physically."

She bites on the corner of her lip.

"I want you too. Maybe we can do the 'friends-with-benefits' thing until this is over? I've never— Yeah."

"Friends?"

"Enemies with benefits," she corrects, a twinkle in her eye. "You *are* a cop."

"Why do you hate cops? Because of Deputy Dingleberry?"

Marci chokes out a laugh, but then her expression sobers. She picks off the corner of the pancake and nibbles on it.

"It's a lot of things," she says. "Some of it's because of Billy. Because I always felt like I was a mother to him in a weird, unhealthy way. I was all he had, and when he started getting into trouble, it was difficult to blame it on him. It still is. It's difficult to accept that I couldn't be what he needed. So, yeah, that part of me blamed you for arresting him."

There's a lot to unravel there, but Marci picks up the spatula and turns back to the stove.

"Why else?" I ask.

"Sheriff Davis hates Billy, and he hates me. Especially after Dad. After—" Marci trembles so hard the spatula shakes in her hand.

I'm at her side in an instant. I switch off the gas, take the utensil from her, and turn her around.

"What's wrong? Why are you shaking?"

"I need to sit down."

I guide her to Mr. Skitters' recliner and dust off the ginger hairs.

"What can I get you? More tea? Water?"

Marci shakes her head.

I sit down on my coffee table, bracing my forearms on my thighs.

"My father died in a car accident," she says.

"I'm sorry."

I touch a hand to her knee, stroking my thumb over her skin. I was aware of the accident, but there's more to this.

Tears gather in her eyes. "He… He had a head-on collision with…" She chokes on the words. "Sheriff Davis."

My eyes widen.

"What?"

That's news to me. News that should've been everywhere if it's true. I've never known Marci to be a liar though.

"Yeah. With Sheriff Davis." The words come out broken. "They didn't investigate it because it was the sheriff, but I heard from a few people at the time that—" She shuts her eyes. "He was drunk. Dad was not. Dad was driving home after dropping me off at June's place, and they—"

Marci bursts into tears, and I can't stand it.

I gather her into my arms and hold her to my chest.

"Not your fault," I say. "Not your fault. This is not your fault."

I repeat the mantra to her over and over again. She's carrying so much on her shoulders that shouldn't be there.

She cries hard, clutching me, her tears wetting my chest, and I do nothing but stroke her hair. There's not a damn fucking thing I can say to comfort her. After Mom, I was inconsolable. It's been years, and it still hurts, but at least we had time.

Marci's father was snatched away from her. Both are

bad, seeing a person suffer versus them being taken away, but to carry that weight so young?

And I'm the asshole that made her life more difficult. No wonder she hates me.

I fetch her a tissue and give it to her. Marci wipes her tears and accepts a glass of water.

"Sorry."

"You have nothing to apologize for. You said he was drunk? Sheriff Davis?"

"There were rumors," she says. "There was never an investigation. Never an arrest. And after that, the relationship I had with Nate dissolved fast. It wasn't because of that. There were other reasons. For a long time, I've associated that sheriff's department with what happened to Dad."

Fuck.

This has to be painful for her. Helping me run for office after that? She's the strongest person in this town.

I sit down on the coffee table again and place both hands on her knees.

"If there's anything I can do to help—"

"You can win," she whispers fiercely. "Win and become the sheriff. Because no amount of poking around or asking has led to anything. I don't have any proof."

For the longest time, being sheriff has been my goal, but watching her fall apart has me twisted into knots.

"I'll do everything in my power," I say. "To win, and to help you with your problems. We'll figure it out together."

We get up, and I take over making the pancakes while the sun crests the horizon over the sea.

Thirty

MARCI

"SERIOUSLY," Hannah says, perched on a puffy red stool in the Heartstopper, "you are glowing."

She pushes a pair of black cat eye glasses up her nose, and they slide right down again. Hannah is the cutest without even trying. She sips her chocolate milkshake.

"It seems like my brother is treating you well."

"Must be that newlywed glow." Riley places her tray on the counter and leans on it with her forearms. "Be still my beating heart."

She's finally opening up after weeks of working here, and I already love her. Riley might not be native to Heatstroke, but she's got that same small town, sweetheart attitude with a bit of spice thrown in. And she's mature for a twenty-something-year-old.

"Mine too," Hannah says, with another enigmatic sip of her milkshake and slip of her glasses.

She snatches her glasses off her face and tucks them into the front of her cute knit dress.

Riley smiles before flouncing off to grab another customer's order.

I'm desperate to change the subject. It's been a month of Jesse. A month of us together at night, of his hands on my body, of screaming his name, and things are starting to get too real.

"How are you doing, Han?" I ask.

"I'm fine. I blocked his number, so that's good. Besides, I'm so done worrying about men. I have bigger plans."

"Such as?"

"I want to redo one side of the library," she says. "Like renovate, but I have to get the funding for it, so I want to throw a fundraiser sometime soon." Hannah taps her chin with a burgundy fingernail. "And then there's the 'too cool for school' initiative to think of as well."

"What's that?"

I pour Todd a refill on his coffee.

Hannah swivels her stool sideways as I round the counter to join her.

"So, it's basically an initiative I came up with that will hopefully encourage more kids in Heatstroke High to get into reading books. There's so much great young adult literature available, and I feel like most of their time is spent lusting after classmates or—"

The bell tinkles over the diner door, and Hannah stiffens, her blue eyes widening.

Carter Savage stands just inside the diner, remarkably out of place. He's larger than life with gray hairs in his beard, tattoos on his neck, and dark eyes that give nothing away. The man is built like a tank, and while I don't personally find him attractive, I'd be a dumbass not to notice how appealing he is. His t-shirt clings to his body, the logo for his self-defense course "Savage Self-Defense" stretched across defined pecs.

Hannah gulps.

"Han?" I prompt. "I think you were saying something about high schoolers being too lust-filled?"

"Huh?"

Her cheeks go red.

"Morning, Savage," I call out.

He gives me a dip of his head and a brief glimpse of a smile. Savage keeps to himself, but he's not a grumpy asshole. I've always seen him as the damaged, secretive type. He comes over, and Hannah blinks up at him, slack-jawed, before shaking her head. The rings on her fingers click against the ceramic as she wraps her palm around her mug and peers into its contents.

"What can I get for you?" I ask.

"Two coffees to go."

"Sure thing." My regulars seldom have to give me detailed orders. Savage likes his coffee black and strong. "Both the same?"

"Yeah."

I head over to the coffee machine, amused at the awkward silence I leave behind.

"Who's the coffee for?" I ask, as I whip out two paper cups. "You got a hot date?"

Han's fixated on her mug, the tips of her ears pink.

"At this time of the morning?" Savage asks.

"Stranger things have happened," I say.

"Nah. I had a long night. Got to set up a training course for the self-defense camp I'm running in a couple of weeks," he says. "Going to be burning the midnight oil tonight too."

"You're running a camp?" Hannah squeaks it out.

Savage's gaze moves down to her hands, sweeps up her arms, and comes to a halt on her face. "Yes."

I pour the coffees, put lids on them, and then hand them over. Savage pays me and leaves with a wave. Hannah watches him go.

"Those are snug jeans," she murmurs.

"You perv," I say, and tap her on the arm. "When are you going to ask him out?"

Hannah gasps. "Ask him out? He's— You're kidding, right? He doesn't even know I exist. He didn't even say my name. He—"

"Hannah, you've spent years going to the same potlucks as the guy. He's practically part of the family," I say. "That was no innocent look he gave you."

Hannah tucks back strands of hair that have escaped from her messy bun.

"He's Cash's best friend. I think Cash would murder both of us if anything happened, not that it ever could. He would have to *like* me first. And I'm not sure he does. He sort of glares at me any time he sees me. He gives me real 'go away, kid' vibes."

"You're not that much younger than him," I say. "You're twenty-eight, and he's—"

"Thirty-eight. Let's change the subject."

The door to the diner opens, and Jesse strolls inside in his uniform. He waves at people in the diner, and a few of them wave back. He saunters over, greets Han, then leans across the counter and plants a kiss on my lips that sends heat through my core.

"Hi," I say.

"Hello, Angel," he says. "How's your morning going?"

"Good," I say. "I mean, apart from the lack of customers, it's good. Did you come for your coffee?"

"Coffee?" Hannah pulls a face. "Since when do you drink coffee, Jesse?"

"What do you mean?" I ask her. "He comes in here every morning and orders coffee."

"That can't be right." Han tilts her head to one side. "Jesse can't drink coffee. He gets the runs."

"Really, Hannah?"

Jesse grabs her around the shoulder, pulls her in, and gives her a decidedly teenage noogie, messing up her bun so badly it droops to one side.

Hannah squeals. "Hey! You asshole. It took me forever to get this style right."

"That rat's nest?"

"You can't drink coffee, Taylor?" I ask.

He clears his throat. "Yeah."

"But then why—?"

"Just wanted to see your face," he says, and sits down at the counter.

But Jesse hadn't started ordering coffee after our fake marriage. He's been ordering it for literal years, since I took over from my father at the diner. I stare at him, perplexed.

Jesse gives me a sheepish grin.

My phone blips under the counter. I need the distraction.

I check my notifications, hoping it's a text message from our group chat. I'm desperate to find out what Lily's been up to. It's so secretive, and if she's making a big career move, I'll be super excited for her.

But my stomach sinks.

BILLY
I got a visit from Jonesy today.

There's a picture attached, and I open it then place a hand over my mouth.

"What's wrong, Marce?" Hannah asks. "Oh my God, what's wrong? Are you okay?"

"Angel?"

Billy's right eye is swollen shut, and rimmed with red and purple. His eye itself is bloodshot, and his nose bears a bloody slash over the bridge.

What the hell??? Billy. Go to the hospital.
You could have a concussion.

Not going to help. He said that I've got
two months to get him the money or I'm
done.

What does he look like? Tell me, please.

I dunno. I'm not good with faces. He's got
ginger hair. Marci, I need your help.
Please...

I don't have the money to offer to him.

Strong arms encircle me, and Jesse pulls me close, that smoky cologne filling my nostrils. I shut my eyes and hold back tears. Jesse takes my phone from me and checks the message.

"Shit," he says.

"What do I do?" I ask. "What the fuck do I do? I can't let anything happen to him."

Jesse takes me by the arms, his thumbs stroking over

my skin, and takes hold of me with that blue gaze. Blue as the sky on a summer's day.

"Angel," he says, "I'm going to take care of this."

"How?" I ask. "You hate Billy."

"I don't like the guy, but that doesn't change things between us," he says. "You're my wife, and I'll do whatever I can to protect and help you. So, here's what's going to happen. I'm going to talk to Savage about keeping an eye on Billy."

"Savage?" Hannah perks up nearby.

"For God's sake, Han," Jesse says. "Keep it in your pants for a second, would ya?"

"Dick," Hannah mutters.

"I'll pay him," Jesse says, "to look out for Billy. Savage does self-defense, acts as a bodyguard, that kind of thing. I'll make sure Billy stays safe while I find this guy. Ginger hair. Is that what we have to go on?"

I cast my mind back to the day that stranger came into the Heartstopper and acted so rude. I'd had the fleeting thought that he was suspicious, but I hadn't mentioned it to Jesse because Jesse is a cop. And the cops...

Briefly, I tell him about the encounter.

"All right," Jesse says. "Eyes close together. Do you remember what color they were?"

"No," I say. "Sorry. But how does this help? It's not like I'm sure that's the guy."

"It's a lead. I'm going to find this Jonesy asshole and make sure he doesn't come near you or your family again."

My heart's being pummeled by affection for a man I swore I hated. It's making me dizzy.

"Jesse," I say.

He presses his thumb to my lips and drags them down a little. He captures my lips with his and kisses me.

"Boo!" A crumpled-up straw wrapper hits the side of Jesse's face. "Get a room, happy couple."

But Hannah's eyes glint with excitement.

"The alarm company's coming by today," Jesse says. "Don't give anyone the code. Not even Grant. I'll close up with you. Got it?"

"Are you sure?"

He cups my cheek in his warm palm. "I've never been more sure of anything in my life."

Thirty-One

JESSE

"I'M SO NERVOUS," Marci says, swiping her hands down the front of her apron. "I've never done this before."

I laugh and adjust the camera on the tripod in the kitchen of the Heartstopper.

"You're going to do great. And the best part is, we get to eat it after you're done."

The idea is for Marci to test out new dishes for the menu in the Heartstopper. She's been terrified of making changes because she wants to stay true to her father's original vision, and she doesn't want to piss off Grant, but it's time.

And these photos are going on flyers and a brand new website I'm helping her set up. We're going to spend the weekend traveling to Prickly Poppy Bay, Yonder, and Santa Elena to hand out flyers and drum up enthusiasm with the locals. I'm a *Kitchen Nightmares* enjoyer, and I saw the OG, Gordon Ramsay, do something similar on an episode once.

I'm hoping it will have the same effect.

The bonus is, we get to spend the night together in the diner, the doors locked, and my watchful eye on Marci.

All over Marci.

I trace my gaze over her body. She's in those sinful jean shorts, wearing an oversized sweater and her apron, her shock of red hair tied back neatly. Her bottom lip is caught between her teeth, and her hip popped to one side as she considers the recipes she's scribbled down on her notepad on the steel countertop.

So fucking gorgeous.

How the fuck am I going to keep my distance from her? The thought is terrifying, given that we're planning a future divorce and that I shouldn't have any *feelings* for her.

But I want to protect her from her brother's bullshit, from this Jonesy guy who's lying low, and I'm not ready to face why I feel this way about her.

"All right," she says. "I can do this. I'm going to do this."

She never used to show me this vulnerable side, and I'm honored.

"So do it, Angel. Show me what you've got."

Marci shoots me a glare that's full of a challenge, and I grin at her.

She takes a deep breath, and then she starts grabbing ingredients out of the fridge. I grab a couple of stools from the diner and sit down nearby, watching as she moves through the space. She's determined. Marci's got the type of walk that makes people get the fuck out of the way, and I like that about her.

"What's on the menu, Angel?"

"So, there are a couple of things I want to try," she says.

"We usually serve burgers, steaks, breakfasts, and that kind of thing, and I want to stay in the wheelhouse of like… All-American cuisine. But I want to try new and exciting flavors. I'd love it if we did quesadillas or fajitas. I love Mexican food."

"Me too," I say. "Hold the spice."

"That's so funny," Marci replies. "Your sister loves spice, and you don't?"

"Oh, Han? Yeah, she's a freak when it comes to that stuff. Enters the hot pepper eating contest every damn year. I'm surprised she hasn't won it yet."

Marci laughs, and it's such a joyful sound, I want to wrap her in my arms and take her home.

"I'm excited for you," I say.

"Yeah?" She chops vegetables. "But how excited are you to grate cheese?"

"Bring it on. But first…" I dip out into the diner and return with the same picnic basket we took to the recent event. I bring out a bottle of sparkling wine.

"What's that for?" Marci asks, as she places the cheese on the counter.

"To celebrate."

"Celebrate what?"

"You being my wife," I say.

Marci holds her breath.

Too far.

"And the fact that you're cooking in your kitchen in the Heartstopper. This is right, Marci. This is what you want, right?"

She exhales, and her trepidation dissolves.

"Yeah. It's what I want. Still nervous, though. I don't want to mess this up. And I want to make stuff that's easy to serve. Mac and cheese, quesadillas, sliders, and jalapeno poppers stuffed with barbecued meat. My dad had this old smoker he used to use once in a while, and I want to do that again. But I need the—"

"Don't say money. It's covered, remember?"

Marci squirms. "I—Yeah."

"Angel. We have a deal."

"You're right. I'm not used to people helping me. Especially not people who hate me."

I pour wine into two mugs—Marci doesn't serve alcohol at the diner—and we toast over the cheese and the grater and the tension between us.

"I never hated you," I say. "I liked fucking with you. You make it easy and fun."

"Well, I can't say the same for you." She takes a sip of her wine and presses those lips together. "I hated you with a fiery passion. Such a show-off. Always teasing me. Always in the right. Always more popular. I guess jealousy blinds you."

"What were you jealous of, Angel?"

Marci takes another sip of wine and doesn't answer.

"Were you jealous of me? Or were you jealous of the women who wanted me?"

She sets down her glass. "I'm not at liberty to say."

"Spill it," I reply.

"You'd have to make me."

I get off my seat and stalk toward her like a predator. I take her by the hips, pressing her backward until her ass bumps into the steel counter. I fist that ponytail and tip her head backward, then bring my lips to her throat.

"Tell me," I say, "or I'm going to commit a health code violation in your kitchen. Were you jealous of them?"

"Yes," she whispers.

I suck her bottom lip. "You never had to be." I release her and step back. "I spent a long time fantasizing about you."

Marci's pretty mouth pops open in a perfect O.

I return to my seat and take another sip of wine.

"These photos aren't going to take themselves, Angel."

She narrows her eyes at me but doesn't press me for more details. Maybe she's afraid of what I'll say. I don't blame her.

There's a lot on our plates. I've got to announce I'm running for sheriff, attend rallies, deal with Deputy Fuckhead, and protect her. And I've got other goals too. Finding Marci's enemies. Figuring out who would dare threaten her. Most importantly, finding out what the fuck happened on the night her father died.

"What about you?" she asks.

I brush my fingers over my forehead. "What about me?"

"Did you always want to be a cop?"

"No," I say. "I wanted to be a photographer for *National Geographic*. Travel, take pictures, be around wildlife. I went so far as to email them when I was a kid and ask what it would take to become one."

"Did they email you back?"

"Yeah, they did," I say, "but my grandfather caught me taking photos out in the backyard. Normal shit, like birds, and this old beehive. I wanted to set up my camera and try to do a time-lapse of the bees coming in and out of the hive. I had no idea what I was doing."

"And your grandfather caught you?"

I drink some wine. "He broke my camera."

"What?" Marci stops mid-chop of a tomato. "On purpose?"

"Told me that I was too much of a dreamer. That I needed to protect my family and the town."

"Didn't your parents find out?" she asks. Her face is a mask of anger, her lips tight and thin, her nostrils flaring. "How dare he? Did your mom or dad talk to him about it?"

"I never told them," I say. "I was about ten, I think, and I pretended that I broke it by accident. I'm glad he wasn't around to see Cash become a country music hotshot. He wouldn't have approved of that either. He didn't believe in artistic pursuits for men. Which is a crock of shit."

"Yeah. Yeah, it is. Fuck that guy."

I laugh and take a sip of wine. "It's water under the bridge."

But Marci chops the tomatoes furiously. "The audacity of that. I get he was from the older generation, but it's such bullshit."

"Hey, it's over. I turned out fine."

Did I?

"But would you still do it?" Marci asks. "If you could? Become a photographer? Travel?"

"I don't think about it that much."

It's a lie. I do think about it, but I don't want her worrying about me living an unfulfilled life when she's got her own shit to deal with. She already worries about everyone else.

Marci cooks the meal, occasionally humming under her breath, and I grate cheese in the silence. It's a good silence. The kind of silence where you don't have to talk to be happy with each other's company.

She preps the food, and I help her as best I can. Then we take pictures of the food. Me standing behind the counter, snapping the photos, adjusting the lighting apparatus I've brought along. When I'm done, I stand with her, and show her the images.

"What do you think?" I ask.

"They're perfect," she whispers. "So perfect, I could cry."

Just like you.

Thirty-Two

MARCI

I GRAB the jalapeño poppers and carry them into the diner, smiling so hard my cheeks hurt. I've wanted to do this for as long as I can remember—a revamp—but I didn't have the guts. And the fact that Jesse's taken the images and we're going to turn this into a positive outcome makes me giddy.

"This smells amazing," Jesse says, as he sets down a plate of sliders on a table. "You're lucky I didn't eat them while I was taking pictures."

"I appreciate it so much," I say. "This is a huge step in the right direction. It's so simple, I should have done it ages ago."

"Don't be too hard on yourself." He comes over and tucks his arm around my waist, pulling me to his side. "You've been under a lot of pressure, and it's not like any of this stuff is cheap."

Jesse's fingers toy with the hem of my shirt, brushing against the skin underneath. He presses his nose to my cheek.

"You should take off the apron," he says.

I step out of his grasp.

"Since when do you tell *me* what to do, Taylor?"

But it's said without heat or anger.

How can I be mad at him? He's helping me with Billy, with money, with revamping the diner. I'm not even sure how I feel about Jesse anymore, especially after his confession when he thought I was asleep, and it scares the crap out of me.

I move backward through the diner, a smile tugging at the corners of my lips.

Jesse haunts my steps, stalking me again, and I love it.

I love how burly and strong he is, and the glint in his eyes like he's about to lose control, the way his fists clench and release, like he's barely keeping himself together.

"You should see yourself," I say. "You're such a thirsty boy."

"And you're a tall fucking drink of water. Come here."

I laugh. "Or what? What are you going to do?"

Jesse grins.

"Answer me, Taylor. What are you going to do?"

"You forgot the magic word."

I tap my chin, rolling my eyes up and to the side. "Hmm. Oh right. Jesse."

"Fuck." He squares his shoulders. "Fuck."

"Baby," I say.

"I'm going to bend you over this counter," he growls. "In front of everyone."

"There's no one else here."

I've reached the door that leads up to my apartment. I hit the light switch, plunging the diner into darkness.

Lamplight from the street streaks through the front windows, illuminating the front of the diner.

"Are you upset about that, Angel?" he asks. "Do you want an audience?"

"An audience!"

"For when I fuck you until you can't think anymore."

He's so close, his cologne invades my space.

The idea of getting it on in the diner is making me too hot. It's so wrong.

Jesse places a forearm above my head, caging me in his arms, pressing me toward the wall. I stare up at him in defiance.

"I told you," he says. "I want this apron gone." Instead of taking it off, he unbuttons my shorts and tugs them down. "But if you want to keep it on, it's the only thing you're going to wear." He slips the straps of my top down and then tugs. My breasts rub against the material of the apron, and I whimper.

I can't help it. Jesse's got me cornered, and his dominant side does it for me. The way he needs me does it for me too.

He leans in, and I tilt my head upward, waiting for the kiss and the heat.

But Jesse steps back.

"You have two seconds to run."

My pulse races.

He holds up an index finger. "One."

I shriek and kick off my jeans, scramble to swing the door open, and start up the stairs that lead to my apartment, tripping over my own feet. There's enough light from the window on the landing to navigate but—

"Two. Here I come, Angel."

I scream-giggle as he thunders up the stairs behind me. Jesse loops an arm around my waist and pulls me into him on the stairs. He showers my neck with kisses, open-mouthed, sucking and biting, his hand palming my breast over the fabric of the apron.

"Such a good girl," he growls and bends me over.

I grab the step above me, bracing myself.

Jesse spanks my ass, and I jolt and cry out.

"Good?" he asks.

"More."

"You want it, don't you?"

"Yes," I say, heat gathering in my core.

I'm already wet for him, and I'm struggling against a wave of dizziness that rides high with arousal.

Jesse spanks me again. He drags my underwear off and tosses it onto the balustrade.

"Crawl up the stairs for me, Angel. Show me how much you want it."

And I do it. God damn, but I do it.

I crawl up the stairs, slowly, taking my time, swaying my hips, the apron dragging between my legs. I'm going to have to toss it out after this, but it's worth it. It's so worth it.

Jesse makes unearthly noises behind me. He's close to snapping by the time I reach the upstairs landing.

"Stop," he growls.

I glance over my shoulder at him. He walks up the stairs and then drops to his knees behind me. He grasps my ass cheeks in both hands and squeezes, his fingers biting into me.

"You are so fucking naughty," he says, and spanks me again. "I thought you were a good girl."

"I'm whatever you want me to be tonight, baby," I whisper.

"That's right." Jesse releases me, and I watch over my shoulder as he removes his shirt. He folds it neatly, then loops an arm around my waist and places it beneath my knees.

"The apron bothering you?"

"No," I say.

Jesse takes my ass in his hands again, then bends over and draws his tongue from my clit up to my entrance, sending shivers over my body. He leans back and slides two fingers inside me, groaning as he does.

"You should see yourself," Jesse whispers. "You're such a needy girl."

"Fuck me," I say. "Please, Jesse. I need you inside me."

"You need me?"

"I'm craving you. Like a fix," I manage.

Jesse hums his satisfaction. "You'll get your fix," he says. "And then some. But first..."

He fucks me with two fingers at first, then three, using his other hand to focus on my clit. He works my pussy like we've been doing this for years, and I'm already arching toward him, drumming my tennis shoes against the stairs, beating my palms on the landing.

"Jesse, I'm going to come. I'm going to come."

I don't hear his response because I'm already over the edge and squeezing through an orgasm, tense and elated, my body aching, my mind blanking out.

Jesse grabs me around the waist again and lifts me, turning me in his arms like I weigh nothing. I cling to him, arms around his neck, the apron blocking skin-to-skin contact. I pluck at it in frustration, and he laughs.

"You want me to tear this off you too? I've ruined too many of your clothes."

"It's already ruined."

Regardless, he sets me on my feet, lifts the apron strap over my head, then reaches around and unties it so that it falls free.

I'm exposed, my top a band of fabric around my waist, my nipples erect in the cool air.

Jesse unzips his pants and moves toward me. He pins me against the wall, lifts one of my legs, and holds the base of his cock, angling it toward my glistening entrance. "I want to make you come again," he says. "But I can't wait any longer to be inside you."

"I'm on the pill," I whisper.

It's been over a month, so we'll be safe, but this will be the first time I've ever done anything without a condom.

"You sure?" Jesse asks.

"Yeah. I'm sure."

He presses the tip inside me, and I cry out because it's even better without a barrier between us.

"Such a tight fit," Jesse says, working his finger over my clit again. "Fuck." The head of his cock is thick and hard, and it pulses inside me once. "I've got to make you come like this. I want you to come, Angel."

"Baby, please."

We're both transfixed on the spot where we're conjoined. Him inside me, the tip, his finger working my clit, the sounds we make. I'm so close to breaking a second time, it's ridiculous. Jesse and I have been together for thirty days. We should be raw. We should be bored with each other. But I've never been so turned on and ready for him.

He's kept his promise of making me come and never letting me do it for myself.

"I want to watch that sweet, hot cunt come on my cock," he says.

"Jesse."

I pant.

And then I'm lost again, clenching around him in the most satisfying way, arching my back so that I take in more of him.

Jesse slides inside me slowly.

"It's too good, Angel," he says. "You're too fucking delicious."

"Fuck me hard," I say, my eyelids heavy with satisfaction. "I want you to come inside me."

Jesse lifts both my legs and rams me into the wall, manipulating my body to his will and pounding into me so hard it feels like the stairs should be shaking. I dig my fingernails into his shoulders, and he brings his mouth to mine, the kiss messy and wet and hot, our tongues colliding, battling to take more from the other.

He draws back and pounds into me, his abs flexing, glistening with sweat in the half-light from the window.

"Say you're mine," he says.

"W-What?"

"Say it," he says. "Say it."

"I'm yours, Jesse. I'm yours. This pussy belongs to you."

He moans and drives into me, burying himself, holding me suspended as he releases inside me, filling me as I wanted him to. The pressure is too much, and I crash over the edge with him, crying out, grabbing at my breast.

Afterward, he slides his hands around my midriff and

holds me, and I wrap my legs around his waist. He carries me up the stairs and toward my apartment door, but it's locked. We collapse onto the landing together, his cock still inside me, and his lips pressed to my forehead.

"Keeping it inside," he says. "Going to fuck you again in fifteen."

And even that's sexy.

I'm lost with Jesse Taylor, and I'm starting to worry that I don't want to be found.

Thirty-Three

MARCI

I **SIT** on the edge of the bed waiting for Jesse, my belly turning over, my cheeks sore from smiling. We spent today in Prickly Poppy Bay, another adorable beach town down the coast with its own cove that overlooks the sea. We handed out samples and talked to locals about the Heartstopper, and the response was positive. I lost count of the number of people who said they planned on visiting for a burger. Prickly Poppy Bay isn't that far from Heatstroke, and I feel success in my bones.

The shower cuts off, and Jesse emerges from the bathroom, shirtless, toweling his dark hair dry, another towel wrapped around his waist.

"I like it when you smile," he says. "You never used to do that when I was around."

"Are you okay?"

Tomorrow's a big day for Jesse.

It's the first rally since he announced he's running for sheriff a week ago, and he's nervous. He's been working with a personal assistant, Greer, trying to get his affairs in order.

"Yeah," he says. "Nervous. Never thought I would say that out loud."

He chuckles.

"Why?"

"Not what Taylor men are supposed to say."

"You're going to speak in front of the citizens of Heatstroke about being their future sheriff," I say. "Of course, you're nervous. Anyone would be."

"Surprisingly," he says, "that's not helping." Jesse laughs and tosses the towel aside. "You suck at this 'supportive wife' gig."

"Are you kidding me?"

"Yes," he says. "You're amazing."

I lose my train of thought.

Jesse comes over and sits beside me in his towel, leaning his elbow on his thigh and catching his chin in his hand.

"I'm nervous because people might not show up. Or if they do, it'll be because they want to watch the car wreck."

"You're anything but a car wreck," I say. "You're a fantastic person, Jesse."

He straightens, and his gaze goes soft as it lingers on my face, my lips.

"You think that about me?"

"Yes," I say. "I think I was wrong about you. I mean, you can be so fucking annoying, don't get me wrong, and I'm still not about cops in general, and there's the fact that you arrested my family member, but—"

He presses his finger to my lips. "You were doing so well until then."

I place the tip of his finger between my lips, and Jesse groans. I suck his finger from the base to the tip, then kiss it and smile sweetly.

"I was talking," I say. "You can't shush me whenever you want."

"You're going to be the fucking death of me. I nearly blew a load from that."

"So romantic, Taylor."

He grasps my throat and squeezes lightly.

"I'm going to punish that pussy if you keep this up."

"Promises, promises."

But I get up and walk to the other side of the room before things can escalate. I love sex with Jesse. In fact, it's the first time I've liked sex, but fucking isn't going to help him deal with what he's feeling.

He watches me, his gaze hooded.

"Jesse, you're amazing," I say. "You're responsible and kind. You're funny. You care about Heatstroke. And you've gone out of your way to help me."

He shrugs. "I try but I can't get any of this shit right. I spent the past week trying to find leads on this Jonesy guy, and I'm coming up blank, even with the description you gave me. And figuring out what happened on the night your father passed is proving difficult."

My throat closes. "Jesse, you don't have to—"

"I want to," he says. "If Sheriff Davis is responsible, he's going to pay for it. And I won't let that piece of shit son run this town either."

"Why?"

"Because he… Because they hate you, Angel. They've always hated you. Why do you think I wanted to run for sheriff in the first place? Not because of my grandfather, but because of you."

I place a hand over my mouth. "What?"

"I told you," he says, bracing his hands on the bed, and there's this look in his eye, one that sends prickles over my body and makes me tense.

"I told you, Marci. I never hated you."

"I don't want you to do this for me," I say. "Run for sheriff. I don't think you should do anything for anyone but yourself, Jesse. You don't need to impress me or your family. You're great as you are."

His Adam's apple bobs.

A scratch at the sliding door distracts us, and I open it for Mr. Skitters. The ginger cat strides into our bedroom like he owns it. He pauses and meows first at Jesse, then at me. Jesse and I stare at each other, wide-eyed.

"Do you think he wants food?" I ask.

"Already fed him. No way he wants food." Jesse turns to the cat. "Hey, we can't give you food. That's too much food for one cat. You're already starting to gain weight."

"Did you just… fat shame a cat?"

"I would never," Jesse says. "But I can't get him into a carrier without getting viciously scratched in the event we do need to take him to a vet for gastrointestinal issues."

"So sexy. Gastrointestinal. Oooh."

"And they say I'm the immature one," Jesse says, glancing off to one side like he's looking into an invisible camera and he's the star of a sitcom.

"Jesse. The cat."

He slips off the bed and crouches down, holding out a hand to Mr. Skitters.

"Here," he says. "Take affection instead."

But Mr. Skitters merely considers him.

"Can you get me a treat?" Jesse asks. "They're in the kitchen underneath the sink."

"Sure, no problem."

I grab one from the bag and return it to Jesse.

He takes it and holds it out in the flat of his hand. Mr. Skitters comes closer, closer, and then, he crunches the treat over Jesse's palm. The way his face lights up is priceless. I grab the camera off the tripod at the end of the bed and snap a photo of his excitement, capturing the moment Mr. Skitters finally trusted him.

It feels like a sign. It feels like tomorrow's going to be a good day.

Thirty-Four

I AM SHITTING COW-SIZED BRICKS. Not literally, but holy fuck, I'm nervous.

It's the day of my first political rally, and there are actual camera crews for local news stations in the park. The stage has been set up, and I'm one of a few people who are going to talk today. We're not exactly presidential fucking candidates, so it's not like we can afford to host rallies by ourselves.

I pace back and forth behind the divider that separates me from the people out there, sitting or standing in the park.

The last time we were here, it was for the department picnic, and that went to shit real quick.

And after this rally, there's a mayoral dinner with the candidates this weekend. If I can't handle this, how the fuck am I going to handle that?

"Jesse, it's going to be fine," Marci says. "You're fine."

But I'm not fine. I'm not fine at all. I'm sweating, and

I'm wearing a suit, which is not a thing for me, and I cut myself shaving this morning.

Marci grabs hold of my hands and turns me toward her. "Look at me, Jesse."

I find her face. *My beautiful wife.* And the nerves fade. "Angel?"

"You're good," she says. "I'm right here with you. I'll be standing in the crowd. Just talk to me. That's all. Talk to me and pretend it's us two alone in your bedroom."

"I don't think that's a good idea," I say. "Getting a boner on stage would probably fall into line with my fuck boy image."

"Funny."

I capture her lips in a kiss, pushing my fingers into her hair and holding her to me. It helps calm me down. She's here and she's real, and she thinks I can do it.

A woman clears her throat nearby.

"Excuse me."

Marci and I separate, but I keep my arm around her waist, pressed to the side of her knit dress. It's getting cooler with fall on the way, and she feels good against my side.

Annaleigh gives me a tight smile. She's got flowers braided into her blonde hair and is in a professional pants suit. Her gaze flickers toward Marci, and I tighten my grip around her waist.

What now?

I don't need trouble with an ex today. Let alone one who edits *The Heatstroke Hit Piece.*

"We're not taking interviews now," Marci says firmly. "Thank you for your interest, but after the last hit piece you published about Mr. Taylor, it's fair to say that we have no interest in—"

"I'm sorry," Annaleigh says.

Marci and I exchange a glance.

"What?" I ask. "You're—"

"Sorry," she says. "Look, my paper is a gossip column, so we write some interesting pieces, but I've felt like that article about you was out of line since we published it." Annaleigh releases a breath. "I—I've been spending a lot of time over the past month thinking about stuff."

"Stuff?"

Analeigh bites down on her bottom lip.

"What I want out of life. What my father wants from me. That kind of thing. It takes real guts to do what you're doing, Jesse. You don't care that almost everybody in this town thinks you aren't worth two squirts of piss."

"Hey," Marci snaps.

Annaleigh waves a hand.

"Bad phrasing, sorry. I'm doing a crap job of apologizing," she says. "Basically, I'm going to issue a retraction on that article. It will go live later today. I wish you all the luck in the world, Jesse, because I—I'm leaving town."

"No way," Marci says.

"Yeah. I told my father I'm not going to live here anymore. I'm moving to Houston. Got a job as a reporter there."

"Well done." Marci smiles at her, one of those gorgeous, full smiles. "That's amazing. Good for you, Annaleigh."

My ex beams at her.

"And good for you guys. I can tell you're truly in love. I'm happy for you both."

Truly in love?

I glance down at Marci. Her cheeks are pink, and her lips part as if she wants to deny what Annaleigh said.

Annaleigh wishes me good luck then leaves us alone.

"Mr. Taylor?" Greer, with neatly parted hair and a houndstooth suit, taps me on the arm. "It's about time. They're going to call you up to the stage in a moment."

"Thanks," I manage.

"You've got this, baby," Marci whispers and brushes a kiss over my cheek.

It's too real. Baby. I'm hers. She's mine. But how much longer is this going to last? The bubble has to pop at some point, and it's not going to be me that pops it, because I've fallen for Marci. I don't know what love is, but it's got to be this.

This feeling that I will go to the ends of the earth for her.

The realization doesn't come with a lightning strike. It's not because I've almost lost her. It's because she's the only person in my life who has consistently praised me for being me. Who's told me that I can do what I want to do. Who hasn't tried to discourage me from taking risks.

I square my shoulders and walk out onto the stage.

The crowd spreads out through the park, and it's immense. Or it seems that way to me. I stand in front of the podium and adjust the microphone. It screeches and wails, and the folks in the crowd wince.

Fuck. Great start.

I scan the crowd and spot Marci near the front. My gaze latches onto her, and my breathing rate slows.

"I'm sure you're wondering what I'm doing on this

stage," I start. "None of y'all expected Jesse Taylor to run for sheriff." That gets a smattering of laughter. "The truth is, I was inspired by a special woman. My gorgeous wife, Marci." I smile at her, and her cheeks pink. "She's taught me that it's important to go for what you want in the way she does business and cares about the people around her. And that's why I'm running this year. Because I care about this town. I was born here, lived here all my life, and I know what the people of Heatstroke deserve. Less crime. A place that's safe for their kids, their loved ones. Where you don't have to worry that a guy with a knife is going to attack you in the street. Or that the police won't take your requests seriously."

A couple of expressions shift in the crowd from bored to intrigued. To my left, Deputy Dinglefuck shifts in his seat and shoots me a look.

This will hit home. Sheriff Davis isn't batting a hundred. After what Marci told me about the night her father died, I've been doing some research of my own. And I've come up against some pretty substantial barriers.

"As the sheriff, my first duty is to the people of this town. That means I'll be restructuring how things are done within the bounds of the law and weeding out those unsavory elements who are acting with negligence within the department."

Applause.

I grasp the sides of the pulpit, drawing my shoulders back.

"And, of course, small businesses are the backbone of our county and our town. I'll be putting extra effort into ensuring that there are more deputies and peace officers present on the streets to keep crime at a minimum. Currently, our department is severely lacking in diversity. I'll remedy that as sheriff. This community deserves peace officers and law enforcement officials who represent what it stands for." I take a breath. People are paying attention now. There are smiles, nods, even. "I intend on having an open door policy, so that complainants can talk to me directly when they have an issue with how due process is being handled in our town. Heatstroke, and the entirety of Wait County deserve better. I'm the one who'll deliver it to them."

The crowd cheers. It's not deafening, but it's enough, and I leave the stage elated.

Marci meets me behind the screen and throws her arms around me with an excited squeal.

"You were fucking amazing. Are you kidding me?"

"You think so?"

"Jesse, you're a superstar. They couldn't get enough of you."

She brushes a kiss over my cheek that's spontaneous and carries more meaning than our friends-with-benefits arrangement.

"Couldn't have done it without you," I say.

A frown flickers across her brow, and she backs up a step.

"The plan's working," she murmurs. "I'm happy that it's working."

I stare at her. "Me too."

A woman with graying hair approaches us. She's tall and thin, wearing blue and red. "That was a great talk, Deputy Taylor," she says, and extends a hand. "Francis Oakes."

We shake on it, and Marci backs up more. I want to reach out to her, but I don't.

"I liked what you said about diversity in the sheriff's department," she says. "That's precisely why I'm running." She gives me a tight, professional smile. "I was a police commissioner in Austin. Turns out retired life isn't for me."

My gaze moves to Marci again.

"Best of luck to you."

I should be threatened by this woman. She's far more experienced than I am, she's well put together, but I only have eyes for my wife and the way she's moving farther from me.

"I've got some obstacles to overcome," Francis continues. "These people don't know me, but I'm sure I can get them to listen. I'm looking forward to the debate next month. I'll be counting on you being there."

And then she pats and squeezes my upper arm and walks off toward the stage.

Marci's already gotten into her old car and started the engine.

I whip out my phone and dial her number, but she declines the call.

MARCI
Sorry. Emergency at the diner. I'll see you at home.

Angel, we should talk. I can tell something's up.

See you at home. Everything's fine.

I glance toward the crowd and the stage. I have to stay

for questions after everyone's done talking, but I don't want to. I've worked so damn hard to get here, but it seems unimportant now.

Marci's afraid, and I'm not going to let her pull back now that I've had her. I can't.

Thirty-Five

MARCI

I'M FINE.

I'm not in love. I'm fine.

I sing it over and over again in my mind. I unlock the diner, key in the alarm code on the pad and enter it. It feels different. Not like home, but like a memory of home. Like I'm looking in on a life I used to live, and it freaks me out even more.

Because this is Dad. Dad is in this diner and always will be, no matter what I put on the menu, how many alarms get installed, or, or…

"What the fuck is wrong with me?" I squeeze my hand to my forehead. "I'm losing it."

I need space from Jesse. When I'm near him, everything is too raw and clear. He makes life seem simple when it's not. He decides he wants to run for sheriff, and bam, he does it. He doesn't hesitate to take risks and make changes, and I feel stuck in comparison to him.

Coffee. That's all I need. A cup of coffee and a moment.

I head to the coffee station, but the sight of the stack of

paper cups beside it makes me think of him. Because Jesse doesn't even like coffee, but he's been ordering it from me for literal years. Paying for a cup he won't drink.

My pulse spikes.

The last time I experienced *feelings* I wound up humiliated and heartbroken while I tried to raise my little brother and grieve my father. What's scariest to me is that these feelings for Jesse? They're more intense than anything I've experienced.

I fix myself the coffee, losing myself in the familiar motions of everyday life. A comfort zone that's uncomfortable because it's another way to hide from the past.

The diner door bangs open, the bell tinkling wildly overhead, and I fully expect Jesse to stride into the space and demand answers.

But it's Billy instead.

My brother stumbles in and then falls to his knees. He reaches up and pulls back his hoodie. His mouth is swollen, and there's a fresh cut over his left eye.

"Billy? What the—?"

"He found me again," Billy whispers. "He found me. I thought you said your cop *husband* was going to protect me too." The word husband comes out as a hiss.

"How did this happen? When?"

"Twenty minutes ago at my place," he whispers.

Billy's rooming with friends in a small house on Fahrenheit Road, and I've wanted him to move since the day he got there. It's not secure, and his friends come and go as they please. But he won't live with me, because of my no alcohol, no drugs, and no strangers rule.

"Billy, that's impossible," I say. "Jesse's been making

sure that Jonesy can't get to you. You met Savage, remember?"

Billy doesn't answer, but lies down on his side with a dramatic exhale.

"He got in through my back door. Frank left it unlocked, I think. I dunno what to do Marce, I don't think he's going to stop until he gets what he wants."

"But—"

It doesn't compute.

Savage is ex-military. There's no way he would let Billy get hurt. And neither would Jesse.

"It's over," Billy whispers. "He told me that the next time he comes by, if I don't got the fifty grand, he's going to take my head instead."

I go to the kitchen and grab a glass of water then bring it back into the diner. I sit Billy up and give it to him. He sips and winces at the pain.

"You need to go to the hospital," I say.

"No! I don't want this to get worse, sissy," he says. "He told me not to tell anyone. It will only make things worse."

"I don't get how this can get worse if the guy is literally threatening to murder you."

I frown at him.

"Why are you looking at me like that?" He squints up at me, one eye closed. "You're pulling that face like you used to when you caught me with weed in my bedroom."

"Billy, this is starting to get real weird. Maybe Jesse's right, and we should call the cops."

I can't even believe I'm suggesting it.

"No! Hell no! Are you fucking crazy? I don't want the cops on this. They hate me in this town," he says.

"Billy, this is the second time this has happened, and if Savage can't protect you then—"

"Why do you want to get them involved when you can give me the money," he says.

"Huh?"

"If I get the fifty grand, he goes away."

"Because I don't have fifty grand, Billy," I say.

He turns his head, sweeping the diner with his gaze.

"Those new tables over there? Looks like you got the stools reupholstered."

"Yes, with Jesse's help," I say. "It's his money, not mine. He's investing, and I intend on paying him back."

"But he's your husband now, right? So ask him for money to pay the guy off."

"No."

"Why not?"

"Because you don't get someone else's money," I say. "It's not owed to you. You're not entitled to it. You didn't work for it. You didn't earn it."

"Then sell the diner," Billy says and spits blood onto the floor.

I blow out a breath, grab some napkins, and hand them to him.

"Clean it."

He glares at me like I've asked him to count grains of sand, but he cleans up his mess. I'll have to wash the floors again later, anyway.

"Sell the diner," Billy says, his tone taking on a quality I don't like. Rough and demanding. "It's not fair that Dad left it to you."

"We've had this discussion before, and I've made my stance clear. Dad left the diner to me. I am not going to sell it," I say. "Especially not to pay off the debt you took out to buy a stolen car that you've been charged for. When's your court date? You haven't even told me—"

"Because you don't care, Marce," he says. "You care about your new husband more than you care about your real family."

"That's not true," I snap. "I care about you, and that's exactly why I'm trying to help you, but I'm not going to sell our father's diner to enable you."

"You've changed," he says.

"Yeah, well, it was about time."

Billy rises from the floor, steadying himself on the back of a chair.

"I thought you were my sister."

"I am your sister, and that's exactly why I'm not going to sell our family diner so that you can—"

"Bullshit. Don't call it that. Don't call it *our family diner* when you don't treat me like family anymore. It's your diner. It's always been yours," he says, and then he limps off toward the door.

"Billy."

He turns back and looks at me.

"Go to the hospital."

"Don't pretend you care about what happens to me, sissy," he says.

I huff out a breath, biting back tears.

"Billy." It takes everything in me to say it. "Billy, the next time you call me, it better be with an apology. For the way you've acted. And for the things you've done. I've never expected much of you, but now, I need more. I need you to be more than this so that you can be safe, and I won't have to worry about you anymore."

"It's easy for you to say that when you have everything."

And then he slams the door shut and crosses the street, pulling the hoodie back up.

I lower myself into one of the chairs, a new addition to the diner thanks to Jesse's funding and help, and squeeze my eyes shut.

The bell tinkles again.

"Angel."

My eyelashes flutter open.

Jesse has unbuttoned his shirt and gotten rid of his tie, his suit jacket is over his arm, and those eyes consume me with how much emotion they carry. Concern, warmth.

"What happened?"

"I saw Billy."

And then I tell him about the conversation.

By the end of it, Jesse's fixed me a fresh cup of coffee, hugged me, and is already on the phone to Savage to figure this out. He paces back and forth in the diner, eyebrows drawn into slashes above his eyes.

"Yeah? That it? Fuck it. Right, yeah. Thanks, Savage. I'll be in contact. Just keep doing what you're doing, man. I appreciate this. Owe you one, big time."

And then he hangs up.

"What did he say? Did he see the guy?"

"No," Jesse replies.

"But how? It's Savage. His past is kind of like… shady or whatever, but he's ex-military, right?"

"Navy SEAL," Jesse says. "And he's not a slacker. He followed Billy from the house to the diner and back again."

My eyes widen.

"I didn't see him."

Jesse checks his phone and then pockets it.

"Here's the thing," he says. "Savage saw Billy leave through the back door of his house and come over here. But he didn't see anyone else."

"What do you mean?"

"Nobody except for Billy went in or out. Not even his roommates," Jesse replies.

"But— Could he be wrong? Could Savage be wrong?"

Jesse gives me a pensive look.

"Something's up. The fact that no one went into the house makes me suspicious. Could Billy have hurt himself?" he asks.

"Hurt himself?" I shake my head. "He's never done that before. He's irresponsible, but he doesn't hurt people, especially not himself."

"Huh." Jesse's not convinced. "Either way. We'll figure it out."

And then he draws me into another hug that sends me into a tailspin.

"Thank you," I whisper.

"Don't thank me," he replies, brushing a kiss onto the top of my head. "Anything for you."

Thirty-Six

JESSE

I DON'T BELONG in hoity-toity places like the mayor's house. I don't fucking want to be here rubbing shoulders with people like Deputy Dicksneeze or his corrupt father, but having Marci beside me is making this worth it.

She's wearing an emerald green strapless cocktail dress in silk that hugs her curves and has ruched halfway up her thighs. When Marci moves, gazes follow her across the room, and I don't blame a single one of these chuckleheads for staring.

I place a hand on the small of her back as we navigate our way around the mayor's vast entertaining room. Servers sweep by, bearing glasses of champagne and entrees on silver platters.

"I'm starving." Marci groans. "Do you think we can steal one of those trays and mainline it somewhere?"

"Fuck yeah, we can." I scan the fancy space with its thick Persian rugs and chandeliers and spot an unassuming server in the corner, straightening his bowtie and considering the guests.

"There's our mark," I say. "Five o'clock."

"What's the plan?" Marci asks.

I trace circles over the skin on her back where the dress dips low. I love that she breaks out in goosebumps at the light touch. The plan is to get her home and make her come. Marci's been more withdrawn lately, and it makes me want her more.

I've spent my time doing what I can for my campaign, working to find out who's been messing with Billy, and spending as much time with Marci and Mr. Skitters as possible.

I never thought I'd be the type of guy who'd rush home after a long day at work, but this is where we're at. Nothing feels as important as her anymore, and I'm still not terrified.

What if I can keep her? Have her forever. Have this forever?

"Jesse?"

She blinks up at me, those gloss-covered lips parted. Temptation.

"Yeah," I say. "Let's get him. We'll grab more champagne and a tray of snacks."

We start moving across the room together, past folks in their suits and gowns, but Davis steps in front of me, his arm around his wife's waist.

"Taylor," he says.

"Davis."

I nod.

"You've met my wife," Davis says. "Helen, you remember Deputy Taylor, right? He's the guy I told you about. The one who always let his drunk dad off the hook."

Helen, to her credit, colors at the description and smooths a hand over her glittery black dress.

"Nate, that's—"

"It's the truth," he says.

Helen rests a hand on his chest.

"Honey, there's no need to get this angry. Your blood pressure."

Next to me, Marci is stiff and stares off in another direction. I'm tempted to pull her into another kiss in front of these people, but the priority is to get her away from this moment.

"Excuse me," I say. "We were in the middle of a conversation. Nice to meet you, Helen. This is my wife, Marci, since your dickhead of a fucking husband forgot to introduce her."

I say it low so no one else except the four of us can hear.

Davis goes red as a fucking beet.

I sweep Marci away from him, walking her toward the server. She loops her arm around my waist and squeezes lightly.

"Here's the plan," I say. "You distract him with your feminine wiles. I steal the platter. Meet me in the hall with two glasses of champagne in like five minutes. Got it?"

"Got it," she whispers.

I kiss her on the temple, enjoying how real it feels, even though we're doing it for show. Marci taps the guy on the arm and starts asking him questions, and she's got his full attention within seconds. I don't like how fucking jealous it makes me.

I grab the platter from where he set it down on the side table, then make a beeline for the thick wooden door that leads into the hall, checking that nobody's noticed our subterfuge. Thankfully, they're entranced with the mayor's wife, who's taken a seat at a piano and is about to start playing.

The five-minute wait for Marci is painful. I place the platter on a side table and tuck my hands into the pockets of my suit pants. I'm not used to dressing up, but if it means I get to see Marci in a barely there cocktail dress, I'm all for it.

She slips into the hall, shutting the door behind her, and spots me waiting. A smile parts her lips.

"That was fun," she says. "A covert operation."

"You like that?" I take the champagne glasses and her glittery purse and set them on the table. "You should see what else I have planned for you."

I press her up against the door.

"Jesse," she whispers. "We can't. What if someone sees us?"

"Then they'll think that we're husband and wife," I say, my lips against her throat. She's wearing that delicious coconut scent again, and it's driving me fucking wild. "And that's what we're trying to achieve, remember?"

Marci's hands move up the back of my neck and into my hair.

"Oh, Jesse." She sighs. "You're such a mind fuck."

I grind my hard cock against her, hiking one of her legs up. She's wearing a silk thong underneath, and I reach down and slip my finger past it, pulling it forward and then snapping it back into place.

"Why did you wear that?"

"For you."

Words I love to hear.

"For me," I say. "I was going to eat those appetizers, but now…"

She moans, and I capture those gloss-covered lips with mine. They taste like cherry, and I suck and lick, devouring her. Marci's fingernails rake through my hair, drawing pain and pleasure, and I want to tug that thong aside and bury myself inside her right here, right now. Fuck everything else.

"Jesse," she whispers. "Baby, we're not supposed to do this. You should be in there. You wanted—"

"I want you," I say. "Why is it, Marci, that I can't make it through a night without having you at least once? What have you done to me?"

I rub my hard cock against that silk slip of fabric between her legs. It's already soaked through, and some of her wetness rubs off on my suit pants.

She reaches between us and grabs me, stroking me through my pants, and I grab either side of the doorjamb.

"Anyone could come out here and see us," she whispers, her tone needy. "They could catch us."

"Don't care. Do you?"

She bites her bottom lip as she strokes me, and then she fumbles with my zipper.

"That's it," I say. "You want my cum, don't you? You want it dripping down your thigh while you pretend to be my chaste, good little wife."

"Yes."

She's panting as she gets my dick out. She swirls her thumb over the tip, catching beads of my pre-cum and raising it to her lips. She sucks her thumb clean, and I nearly blow.

"You like that? Being my good wife, my good girl?"

"Yes."

I tear her panties to the side and glance up and down the hall.

"This is going to be quick."

I lift her off the door and press her to the wall next to it.

"They could catch us," she whines.

"Not if we're quiet."

Which seems like an impossible task at this point.

I hold my cock at the entrance to her pretty pussy. I'm so fucking hard, and I haven't made her come yet.

"Just do it," she whispers like she can read my mind. "I'll go while you're inside me. Please, baby, I'm so fucking horny for you."

"Fuck."

I press inside her, and she accepts me, making the sexiest mewling noises I've ever heard. The silk of her cunt has me on the brink, and I press my thumb to her clit as we pound it out together.

She clenches around me, arching her back and crying out behind her hand, and I hold her in place as I come inside her, pulsing, my gaze fixed on her face, her mess of red hair, the way her lips are parted on my name.

It's over real fucking quick, and I pull out slowly, then remove a clean handkerchief from my suit pocket and use it to clean her up. I place her thong back over her pussy again, tuck myself away, and hide the mess we've made of my pants with my suit jacket. Marci excuses herself to go to the bathroom. She comes back fucking glowing, her hair tousled and her lips glistening with gloss. I go in after her and wash up, then meet her back at the spot.

"Wow," Marci whispers. "Holy fuck, Jesse."

I grin. "You do things to me."

"And you've done a lot of things to me," she replies with an adorable smirk. "Like ruining several pairs of underwear."

"Yeah, well, you haven't learned your lesson," I say.

"And what lesson is that?"

Marci accepts a glass of champagne from me.

"That you need to stop wearing underwear around me."

We toast to that and then set to work on the appetizers, both hoovering them at a rate that would put speed eaters to shame.

"Oh my God, these are good," she says. "What are these things? Like little crab cakes?"

"Crab? I thought it was fish," I say, shrugging. "You're the expert."

"It's got this great, lemon zesty kind of—"

Her phone rings, and I get it out of her purse for her and hand it over.

She answers the call and walks away a step. Before I can follow her, the door opens, and the mayor himself steps out. He's wearing a golden pin on his navy suit lapel, and his jowls move when he talks.

"Mr. Taylor." He claps a hand on my shoulder. "I've been looking for you everywhere."

Thirty-Seven

MARCI

"BILLY?" I answer the phone. "I told you not to talk to me unless—"

"I'm sorry," he says.

I walk further away from Jesse and the mayor, who are locked in a conversation that looks pleasant and I hope, is fruitful.

"You're sorry," I say, and I can't help that my tone comes out flat. "Billy, I've heard this from you a hundred times before. What makes this time different from any other in the past?"

"Because I get what you were saying," Billy says. "I messed up. I haven't been easy to live with. I— I've been scared lately cos of Jonesy. I hear what you're saying."

"All right."

I'm dubious about this. My brother has a history of asking for forgiveness rather than permission. It's taken Jesse to help me realize that. That I'm worthy of being treated right by my family and friends.

"Can you meet me?" Billy asks. "I can tell that you

don't believe me, but I want to prove it to you. Do you think you can come by my house? I've got a gift for you, and I want to show you that I'm going to change. I'll quit alcohol and everything. Maybe that husband of yours can help me, uh, find a place where I can get help."

Jesse smiles at me from across the hall. He's happy, doing what he said he would do, shmoozing, rubbing shoulders with the people at this party, and he's finally got his opportunity with the mayor. A guy with a camera exits into the hall and snaps a photo of them together.

"Please?"

"I'm kind of in the middle of something, Billy," I say. "I can't run out to—"

"Please, Marci. I promise, it will be worth it. It's a real gift. And it's not a stolen car this time. And I've got news about Jonesy too. I managed to strike a deal with him."

"You're kidding," I say. "How?"

"It's too complicated to explain over the phone, but please, Marci. I—"

"Everything okay?" Jesse places a hand on the back of my neck and squeezes lightly.

I like the gesture too much. "Yeah," I say, looking up at him. "It's Billy. He wants to meet me at his place. He's got a gift for me, and news about Jonesy. Apparently, he's managed to get him to back off."

Jesse frowns. "I don't think that's a good idea."

"Yeah," I say.

"It *is* a good idea," Billy says, on the other end of the phone. "Look, let me talk to your husband. When he hears what I have to say—"

"You don't need to talk to him, Billy. I can make decisions on my damn own," I reply.

Jesse turns his head toward the open door and the party. The mayor beckons him over.

"Go," I say. "Go do what you've got to do. I'll deal with this. If I leave to see him, I'll be quick, all right?"

"I don't want you going alone," he says.

"Billy, I'll see you soon." I hang up on my brother and then brush a kiss across Jesse's cheek. "Look, nothing bad will happen. Savage is out there doing ex-military things, remember? I'll be fine."

Jesse gives a half-satisfied grunt.

"I should come with you."

"No," I say. "You do what you've got to do. We're wasting time with this. I'll be back before you know it."

Jesse draws me into a hug, his hand traveling down my back, fingers stroking the line of my spine.

"Fine. But if you need me, call. If you're not back in an hour, I'm going to find your brother and give him some extra bruises."

"Jesse, he's harmless. I'll call Todd to give me a ride."

Jesse kisses my forehead, and I leave him to party with the mayor. I hope things go well for Jesse, I do. He'll get what he's always wanted. But if what Billy's saying is true, then I don't need Jesse's protection anymore.

The only thing keeping us together is his bid for sheriff. The diner's already doing way better thanks to the menu revamp, which Grant *likes* by some miracle, and the work we've done to drum up excitement in the county.

But the thought of returning to my tiny apartment, of leaving Jesse and Mr. Skitters, and missing out on nightly photos, makes my throat hurt.

I accept my coat from a butler near the front door, then head out into the night. Jesse and I came in his squad, so I whip out my phone and call up my favorite customer. Todd's more than happy to stop by and pick me up, and he arrives five minutes later.

I get into the back of his car, put on my seatbelt, and sit back. "Thanks, Todd."

"No problem, Marci."

"The taxi business treating you well?" I ask.

"It's not too bad," Todd says, glancing in the rearview mirror. "Soon enough, I'll be able to pay off that tab at the Heartstopper. Kind of looking forward to it. I've been avoiding the new menu items until I can afford to pay for 'em myself."

"You don't have to do that, Todd."

"It's the right thing to do," Todd says. "You've been nothing but good to me. So, where are you headed?"

"Billy's place on Fahrenheit," I say.

"Oh yeah? How is that brother of yours?"

"Causing trouble as per usual."

I sigh.

Todd grumbles.

"You're the last person who deserves trouble, Marci. But looks like you're finally getting the goodness you deserve. You and Jesse together have got people talking. In a good way. Folks in this town know true love when they see it."

My stomach tumbles, and I clutch the door rest.

"Thanks, Todd."

We arrive at Billy's place, a boxy house with a chain-link fence, and a messy front yard. The lights are on inside.

"How much do I owe you?" I ask, lifting my purse.

"Are you kidding me with that? Free of charge."

"Todd."

"You've got free rides for life after the way you've helped me. Now, go on, get. And if you need a ride back to the mayor's house, you let me know."

"Thank you."

I exit the vehicle, swallowing emotion. This town is everything to me, and after the struggles, I can't believe how good I feel. Even if it's *fake*.

The word hurts.

Todd waits until I'm on the front porch, knocking, before he starts up his engine to leave. I scan the street, but I don't see Savage. He's got to be parked in a car somewhere, watching, because I doubt that he's hiding in a friggin' bush.

The thought of Savage with his beard and neck tattoos peering at me from between leaves brings a giggle to my lips. I knock on Billy's front door a second time.

Finally, the door clicks open.

My brother's eye is badly bruised, but his mouth isn't swollen anymore, and he's got an ice pack in his left hand.

"Marci. You came." He gives me a smile. "Thank you."

I take a hesitant step inside.

Billy closes the door behind me. He hurries through the open-plan living room and grabs empty pizza boxes and beer bottles, clearing off a space for me to sit on the sofa. He drops his ice pack onto the coffee table and fiddles with the hem of his oversized gray sweatshirt.

"You gonna come sit down?"

I circle him and stand behind the sofa instead. He turns to face me, his back to the door.

"I came out here because I still have hope that things can change, Billy," I say. "You didn't get it easy in life, but I don't think that's an excuse for the way you've been behaving lately. We need to have some boundaries."

"Boundaries?"

"That's right. You can't call me and expect me to drop everything."

The corner of his lip lifts. I don't like that smile. It's cocky.

"That's what you did now. You came running over the minute I asked for help."

"You didn't ask for help," I say. "You told me that you wanted to apologize, talk it out, and that you had a gift for me."

"So you came for your own selfish reasons. Because you wanted your gift."

"No, I came over here because I wanted you to know that you're still my family, even if things have been tough lately," I say. "Also, how the hell did you get Jonesy to back off?"

"It wasn't that hard," Billy says. "You want a drink?"

More fiddling with his sweatshirt.

"Why are you twitching so damn much?" I ask. "What's going on?"

"I'm sorry, Marci."

"Sorry?"

Billy removes a gun from the waistband of his jeans and points it at me.

Thirty-Eight

JESSE

I DON'T LIKE that she's not here with me one damn bit.

I don't like that she left to go see her brother on her own, and I don't care that Savage is there to protect her. I should be there.

The mayor taps me on the arm. "Jesse?"

"Huh? Sorry, Mayor Williams," I say. "You asked me a question?"

"Sure did," he says. "I was talking about that ranch on the edge of the town, the one owned by that the, uh, what's his name?"

"Carter Savage?" I ask.

"That's the guy," the mayor says. "Now, don't you think that's a waste of land? Could be used for actual cattle, not these, uh, self-defense courses and camps and whatnot."

The mayor's wife, Trudy, laughs.

"Bless his heart. He thinks he's doing the town a service. Isn't that what the police are for?"

"Always good to have an added layer of defense," I

say. "The more prepared people are to protect themselves, the better. That's the Texan way."

The mayor makes a noncommittal noise.

"Excuse me," I say.

In the past, I would've pissed myself at the chance to talk to Mayor Williams about random shit or relevant shit. I would've agreed until I was blue in the face, but too much has changed for me to do that.

I walk out into that hall again with its paintings and nooks, parquet floors and chandeliers, and whip my phone out. I call Marci.

She doesn't pick up.

"Fuck."

I call Savage instead.

"Savage," he answers.

"It's Jesse."

"Yeah, I can tell from my caller ID," he says.

"Right. Fuck. Is Marci at Billy's house?"

"She is," he says.

Savage has got that unreasonably deep voice that most men would give their left nut to have. It makes him sound like he could wrestle a bear and win.

"Have you got eyes on them?" I ask. "Can you see them?"

"Curtains are shut, but I'll try to get a closer look. You worried? You want me to get in there and find out what's going on?"

My gaze flickers across the gathered partygoers and lands on one in particular. My eyes widen.

"Get closer if you can. I'll be on my way there, shortly."

"Got you."

Savage hangs up.

I pocket my phone and enter the living room. I grab the guy with the ginger hair and spin him toward me.

"What the—?"

The guy's wearing a suit, his eyes are close together, and his upper lip curls into a sneer as he pulls his arm out of my grasp.

"Are you having an aneurysm, Taylor?" That comes from Davis, who's standing with him. "What the fuck's wrong with you?"

"Jonesy," I say, staring at the ginger-haired guy. "What are you doing with him?" I ask Davis.

"This is my cousin," he replies, his head pulled back as he studies me like I'm unhinged.

"Jonesy," I repeat.

"No, not Jonesy. What kind of name is Jonesy, anyway?" Davis asks. "Are you having a stroke? George is a doctor. He can help you if you need medical attention." He gestures to the ginger-haired guy. Davis laughs. "Then again, when don't you need medical attention? Anyone who marries a Walsh needs—"

I turn toward the guy I'm pretty sure threatened Marci, and he lifts a palm.

"Hello," he says. "And you are?"

"Marci's husband," I snap. "What were you doing in her diner, threatening her?"

"I'm sorry, what?" George, Jonesy, whatever the fuck his name is, glances at Davis and back to me again. "I have no idea who you're talking about."

"A couple of months ago, you stopped in at the Heartstopper Diner, and you threatened my wife," I say.

"She wasn't your wife a couple of months ago," Davis says pointedly.

"Look, dude, I didn't threaten anyone. I was in town visiting family," he says, gesturing to Davis, "and I happened to get a drink from a diner. I think. What the hell? It was so long ago I can barely remember."

"So, you—" I cut off, dread tunneling through my stomach.

Oh, fuck. Oh, fuck no.

I grab the guy's hands and lift them. He flinches and tries to pull back, but I don't let him go. I examine his knuckles. Nothing. No signs that he was in a fight or that he battered Marci's brother. He's got manicured fucking fingernails for fuck's sake. This guy isn't a threat. He's an asshole.

I step back, running fingers through my hair as I click everything into place in my mind.

No fucking wonder I couldn't find this Jonesy guy. No wonder.

He doesn't fucking exist.

I should have trusted my gut instinct, but I was too close to Marci, to the issued, to follow through.

I'm moving toward the door in a heartbeat, brushing past people, my phone out. I try Marci's number again, but she's not answering. I call Savage, but he doesn't pick up either. I leave him a voicemail.

"Kick the door down if you have to. Something's wrong. I can feel it."

Thirty-Nine

MARCI

"BILLY, WHAT THE FUCK?" I stare at the gun, a matte black pistol, that's shaking in his grasp. "What are you doing?"

"I'm pointing a gun at you, sissy, what does it look like I'm doing?" he asks.

I can't comprehend how or why he would do this. It's — This is Billy. Billy, for fuck's sake.

"Why?"

Billy's back is to the door, blocking me from an easy escape. I could try make a run for it through the kitchen and out the back, but we are in close quarters, and if Billy wants to shoot me, he can do it while I run away.

"Why do you think?" Billy asks.

"Billy."

"You treat me like trash," he says. "You act like you're better than me. You won't give me what I want. But now, I'm going to get what I want anyway. You're going to sell the diner and give me my half of the money. If you don't, I'll shoot you."

I frown at him.

It's the weirdest thing, but I'm not afraid. I've gone completely blank inside as I study my brother. I've spent years trying to protect him, raise him, make him comfortable, and it's at this moment that the stark realization hits home.

If I'd never blamed myself for what happened to Dad, I wouldn't have taken my guilt out on Billy. I would have raised him better. He wouldn't be this entitled.

But I also can't blame myself for the past anymore. I have to figure this out. Now.

"Say something." Billy rattles the gun, and it sounds odd.

"What do you want me to say?" I ask. "I can't sell the diner on the spot. How did you think this was going to go, Billy? Did you think you'd point a gun at me, and I'd cave?"

His bottom lip quivers.

"Billy, was there even a Jonesy? Or was that you in the diner?" I'm cold as the words leave my mouth. "Was it you with the knife?"

"I wanted to scare you a little," he says. "I wanted you to sell so that we could share the money."

"Why?"

"Because you owe me that money," he says. "We could've split it, and I could've left town and started a new life. Everyone hates me here. They hate you too."

"I don't care what they think."

But that isn't entirely true anymore. I care what Jesse thinks. And my friends. And even the rest of the Taylor family. They've been a family to me when Billy couldn't be. They accepted me with open arms, and when Billy made a scene at the wedding, they didn't mention it afterward. They supported me.

"I need the money, sissy," Billy says, his voice taking on a pleading quality.

"Why? There's no loan shark. So why do you need the money?"

"Because I can't go to jail again, and I've gotta get out of here. Leave the country, maybe. Start a new life."

"What the fuck, Billy?" I say. "You can't run away from what you've done. You broke the law. You've broken the law multiple times now."

"I thought you were on my side."

"You gave me a stolen car, for fuck's sake." I can't hold it in any more, gun or not. "You got arrested because you had a warrant, and I spent so much damn time being angry at the wrong people, when I should have held you responsible, but I was afraid to do that. Because holding you responsible meant taking a closer look at myself. I wasn't ready. I wasn't ready to admit that you are who you are. But I am now."

Billy gulps. The neck of his sweatshirt is wet.

"Did you do that to yourself?" I ask, pointing at his face.

He doesn't answer.

I'm trying to stall so that I can think of a way out of this. Savage is outside. If I yell loud enough, will he hear me?

I can't let this go on any longer. Not the lies I've told myself or the way I've helped him escape responsibility. Billy has to look himself in the mirror like I've had to.

Jesse, please.

But he thinks I'm safe.

I've got to figure this out.

"Answer me, Billy."

"Yes," he says. "I did it myself. Stop changing the subject. Are you going to sell the diner or not?"

"Are you going to shoot me if I don't?"

"Who did you leave the diner to in your will?"

Shit.

"To my husband," I lie. "I recently had my will altered so that he'll get control of it when I pass."

"Are you kidding me with that?" Billy snaps. "I'm your own flesh and blood. And you're going to leave it to the guy who arrested me, who—"

"Jesse would never hurt me," I say, and my stomach twists. "But you would. So I don't think that flesh and blood is up for debate. Are you going to shoot me, Billy?"

My brother trembles. His finger inches toward the trigger.

"If you don't give me money, I'll have to."

"Help!" I scream as loud as I can. "Savage, help!"

I dive down, hoping that it will be enough in case he fires. If I can get behind the sofa, I can at least take cover until—

A bang sounds out, and I look up, sure that I've been shot.

But no, the front door of the house is open, and Jesse charges into the room, gun at the ready. Billy turns, and there's a *pop* that chills me to the core.

Forty

JESSE

THE SHOT HITS me in the solar plexus, and I lose my breath. Pain threads through my stomach, and I stumble, bringing my gun up.

"Mother *fucker*," I wheeze, aiming the weapon at Billy. "Drop your—" But I don't have enough air to say the words.

Marci screams from the floor. My ears ring.

Billy drops his gun and clutches the sides of his head, eyes wide, horrified.

Savage blows past me and tackles him to the ground.

It happens within seconds, but it's like time has slowed to a seep.

I fall onto my knees, my hand pressing against my shirt. This doesn't feel right, doesn't feel as bad as it should. I've never been shot before, so maybe it's shock? I lift my shirt and check my stomach, but there's no bullet wound, only a graze and a nasty bruise. I try to suck in breaths, but nothing comes. Nothing. Nothing, and then—

My inhale rattles through my chest.

Thank fuck.

"Jesse." Marci's next to me. "Jesse, oh my God. Jesse. An ambulance. I'll call an ambulance. Jesse, talk to me, please."

"It's okay," I manage. "I'm fine."

"You're not fine." Her face is streaked with tears. "You were shot. You're not fine." She takes her phone out with shaky fingers. "I'm calling 911."

"I'm fine," I repeat, and lift my shirt. "Look."

Savage puts his knee on Billy's back. He's got the guy's arms pinned in one hand, and is holding up Billy's weapon in the other. He unloads it.

"Rubber bullets," he says. "Strong enough to knock the wind out of you, maybe even kill a deer. You good?"

"Yeah," I say.

Man, I love breathing. Never appreciated my lungs this much. Or the woman next to me.

"I don't have my cuffs," I say. "You got him?"

"I've got him."

"Probably drop the gun," I say. "That's evidence. Marci, Angel, I'm fine. I'm not shot. Not with a real gun, but we do need to call 911 and get the cops over here."

She's shaking from head-to-toe, kneeling next to me in that green dress, her mascara running down her cheeks, and she's never looked as beautiful. I sweep her hair back from her face and cup her cheek then take the phone from her hand.

I make the 911 call, then holster my gun and get to my feet. I head into the kitchen and root around, coming back with a cable tie to restrain Billy's hands in the meantime. Then, once I'm sure he's taken care of, I bring my woman into my arms and hold her tight.

"I'm sorry," she whispers. "I should never have come here. This is my fault."

"It's not your fault for caring about your family or wanting to help them. It's your brother's fault for taking advantage of you. I'm fine." This could've gone a lot worse.

Threatening me or anyone else with a gun, rubber bullets or not, is a serious fucking offense. He's going to be put away for a long time because of this, and I can't find an ounce of pity for him in my cold soul.

I inhale and wince.

"What's wrong?" Marci asks. "What is it?"

She places a protective hand over my midriff.

"I think he might've cracked a rib," I say.

Savage nods. "Possible."

He sits on the sofa, one foot up on the coffee table, his arms folded, and one gray-speckled eyebrow arched at Billy.

"What was the kid thinking? What were you thinking, kid?"

Billy doesn't say anything. He lies on his front, head turned to the side, staring out the open front door at the street, blinking slowly.

Sirens wail in the distance.

The next hour is a blur of motion, and at its center is Marci. She's all I care about. The EMTs get here and check me out, but I'm more worried about her mental state. This can't be easy for her to take, and I do *not* want her to blame herself for this.

Finally, once everything is done, Billy has been removed, and statements have been taken, I place Marci in the front of my squad and drive her home.

She rests her forehead against the glass, peering out at Heatstroke as it passes by, storefronts illuminated like snapshots in a toy viewfinder.

We arrive home, and I open her car door for her, and guide her into our cottage. Once inside, she lets out a breath at the sight of Mr. Skitters curled up on the recliner.

"It's good to be here," she whispers. "It feels…" Marci licks her lips. "It feels like home, Jesse. I can't believe that tonight happened. It was a lie. Billy lied to me about being in debt. He lied to me and used me, and you were fucking right. I'm an idiot."

"You're not an idiot," I say, shutting the door and hanging up my suit jacket.

I guide her through to the bedroom and sit her down on the bed. I remove her shoes and massage her feet.

"You are not an idiot. You're a good person, and he took advantage of you, and that doesn't make you any less. Being taken advantage of is a reflection on him, not on you. It doesn't make you weak or him strong. It's the opposite."

"Stop." Marci pulls away from me. "I'm not the one who needs care right now. It's you."

"Angel."

"Get up on the bed," she says. "Now. I'm going to take care of you."

Marci gets off the bed and sets up the tripod. She places the camera on it, and then she strips off every piece of clothing. She sets the timer and comes over, climbs into my lap, clasps my head in her hands, and hugs me to her chest.

"Are you sure?" I ask.

"I'm tired of fighting you," she says. "Fighting you in real life and in my head."

I want to press her and ask what that means.

"Tonight," she says, "I want to pretend that what we have is real."

She presses me backward onto the bed, straddles me, and kisses my face, peppering me with affection I crave but never get.

Forty-One

MARCI

I'M FALLING FOR HIM.

Falling for a man I thought I hated. Because he's treated me better than my own family. He's cared more than anyone ever has, and that's not an indictment on my friends. More like any man I've met. None of them compare to Jesse Taylor.

I want him to feel it. I don't want to scare him off, but I can't hold back tonight.

"Angel," he says, and there are other words on his lips. Ones he doesn't say. "Angel, you do incredible things to me."

Goosebumps break out over my skin.

I straddle him. I unbutton his shirt carefully, and he winces as my fingers brush past the bruise spreading across his ribs. My pulse races, and I force myself to keep my anger under control because I want Jesse to feel *us* tonight.

I want to erase our doubts, even though I'm not sure I

can wipe away years of history between us, or my own fear of commitment.

"Marci, Angel," he says, his tone gravelly with desire. He cups my breast and pinches my nipple. He winces and groans. "Fuck, that hurts. I can't do much. Don't think I'll be thrusting any time soon. Cracked rib."

I squirm on his lap, against his hard length.

"Baby," I say. "Just hold still. I'm going to take care of you."

Gently, I remove his shirt. I get up, remove his shoes and socks, then strip off his pants, those fitted boxers. He lies naked on the bed, one arm propped behind his head, bicep flexed, watching me with hungry eyes.

"You're killing me," he murmurs. "I want you, Angel. I promised I'd make you come when you needed me, and I can't tonight."

I crawl up the bed beside him, running a hand up his thigh.

"You've been making me come for longer than you realize."

He turns his head.

"What?"

"You have no idea how many times I've fantasized about you, Jesse," I say. "About your hands on my body, your lips on my throat, your cock in my mouth."

He drops his head back and groans, covering his eyes with his hand.

"Holy fuck."

"Hold still."

I position myself over him, careful not to put my weight anywhere that will hurt him, and lick my way up his shaft. His dick pulses, and the tip is moist with pre-cum.

"Marci, are you sure you want to do this? I can't fucking—"

"Yes. Stop worrying," I say, and then I lift his cock and suck the tip into my mouth, lapping him up.

Jesse makes a noise halfway between choking and moaning, and it makes me so wet I squirm. Because I have this power over him, because he desires me this much.

"How many times have you come because of me?"

He hisses.

"Fuck," he says. "Fuck. Countless times. I wish I could make you come. This is torture."

"You *are* going to make me come. How long has it been since you started touching yourself and thinking about me?"

Jesse swallows.

"How long, Jesse?" I ask.

"Years."

"Years?"

"Years. I've wanted you for years, Marci," he says. "I've dreamed of you looking at me like you need me rather than hate me."

I pop the tip of his dick into my mouth again and suck, tracing my tongue over the underside of his head, finding the sensitive ridge.

"Fuck, fuck, fuck, fuck."

He grips the white bedding and balls it up in his hands.

"Relax, baby," I say, brushing my fingers over his toned abdomen. "Relax."

"How can I fucking relax when you've got my cock in between those pretty lips?"

"Because I asked you to. I can't keep doing it if you're going to hurt yourself," I say. "No matter how much I want to." I drag my tongue over the underside of his dick. "Tell me how you like it."

"Slow and steady."

"I need more than that. I've never... I've never done this before with anyone," I say.

His dick throbs in my hand.

"You've never— I'm your first?"

"Yes."

A darkness flickers through his eyes.

"Spit on your hand and run it up and down my shaft. Suck my head as deep as you can at the same time, in a rhythm."

I do as he's asked, and he uses one hand to help me find the right rhythm.

"Yes, Marci, that's it. That's so fucking good. Just go a little slower," he says. "You're so good at that, Angel. How are you so good?"

I color at the praise. I bask in it. I want to give him as much pleasure as he's given me. Jesse's impossibly thick, but I do as he tells me, and I love that he's putty in my hands. He's ready to fall apart, his thigh muscles twitching the closer I bring him to the edge.

"I'm so close. I'm so fucking close," he groans.

His cock pops free of my lips, and I hover over him, holding him by the base of his dick. I lower myself onto him, carefully, so that he doesn't get hurt.

"Marci, what are you doing to me? I'm fucking lost."

I play with myself as I ride him, focused on his face, the

way his eyes flicker up and down, left and right, taking me in, hazy with his desire.

"I'm going to come, Angel," he says, words halting. "I'm going to—"

"Me too, baby."

And then he's rock hard inside me, his hand on my breast, squeezing as we ride through our orgasms together. I cry out, and he moans my name, over and over again.

Afterward, I get up gently, then go to the bathroom, clean up, wet a towel, and come back to the bedroom. I wash him gently, and he stares at me.

"Angel," he says. "You're amazing."

"You are too."

And I'm afraid, so afraid of what that means and how much things have changed, but not scared enough to stay away from him. Once we're clean, I lie down next to him and press gentle kisses to his cheek and temple and earlobe.

We fall into an easy sleep together, the lights still on, and our bodies touching.

Forty-Two

JESSE

IT HURTS to breathe too deeply, but I can move around fine. The medic gave me strict instructions not to avoid breathing fully, which seems counterintuitive, but the woman knows better than me.

I stand in the kitchen and force myself to take a deep breath, then wince and exhale.

"Ah, fuck," I murmur. "That's not fun."

Mr. Skitters meows at me from the recliner.

"And good morning to you too," I say.

He hops off the recliner and shocks me by coming into the kitchen and standing close by, expectantly.

"Food, huh? When isn't it food?"

I grab a treat from the cupboard under the sink, then bend and place it in the palm of my hand.

Mr. Skitters comes over and eats it, crunching loudly and spattering my palm with little chunks. Both gross and cute. Afterward, he licks my palm and then rubs the side of his face against my hand, and I'm so excited I want to yell for Marci. But she's still asleep.

Instead, I put out water and food in the kitchen, then open the windows to let in fresh salty air while Mr. Skitters has his breakfast.

"Right. What are we going to make our woman for breakfast?" I ask him. "Waffles? Pancakes?"

Mr. Skitters flicks his tail and meows, then returns to his crunching.

"Let you in on a secret," I say. "I did something I swore I would never do."

I peek at the bedroom door and then open that cupboard under the sink again. I've got a brand new coffee machine in there in the box, and I reach for it and then cry out at the pain in my rib.

The bedroom door slams open.

"Jesse?" Marci hurries into the kitchen. "What are you—?"

"Trying to get the damn coffee machine out and make you breakfast in bed. The rib has spoken. I've given in to its demands."

Marci's fingers brush her lips. Those lips. Oh God.

"You bought a coffee machine? But you hate—"

"For you," I say.

"I'll get it," she says and takes it out.

She's still naked from last night, and I love that she's comfortable enough to walk around in my kitchen with her tits and ass out. It's a treat, and it makes me feel special.

Marci sets the coffee machine on the counter and places her fists on her hips.

"You shouldn't have done this. I have coffee at the diner."

"Yeah, but you like to drink coffee first thing like a heathen."

She sticks her tongue out at me, I slap her naked ass.

"I can take it from here," I say. "Let me make you coffee and breakfast. I like it."

"Thank you," she says. "I appreciate that so much, Jesse."

Feels like I'm glowing from the inside out. It feels like… It feels like every picture I've taken on my own in my bedroom was a lie, and like the ones with her in them are the real thing.

Like my life before this was fake.

Fuck.

Fuck.

I am fucked.

I make the coffee and fix her pancakes with crispy bacon and maple syrup. Marci comes out with her hair damp, wearing a fluffy sweater and a pair of shorts. She plops down, smelling like heaven, and grins at me.

"This looks amazing," she says.

"I hope it tastes as good."

And then we hoover our food down. My phone blips on the counter, and I lift it. I haven't answered any of the concerned texts or calls from my family yet, and I take a minute to shoot off a few now.

CASH
Are you all right, brother?

I'm good. Cracked rib.

That's fucked up. How's your wife?

I like that a lot. I grin as I shoot off the next text.

> She's mine.

My phone rings in my hand before Cash can text back, and I frown.

"Mind if I take this?" I ask.

"Of course not."

Marci looks about ready to lick her empty plate, so I dish up another pancake onto it and shift the maple syrup toward her.

"This is Jesse Taylor," I say.

"Mr. Taylor. Sorry to call you this early in the morning, but I wanted to get ahead of the curve. My name is James Tremere, and I'm calling from the *Prickly Poppy Bay Times*. Do you have a minute to talk?"

I glance at Marci.

"I'm in the middle of breakfast with my wife."

Is it bad that I don't care whether this is about me running for sheriff? My priorities have shifted. I'm torn between sticking to the plan and following my gut.

"I'm sorry. I can call back later."

I can't lose Marci, and if I don't run for sheriff, she won't have a reason to play pretend. It's fucked up, but it's the only way I can keep her. And there's the fact that I can't let Davis become sheriff. I step around the counter.

"I can talk," I say, and put the phone on loudspeaker.

"Great. Great. Listen, Mr. Taylor, I understand you're running for sheriff. I'd love to interview you about your campaign and last night."

"Last night?"

I scratch the wrinkles on my brow.

"Yeah, it's come to our attention that you put yourself at great risk to save the citizens of Heatstroke. And your wife. It'll make for a great article," James says. "Small town deputy saves his wife and the town from a criminal. Okay, on second thought, that title needs work." He gives a self-deprecatory laugh. "But we can come up with a title."

Marci perks up at the counter and gives me an excited double thumbs up.

"I'd be happy to do a telephonic interview now."

"That's amazing, Mr. Taylor. I appreciate this. It's safe to say that this is going to make waves in the county. I wouldn't be surprised if this reaches the national level. It's such a sweet story."

I sit down in the recliner.

Mr. Skitters eyes me from the kitchen. He darts into the living room and jumps up onto the armchair then sits there, watching me. I lay my arm down and let him sniff my fingers, but don't stroke him yet. He's not ready.

"Fire away," I say.

We chat for fifteen minutes, and after I've hung up the call, another one comes through, and another. Another.

Marci brings me water. She paces back and forth as she listens to the calls.

She wants me to run for sheriff, but she'll never stay married to a cop after her past.

If I don't run for sheriff, I can't stay married to her.

Fuck. Fuck. Fuck. What the hell do I do?

I'm barreling down this road without lights. I can't lose her, and I will do whatever the hell it takes to keep her where she belongs.

In my arms. As my wife.

Forty-Three

MARCI

I DELIVER Todd's coffee with a smile, but I can't focus on small talk today. It's a blustery day with gray skies and the chill of fall, which means the customers in the Heart-stopper want to discuss the weather. And there are more of them than usual.

More Heatstrokers and new faces from the surrounding towns. I love talking to people, hearing their stories, but I can't focus.

My brother's in jail. My brother pulled a gun on me last night.

And I'm in love with Jesse. Or infatuated with him.

The thought makes a fine sheen of sweat break out on my brow, because as much as I'm afraid, I will *never* forget what it felt like last night when I thought he was dying. Shot. Because of me.

"Are you good, Marci?"

Riley stops beside me, touching her fingers to my arm. She's tied her golden locks high on her head so that they fountain down, and she looks delicate, almost fragile.

"You seem scattered. Are you sure you want to be here after last night?"

News about the incident has traveled far and wide, like a flash of lightning or like the townsfolk absorbed it via osmosis.

"I'm..."

"Not fine," Riley finishes, and gives me that broad grin. She's got a tiny gap between her two front teeth and it makes her look like one of those freckled, catwalk models. "Come on. Sit down and have a cup of coffee. Take a load off. I've got things under control."

"I don't want you overwhelmed. We're finally filling up again."

She brushes a hand over her cute Heartstopper apron with its red frill.

"I've got it. You can count on me."

And then she pats the stool on her way past.

I prepare a coffee for myself then plop down and take a few sips. Thankfully, Todd must sense I don't want to talk, and the rest of the regulars are too invested in their own gossip to worry about me too much.

The coffee is good, but it doesn't solve my problems.

Jesse is amazing. Flawless. Unreal.

He's annoying and sexy.

What's going to happen when he eventually breaks my heart? The last time, I had to collect the pieces of myself together again and focus on my family. But what I thought was love with Davis was a cheap illusion. This is the real thing, and it is fucking scary.

"Mrs. Taylor?"

I turn around and find a short man wearing jeans and a

shirt, an unlit cigarette hanging from the corner of his mouth.

"There's no smoking in here," I say, pointing toward the sign. "Can I help you?"

"No problem," he says, plucking the cigarette out of his mouth and tucking it into the pocket of his shirt. "My name is Drake Star from *The Yonder Report*. Do you have a minute to talk to me about your husband? There's been a lot of talk about what happened yesterday. I understand he's already been contacted by reporters from our paper, but we thought it would be nice to get your perspective."

I *do not* want to talk to reporters. They're as bad as cops most of the time. *Apart from Jesse.* And the other cops who do the right thing in this town.

But if this is going to help Jesse become sheriff and achieve his goals, then I'll do it, because in spite of the last bit of debt I have with the bank for a business loan, things are getting better. The Heartstopper has new furniture, the menu has been replaced, and we've redone the entire kitchen. Grant's always whistling lately, and he's compli-mented the new gas burners five times in the past two hours.

"Ma'am?"

"Sorry," I say. "It's been a long morning."

"Of course," Drake says. "I understand you were involved in last night's incident?"

"I wouldn't say I was involved. Why don't you take a seat, Mr. Star. We can talk about it. I'll fix you a coffee."

"I'd appreciate that."

He's peppy and bushy-tailed as he takes his seat. He smells a good story coming.

I circle the counter and make him a coffee, thinking

about Jesse. I'll never be able to make a cup of coffee without thinking about him now, and that's a problem since I make about fifty million of them a day.

I deliver the coffee to the reporter and sit down beside him, taking my mug into my hands.

"What do you want to know?"

The reporter sets his phone on the table. "Do you mind if I record this?"

"Go ahead."

"What happened last night? I heard the sheriff saved you from being shot."

This morning, Jesse had avoided the nitty-gritty details for my sake. Because of Billy, my family, and how it would reflect on me. He'd chosen to play that part down so I wouldn't feel any pain. I can't believe I hated that man.

"My brother tried to kill me," I say. "Actually, that's not technically true. He threatened me with a gun containing rubber bullets."

I break into the story, telling him as much as I can and painting Jesse in the best light possible. Not that it's difficult.

"Wow," Drake says, when I'm done. "Wow. That's quite the story, Mrs. Taylor. You—"

"It's a lie." Davis' familiar voice penetrates the diner.

Adrenaline rushes through my veins, and I turn on my stool.

"What do you want, Davis?" I ask.

"I came for coffee," he says, leaning a hand on the counter and smiling at me. "But I'll stay to be the truth-teller that this town needs."

"Nope," I say. "Mr. Star, we'll have to finish up this interview, unfortunately."

But I don't like the look on the reporter's face. He considers Nate from head to toe. "Who are you, sir?"

"I'm Deputy Nate Davis," he says. "Soon to be Sheriff Davis." He chuckles. "Because the people of this town know what's good for them, you see, and it's not a deputy who lets people off the hook. Miss Walsh here was arrested not long ago. For stealing a car."

"It's Mrs. Taylor," I say. "And I wasn't arrested, I was detained. And I wasn't charged."

"Her family has been a dark mark on this town, and I'm sure that the townsfolk are aware of that. They wouldn't want the Walsh family to be anywhere near the top."

The diner is quiet.

Todd drops his fork with a clatter.

"Don't you talk about Marci like that."

Nate folds his arms over his uniform.

"Come now, Todd, she's no good. Same as her brother. And her drunk father."

I suck in a shuddering breath.

"What did you say?"

"Your drunk father. Not many people know that he was drunk when he had that accident," Nate says. "The one that killed him. And I think the townsfolk deserve the truth."

"Out."

Nate tilts his head.

"Out," I repeat. "Get out. Now. You're officially banned from the Heartstopper. Permanently."

I never had the balls to do it before. I was too afraid Nate would find some other way to make my life hell, with the help of his powerful father.

"Look who grew a pair," Nate says. "That's fine, Marci. You can ban me from your diner, but it's not going to change anything. Not who you are or what this town needs. And it's the Davis family."

"You have about two seconds to get out of here before I call the cops and have you removed."

My voice doesn't shake.

Nate laughs like it's the funniest thing he's ever heard, and like I'm doing exactly what he wants me to. Acting irrationally in front of the reporter.

"Have a good day folks. Enjoy this diner while you can."

The words have a hint of promise.

He saunters out of the diner.

Sound resumes slowly after he's gone.

"That was *interesting*," Mr. Star says.

"Sorry about the interruption," I reply. "More coffee?"

I'm shaking.

Riley comes over and places a hand on my back. Todd stands next to his stool, glaring out into the street.

My phone rings behind the counter.

Forty-Four

JESSE

ALL I'VE EVER WANTED IS to be accepted by this town, but Marci has taught me how to accept myself. And that feeling sticks with me as I enter Longhorn's.

It's taken forever for me to find this lead, but after a lot of digging and research, a visit to the Heatstroke Public Library, and browsing through their newspaper archive, I've found the person I need. I knock on the wooden bar. The glass folding doors that open onto the beach are closed because Longhorn's isn't open to customers this early.

A few servers have arrived and are getting things ready for opening time at noon, loading up music, wiping down the menus, or organizing the tables and chairs around the wooden dance floor.

The space smells of wood and leather, and I like that about Longhorn's. It doesn't smell like last night's regrets.

A bartender pops up from behind the bar. It's Luke, a hoop earring piercing his right ear.

"Deputy Taylor," he says, flashing me bright white

teeth. He tucks dark hair behind his ear. "You're here to see Missy, right?"

"Right. She around?"

"Sure is. She's in the back somewhere. Hold up. I'll get her for ya."

Luke hurries through the back door, and Missy comes through a second later.

She's in her sixties now, must be, with her hair dyed Dolly Parton blonde, always wearing red lipstick and tight-fitting tops and jeans.

"Hey, honey," she says in her raspy, familiar voice. She flutters a kiss on my cheek. "It's good to see ya in daylight. And to see less of you at night."

"What's that supposed to mean?"

"That a good woman makes a good man even better and vice versa. You want to talk in the office?" she asks.

I follow her through to the spacious office, with leather armchairs and a view of the sand and beach scrub that lines the path past the bar. Missy sits down in her big executive chair and gestures for me to do the same in the comfy chair opposite her fuck off big desk.

She deserves it. Missy's been running this place for years, ever since her mother left it to her when I was a kid.

"What did you want to talk to me about?" Missy asks.

"Sheriff Davis," I say.

"What about that asshole?"

"I'm doing some research about the night Kevin Walsh died," I say. "I've heard rumors saying he was drunk, others saying that it was the sheriff who crashed into him, also drunk. I've done some, uh, research, and the only information I can find is a vague reference to a bar. And I've checked with the other bars that were around at the time. All of them are closed, except this one."

Missy purses her lips and moves them from side-to-side.

"I've tried speaking on this before, y'know. Every time, it's been squashed."

"Squashed?"

"That's right," Missy says. "Went to the papers with it at the time too, and the story never got published. Got so bad at one point that Longhorn's nearly went under." She lets out a rough sigh. "I'm pretty darn sure that the sheriff's responsible for the fire here back in the day."

"You're fucking kidding."

"I wish I wasn't. After that, I realized that trying only endangered my business, my family, and the people I care about," she says. "I feel a lot of guilt about it, but I had no choice. It's been so long, though, so long. I— Why are you looking into this?"

"For my wife," I say.

"Congratulations, honey. Like I said, good men and good women."

I nod. "And you're comfortable talking with me about what happened now?" I ask. "Because Davis is on his way out as sheriff, and I'm not going to let him go easy. I want him to pay for his crimes. I want his family out of power in this town."

"You've got no idea the shit that he got up to back in the day," Missy says, and taps her red fingernails on her desktop. "He got away with murder, Jesse, honey. He got away with everything because he's got that position of power. It's no wonder that some of the people in this town have a hard time trusting the cops."

"What changed?"

"Time," Missy says. "Time passed. New people came in. The sheriff got better at playing the part."

I haven't killed anyone, but knowing that Sheriff Davis is faking it makes me fucking ashamed. This town deserves better. So do people like Marci.

"What happened that night?" I ask. "Was Mr. Walsh here?"

"Nope," Missy says. "Kev didn't come by the bar often. I remember he was trying to be responsible at the time. Before his wife left him was a different story, but once she was gone, he took being a father real serious. He didn't want anything in the way of his family or his diner. I think the sheriff resented him for that. At the time, there was talk of Kev running for sheriff. Back then, you didn't need to be a peace officer to do it."

"And did he want to run?"

"I don't think so," Missy says. "He was a family man through and through. Kids came first. I think that's why Marci turned out the way she did, even through the shit that went down." She takes a breath. "You know who *was* here that night?"

I wait, tense. I want to rip the sheriff's head off. I want to make him pay for what he's done to Marci, her family, this town. He ruined their lives.

"Sheriff Davis," she says. "He was here. Drinking. Grabbing the asses of my barmaids and servers. Acting the fool as usual. I watched him get in his car and drive off."

"How many drinks did he have?"

"Musta been five or six. Whiskey."

"And he left at about what time?" I ask.

"Just after midnight." Missy sniffs. "And I heard the crash."

"What?"

"I heard it happen. When he crashed down the street. I ran out, and I saw the scene. Sheriff Davis killed Kevin Walsh. He killed him while drunk driving, and he never paid the price for it. And it didn't matter what I said or who I talked to, it didn't make a damn whit of difference." Missy's eyes fill with tears. "Jesse, you got to understand, I didn't want to keep it to myself. I tried. I tried."

I reach over the desk and squeeze her hand.

"I believe you. But I've got a tough question to ask you, Missy."

"Go on, then."

"Will you testify about this in court?" I ask. "Because I'm going to build a case against him and make sure this goes there. I'm going to make sure that this town knows what the sheriff did to Heatstroke and, most importantly, to the Walsh family."

"You do that, you'll go down in flames," Missy whispers.

"I don't care," I say. "I'll burn the world down for her."

"All right, honey," Missy says. "Then I'll stand next to the bonfire. Just you tell me what you need from me."

I nod.

"We play our cards right, nothing bad will come of this. I promise you that. I'll make sure that Longhorn's makes it through. Times have changed, Missy. Men like Sheriff Davis will pay for what they've done."

"I hope you're right, honey."

Forty-Five

MARCI

I DON'T RECOGNIZE the number on the screen, but I excuse myself and head into the office. The pictures on the wall, my father, me, make me smile. The ones with Billy turn my insides into mush, but the path he's taken is one I can't follow him down.

"Hello?"

"Marci, it's Billy."

My skin goes cold.

There's a storm gathering outside. Thunder rumbles in the distance, the sky bruised, ready to weep on Heatstroke. I clasp my phone to my ear, locked on that view out of my office window.

"Sissy, I don't have much time to talk."

I can't believe he's calling me after everything.

"What do you want, Billy?"

"I need your help," he says. "These cops are talking about charging me with a lot of real serious stuff, and I don't want to—"

"Billy, you threatened me with a gun."

"Yeah, but it was like a fake gun."

"You shot a police officer," I say.

"He's a deputy."

"It's the same thing," I reply. "Billy." My throat works. Hot tears spill down my cheeks. "Billy, I can't help you. I can't help you anymore."

"What do you mean, you can't help me? We're family. You help family."

But it's another of those empty phrases he's used on me over the years to get what he wants. He doesn't want to help anyone else. He wants to help himself, because Billy never got over our father's passing and his shattered childhood. I can't blame him for that, but I can choose to step into the light rather than dwell in the dark with my brother.

"I'm sorry," I say. "But don't call this number again, Billy. I have nothing to offer you anymore. I've tried, Billy, I've really tried. I hope that you'll understand that one day."

"Marci, wait."

"I can't do this with you."

"You— Marci. You can't be serious."

"Goodbye."

And it pains me to hang up on him, but this is over. There is literally nothing I can do to help him. I doubt he'll get out on bail after what he did, and even if he does, I don't trust that he'll do what it takes to get his life together.

I squeeze my eyes shut, remembering everything. The pain, the good times, the therapy, the work, and the way it never made a difference.

The phone buzzes in my hand, and I check it, but it's

not Billy calling back. This time, it's a notification from the bank, informing me that my loan has been paid off in full and the account with them will be closed.

"What the hell?" My heart leaps. "What?"

Another message comes through.

> **JESSE**
> Hey, Angel. You're going to get a notification from the bank some time soon. I paid off your loan. See you later today.

I suck in breaths.

Is he kidding me with this? He paid it off? That wasn't his job. We're married, but it's still—

I can't even think the word *fake*, and it's making me even more panicky.

Outside lightning flashes and there's an accompanying crack that sends a jolt through my body. I try calling Jesse, but he doesn't pick up.

> Why aren't you answering my call? I need to talk to you about this.

> Sorry, Angel. I'm in the middle of something important. I'll meet up with you later and we can talk.

> You can't pay off my debt for me.

> I've already paid it. So I guess I can.

> Are you trying to infuriate me, Taylor?

> The opposite.

His answer. Oh God. His answer is too much. What am I going to do about this? Jesse is too good to be true, and the last time that happened, I wound up in the front of Nate's squad car with my heart shattered into pieces, humiliated.

But Jesse is nothing like Nate. Nothing.

I squeeze my eyes shut and take as many deep, soothing breaths as I possibly can.

A knock rattles the door to my office, and it opens. Hannah steps inside.

"Can we talk, Marci?"

I struggle to respond.

"Oh my God, Marci, what's wrong?" Hannah asks, circling the desk and pressing her glasses up her nose as she does. "Did my idiot brother upset you?"

"He paid off my debt," I say.

"Oh. Yeah, that's surprisingly nice of him."

I swallow.

"No offense, but I'm kind of failing to see what the problem is," Hanna says, grinning. "Was it... Was he aggressive in his payment of your debt?"

"Huh?"

"Maybe he paid it off after a fight? Or to get on your nerves?"

Hannah scratches her ear.

"Nothing like that."

"Oh."

Quiet.

"Okayyyy?" Hannah turns her head to the side. "Do you need a drink?"

"I think so," I say.

"Let's go day-drinking at Longhorn's. It'll be fun. We can have mimosas and read books. And talk."

I love that *that's* her idea of a party. Hannah is one of my favorite people in the world, and I draw her into a hug.

"Han?"

"Yeah?"

"I'm in love with your brother."

"Yeah," she says. "You're married, remember? Do you need to go to the hospital?" She checks my temperature with the back of her hand on my forehead, her tongue poking out of the corner of her mouth. "One of the first signs of stroke is discombobulation."

"Hannah, I told you to stop self-diagnosing online," I say.

"I wasn't self-diagnosing," she grumbles. "I was diagnosing you. There's a difference."

I laugh, and it feels good. Like a break in the tension. Like I can get through this day and figure things out until I see Jesse tonight. I can't tell anyone about our deal, not even now, especially not with the debate for the candidates a few days away. But it's good to say it.

"I love your brother," I repeat.

"Yeah."

"I love him. I love Jesse Taylor."

"Yeah," she repeats.

"Hannah, I'm scared."

"They say you're meant to get the cold feet before the wedding," Hannah replies, tapping her chin, "but you've always marched to the beat of your own drum."

"What if he breaks my heart?"

"Then you can take him to the cleaners," Hannah says.

"Han!"

"That was a joke," she says. "Kind of. Maybe. But if he breaks your heart, then I'll ask Cash to break his arm in the next potluck wrestle-off."

"You're hilarious."

It helps.

"Seriously, though, Marce, you've been through a lot, but he's not going to break your heart. I've never seen Jesse like this with anyone before, and I've *never* known him to be dishonest with women. Our father taught him better than that."

She's right about that.

"Okay," I whisper. "Okay. I'm ready for that mimosa now."

Hannah reaches into her tote and lifts two paperback books out.

"Great. Because I just got these babies and I'm ready to dive in." She hands me one. "Remember, broken spines beget broken spines."

"You scare me," I say.

"But you love it," she replies, and tucks her arm through mine.

She drags me toward the exit, and I feel lighter. Lighter after saying no to Billy, lighter after my realization, but still afraid.

Forty-Six

JESSE

THE ROADS ARE SLIPPERY, the rain pelting down on the top of my squad. I park outside of Longhorn's for the second time today, checking my phone with a frown.

Marci's in there with my sister, and Hannah's got to be involved in her sudden day-drinking. That or Marci's angry with me for paying off her debt.

I leap out of the car and run inside, the rain soaking through my shirt.

Marci and Hannah are the only ones at the bar, both of them in hysterics, leaning on each other, with a bemused Luke in the background looking over them. He gives me a thumbs-up as I approach. He's the one who called me when they started getting a little too loud. There's soft music drifting from the speakers in the corners.

I place a hand on Marci's arm, and she jerks away.

"Hey, watch it, buckaroo. I'm a married woman."

And then she spots me, and her mouth drops open.

"I'm aware. Given that I'm the guy who put the ring on your finger."

She blushes and wets her lips.

"What are you doing here, Taylor?" There's a little slur to her speech, but it's not too bad. "Can't you see a girls' day out when you hear one?"

"Shit," I say. "How many mimosas, Han?"

My sister isn't much of a drinker, but she's partial to a mimosa. She winks at me.

"As many as it took, big bro. You seriously came to ruin our fun?"

"It's time to go home," I say. "For both of you."

"In the words of *Mean Girls*," Hannah says, "'Boo, you whore!'"

"My God."

"They've been like this for an hour now," Luke says.

"Hey, you," Marci says, "Lance. Let's do some margaritas. It'll be fun."

"Mixing drinks isn't fun."

"Come on, Jesse," Marci says, turning toward me. She gets off the stool and grabs the front of my shirt. "It'll be fun. For both of us. Don't you want to have fun with me?"

"I think I've made it amply clear that I like having fun with you."

"Boo. You're in love. Gross!"

Marci colors, and looks back at Hannah then makes a shushing noise.

"We spoke about that in confidence."

"About what?" I ask.

Hannah opens her mouth, but Marci draws her hand through the air.

"I swear to God, Hannah, I'll call Savage if you don't shut up right this second."

Hannah claps her mouth closed and zips her lip.

"I don't know what fresh hell this is," I say, "but we're leaving."

Marci folds her arms and pouts at me, and I back up and grab my phone out of my pocket. I call Cash, but he's not picking up, so Savage is my next best option. I arrange for him to come fetch Hannah then wait for him to arrive before collecting my wife.

"Hey, wait, we were going to have water next, I swear," Marci says. "I swear." She crosses her heart.

"We can have water at home."

"Taylor, do you have to be such a buzz kill?" She digs in her heels, and I scoop her into my arms then lift her and walk her out into the rain. She shrieks at the deluge and kicks her feet. "Are you crazy? It's freezing!"

I feed her into the car, buckle her in, and shut the door.

I'm not angry, I'm worried. Marci is *not* a drinker. She's made it clear that it's not her style, so why now? Why today? There's nothing wrong with some fun once in a while, but on a work day?

I start the car and take the drive home with Marci, quiet beside me.

Might be the rain sobered her up, or she's on the brink of falling asleep.

"Why did you have to do it?" she asks as we arrive at the cottage.

I hop out in the rain and go to her door. I open it, and I'm about to bring her out, when she unclips her own seatbelt and hops down. She wobbles on the spot then rights herself.

"Come on," I say. "It's warm inside."

"Why did you have to do it?"

"Because I want you to be safe," I say, and then it

dawns on me. Marci probably thinks I'm worried about what others will think of the potential sheriff's wife getting drunk. "I don't care what anyone thinks. I wanted to make sure you were okay, Marci."

"Not that."

"Huh?"

Thunder rumbles, but it's further off. The rain hasn't slowed, and it plasters our clothes to our bodies. I take her hand. "Inside. We—"

Marci pulls out of my grasp. "No. I want to know why."

"Why what?" I ask. "You're going to catch your death out here."

"Why did you pay off my debt?"

"Because we're husband and wife," I say. "Because I want you to be happy and successful."

"But—" She licks raindrops off her lips, her lashes fluttering as she peers at me through them, those emerald green eyes capturing my heart. "It's fake. It's supposed to be fake, so why do it?"

"I committed to you."

Fuck. I'm not ready to tell her yet. I need to prove it to her instead, to show her, because words are not my thing. I'm not Cash. I'm not the type who writes letters and songs.

"Why?" she asks.

"Because I take this seriously."

"Why?"

"Fuck, Marci," I snap, taking a step back. "This isn't the time to talk about this. You're half-drunk, soaking wet, and we need—"

"I want to know," she shouts at me. "I want to know why you're taking this seriously."

Don't be a little bitch.

"You are important to me. The most important to me. So help me God, if you ask me why again, I'm gonna lose it."

"We hated each other," she says. "This doesn't make sense. It doesn't make sense that you want things to be real between us."

I freeze.

"Or that you're worried that I could never love you."

So, she wasn't asleep that night. I'm fucking mortified, but I push through it.

"It's always been you," I say it softly.

"What?"

"0120."

"Okay?"

"That's my code for my phone."

"Yeah. You gave it to me."

"0120, is the day." Fuck. The rain drips down my face, runs over my lips. "The day you served me coffee in the diner for the first time. It was January twentieth. You were dressed in one of those silk camisoles, and your hair was down. You had on red, fuck off lipstick, and you told me I could order a cup of coffee or get the fuck out of your diner."

"You—"

"So, I ordered the cup of coffee, and I went and sat down in the corner, and I forced myself to drink it, and I hated every fucking sip, but it didn't matter because I got to watch you. Talking to people. Laughing. Smiling. You didn't see me leave, but I came back." The thunder booms closer, and I raise my voice. "I came back every day and got that coffee so I could see your smile. Does that answer your question, Marci Taylor?"

She releases a breath, and it mists in front of her face.

I take her by the hand and lead her into the cottage, and she follows me this time. I get her in the shower and wash her body, warm her up, dry her, dress her, and tuck her into the bed. She's half asleep by the time I get her into it.

"The photo," she murmurs.

"It's two in the afternoon," I say.

"I wish you never had to take any of them on your own."

And then she drops off, and I'm left alone with that, and the determination to find a way to express myself to her.

Forty-Seven

MARCI

IS THIS A HEADACHE?

No, it's hell. It's a fucking hell in which I am the only occupant, and the cause is my own stupidity. I roll over in the dark, my arm searching for Jesse in bed, and my mouth dry as a dessert. The other side of the bed is empty, and I sit up, then instantly regret it and flop back down again with a groan.

"What have I done?" I murmur. "What have I done?"

The bedroom door opens, and I'm greeted by a meow, and the scent of Jesse's smokey cologne. "The princess awakes," he says. "Mr. Skitters and I come bearing water and disdain for your terrible taste in alcohol."

"What century is it?" I ask, scraping hair back from my forehead. "Don't come too close. I smell like a brewery."

"You smell good to me." He places the glass on the bedside table and turns on the side lamp then dims it. "Like a refreshing Marci flavored beverage."

I groan. "Don't say beverage."

"It's midnight. And you need water and to sleep it off."

"Why aren't you in bed?" I ask.

"I've been struggling to sleep. Thinking about the debate and stuff."

I don't want to ask what stuff. I'm not sure if it was an alcohol-induced fantasy, but the things Jesse said earlier are… They're difficult to process. That he liked me. That he bought coffee that he hated so he could see me.

Jesse sits down on the edge of the bed.

"You need anything? Some Advil, maybe?"

"Yeah, that would be great."

He gets it for me, and I drink it with the full glass of water. He gets me another one.

"How about some greasy food?"

"Not at that point in the hangover yet," I say. "We're squarely in the regretting the existence of alcohol and self portion of the festivities."

Jesse joins me again, this time with his back propped up on the headboard. Mr. Skitters jumps onto the end of the bed and settles in, purring and kneading the comforter. It's a cozy vibe.

"The picture," I say. "We've got to take the picture."

"You want to take one now?"

"I mean, I can't get any lower."

Jesse sets everything up then returns to my side. He loops his arm around me and pulls me in close, pressing a kiss to my temple. The shutter clicks, and I relax into his arms. It feels like a forbidden fruit, being this happy with a man.

"Jesse," I murmur.

"Yes."

"Can I tell you what happened?"

"What happened? What do you mean?"

"With Nate."

Jesse goes stiff as a board. "What happened? When? I'll kill him. What happened?"

I brush my fingers over his chest, appreciating how broad it is, how warm and good it feels when I touch him.

"When I was young. After my dad died. The break up."

He relaxes, but only a tiny bit.

"Yes. If you're ready to tell me, Angel, I'm here to listen."

My stomach flutters, and I take a deep breath. I'm going to need it after this.

"Nate and I dated publicly for a while, but everyone thought we broke up way sooner than we did," I say. "He — God, this is hard."

"You don't have to do this."

"I want to." *Why I'm struggling. Why I'm afraid of loving you.* "Nate and I agreed that we would publicly break up after my father died," I say. "He told me that his father *made* him agree to do that, so all we had to do was play pretend until things had blown over."

"Fuck."

I keep stroking him, and he strokes my arm too, pressing a kiss to my forehead again.

"So, I agreed because I felt… I felt like I didn't have anyone. I had my friends, sure, but they had their own lives, and I wanted support. I wanted to feel loved. And I thought that Nate and I were in love. So I agreed. We used to meet—" I cut off. "We used to meet in his car. And then, eventually, in his squad car once he had joined up. It went on like that for over a year before I started getting annoyed. He kept feeding me the same story that it was his dad we were hiding from."

You can do this. It's not that bad.

"Until I found out that he had been lying to me." I suck in a breath. "And that he'd been dating around for years. We had spent years fooling around in his squad car, with me hoping that it would lead somewhere. He promised me a ring. A place in his family."

"That's fucked up."

"Yeah. So I spent years with this guy, the only guy I'd ever been with, only to find out it was a lie. I confronted him when we met in his damn squad car that weekend, and he—"

"If he touched you, I'll fucking kill him."

"He didn't touch me," I say. "He told me that if the news gets out about us, he'd make my life a living hell, and he'd make sure that my brother never saw the light of day. He married Helen two months later. I'm not even sure about the logistics of how he kept us apart, but I've always wanted to tell her. She deserves to know, but I feel like it's too late."

"He has no power over you anymore."

The words make me feel good.

Nate *doesn't* have power over me. And Billy's made his choices.

"I wish things were different," I say. "I wish I'd never met Nate. I wish—"

"Your dad?"

"Yes. Yes. I wish that," I reply. "But I can't go back in time and change things. I have to live in the present. It's not a bad place to be."

Jesse kisses the top of my head, strokes a finger along my cheekbone.

"You're more than what you've been through. You're more than what he said you were. You have a steel spine, Marci. You hold your head tall when most people would crumble, and I— You're amazing."

He kisses me again.

"Thank you." I've never felt it until now, lying here in his arms.

Jesse reaches over and clicks the light off, settling in beside me. He pulls me to his chest, his nose nestled against my neck.

"I'm going to make sure they pay for what they've done to you."

"What do you mean?"

"Those Davis fuckheads. They're going to pay."

"But how, Jesse? There's nothing you can do. Nothing I can do," I say. "The only thing that will help is you becoming the sheriff so they can never hurt anyone again."

Jesse doesn't say anything more, but he brushes kisses up and down my neck, gentle and sweet. Caring. It's affection that I've never felt before, and it sends goosebumps racing over my skin, and prickles of anticipation.

How can something that's fake be better than anything real I've felt before?

It can't.

If Jesse loves me too, I wish he would say it. He says I have guts, but I'm afraid to turn over and ask him if he feels the same way I do. Instead, I lie there, his breath on my neck, and his ring on my finger, my thoughts on a future I wish we could have.

Forty-Eight

JESSE

THE TOWN HALL is set up for the debate with a podium on the stage, curtains drawn across it in the meantime. A technician mics me up while I sit in a chair, waiting for the event to start. Under different circumstances, I would have been nervous about this, but everything has changed.

Marci is out there, in the crowd, waiting to hear from me, and today is my shot to prove to her that I'll do whatever it takes to be with her.

Francis Oakes, my "rival" for the sheriff position, gives me a thumbs up from the chair over and mouths the word, "Ready?"

I nod.

Deputy Dickfuck arrives late, buttoning up his pants and straightening them. He sits down in a chair in between us, casting a look left and then right. He leans over to my side.

"You ready to get your ass handed to you?" he murmurs. "That little slut wife of yours is going to regret—"

I grab the front of his shirt and pull him out of his chair so he's in my face. Davis chokes on his own saliva.

"I'm done playing nice with you," I say, covering my microphone. "If you talk about my wife like that again, I'll remove your tongue."

And then I shove him backward so he sprawls on the stage.

Davis rises, pulling his suit straight, opening his mouth, but he's interrupted by the moderator in front of the curtains, welcoming everyone to the debate.

Davis gives me a look, bottom lip quivering in its sneer, and sits in his chair. He composes himself and puts up a fake ass smile.

Maybe there's some part of this motherfucker that's desperately seeking approval from his bully of a father. Maybe he has his own deeper reason for doing what he does, but I don't care. Sometimes, people are bad, through and through, and there's no helping them.

But I'm going to make sure his family never hurts this town or my woman again.

The curtains open, and there's a round of raucous applause from the gathered townsfolk. There are plenty of familiar faces and others who are likely from the other towns in the county. I scan them until I find *her*.

Marci's in the third row, a nervous smile parting those kissable lips. Her red hair falls around her shoulders in waves, and she's chosen another of those fitted knit dresses for today. She's an angel. An actual angel, and she makes doing this worthwhile.

"We're going to hear from our candidates on important issues today," the moderator says. "And we'll have a chance for questions at the end of our debate. First, let's hear from each of the candidates before we get into the relevant issues. I'm going to ask that the audience behave respectfully. Anyone who interrupts the candidates while they're talking will be removed. Thank you."

A polite smattering of clapping. Someone coughs in the back of the hall.

"First, we'll hear from Deputy Davis."

Dickhead spends the next eternity talking about the legacy of Heatstroke and how his family has been at the forefront of keeping the town safe. The audience seems warm, particularly the younger people in the crowd, but the older folks are skeptical, arms crossed. I pick them out in the crowd as Davis talks. They don't buy it based on the glares they're shooting at him.

Davis is a master manipulator. By the end of his speech, people cheer and stamp their feet. He returns to his seat with a vicious smile.

"Follow that," he mouths.

"Deputy Taylor will talk about his campaign next."

Fuck. This is it.

I get up and approach the podium.

Marci cheers.

"Go, Jesse! Let's go, you've got this, baby."

She claps and whoops, and I grin at her, drawing my shoulders back.

"Thanks for being here today, everyone," I say. "There are many reasons I want to run for sheriff. Because I care about this town and its people, because I believe in doing the right thing, and because of justice. A lot of you, especially those who have been around the county and specifically in Heatstroke for many years, are aware that justice has been elusive in this town."

Davis' chair squeaks behind me.

Marci frowns and glances at the others in the crowd. They're listening. There's a silence in the hall that verges on uncomfortable.

"For a long time, Heatstroke and the county have been under the care of the Davis family," I say. "I use the word 'care' lightly, because while they may have kept criminals off the streets, they've also used their position to abuse this town's justice system."

More shocked faces.

"The sheriff's department is fraught with nepotism and corruption. It's not diverse. It hasn't been audited in years, and because of that, Sheriff Davis has had free rein to commit crimes and hide them. To take advantage of the people of this town and play by his own set of rules. Rules that only apply to his family."

Davis' chair scrapes back.

"Hey, what the hell? Moderator, are you going to allow slander on the stage?"

"Quiet down, Candidate Davis," the moderator says. "You will have time to rebut. Deputy Taylor, please continue without defamatory claims."

"That's the thing," I say. "They're not defamatory. I can prove them, and I will prove them in a court of law. It's never been my intention to run a smear campaign to get my way. And the past few months have helped me come to a clear realization of what I want for this town and my own life. I've realized," I say, my throat drying, "that I care more about my relationship with my wife than I do anything else. It's for this reason that I will be withdrawing from the running to be sheriff. I yield to Candidate Oakes."

Marci's gone pale, her hand flies to her throat.

"Jesse?" she mouths.

Mrs. Oakes walks up to the podium.

"Thank you, Mr. Taylor," she says. "I appreciate your speech. As my first order of business as sheriff, I will see to it that cases that have fallen by the wayside or that have been purposefully brushed under the rug by the current sheriff will be brought to light and re-investigated. I am, of course, referring to the accusations of intoxication manslaughter that have been leveraged against him."

"This is bullshit," Davis leaps out of his chair.

The crowd breaks into whispers that become a hum of anger. People stare at Davis like he's a stranger. Tears roll down Marci's cheeks. She swallows. She realizes what Oakes means.

Investigating her father's case.

Her gaze flickers to my face.

"I will be ensuring that a full audit of the entire department takes place. That audit will be implemented on the day I'm voted into office," Oakes says, and then she turns and gives me a tight-lipped smile, her eyes crinkling at the corners. Determined. "As for references to diversity in the department, on this point, Deputy Taylor and I are in agreement. I'll be inviting new officers of every creed, color, and gender identification to apply to the department to become a deputy. This town's peace officers should be representative of its people."

That brings cheers, especially among the younger folks in the crowd.

"You fuck." Davis turns toward me. "I'll kill you for this. I'll kill you!"

He's red in the face, his body shaking with rage.

I get up and take a step back so that everyone can see what's going on. The moderator perks up, tapping her pen on her desk near the front of the stage.

"Candidate Davis, take your seat. Threaten a candidate again and you will be removed from—"

But Davis can't stand it.

He can't stand being told what to do by a woman. Can't stand that his world is crumbling around his ears.

He roars and dashes toward me, winding up his fist. He punches, and I dodge, then grab him around the throat and put him in a headlock. I hold him there, rip the microphone free from my lapel and drop it to the stage, then lean in and whisper in his ear.

"I told you not to fuck with Marci. I warned you. Now you're going to experience the full weight of your actions, you little good-for-nothing weasel, and I am going to watch you *burn*."

Security runs up on stage, huffing and puffing, and takes Nate from me. He howls and kicks as he's dragged away, and the town hall is thrown into complete disarray.

Forty-Nine

MARCI

I CAN'T FIND JESSE.

He's not at the town hall anymore, and his squad car is gone. He left his cell phone at home, so that's out of the question too. I'm stunned by what's gone down.

Jesse's pulled out of the race. He doesn't need me anymore, but his words on the stage said different. That he cares about his wife? The lines are so blurred, they've ceased to exist, and I'm struggling to catch up.

I love him, and he's doing everything in his power to give me what I want. Freedom, justice, and love. And now he's given up on being sheriff, on, essentially, the approval of the town and his family for me.

I get in my car and ride out to the cottage, hoping to find him there.

My heart sinks.

The squad car isn't outside.

But the front door is open.

I park and get out, twisting the ends of my sleeves into my palms. "Jesse?" I call out. "Jesse, are you home?"

The sea breeze brushes my hair, and sunshine slants down from the heavens, illuminating the quaint cottage. I walk up the stepping-stone path and enter the open-plan living room and kitchen. I make it two paces before I stop.

My pulse races, tears gather and spill over.

Mr. Skitters is on the recliner, wearing a cute green collar. He meows at me impetuously, as if asking me to hurry up and feed him already. He's adorable, but he's not the reason I'm crying.

The walls are plastered with pictures.

A slow progression from one side of the room to the bedroom door. Images of Jesse sitting alone on his bed. Head in his hands. Expression pained. Lying back on his bed with his face covered. Hunched over, one heel elevated off the floor. Standing in front of his bed, his fists balled at his sides.

Most of them are of him seated, staring blankly at the camera.

And then us.

The first picture of me sitting next to him, both of us looking serious. The next with his arm around me, and then every day for months, us together, going from somber to smiling. Jesse's eyes shimmering with excitement as he talks to me, or me laughing, my head thrown back. Me in his lap, naked, clutching his head to my chest, his eyes penetrating through the picture as he stares past my shoulder.

I stumble a little as I track us through the pictures. As I witness the way his face changes, the worry and sadness fall away, replaced by joy. It's like we're both shining from the inside out.

There are more photos too, of me alone. Pictures taken

of me in the diner, in the mornings, laughing with a customer, serving coffee, or leaning my elbow on the countertop and staring pensively out of the windows of the diner into the street.

Pictures I didn't know he'd taken of me.

My heart flips as I enter the bedroom and find more of them, me with his family at potlucks or wrestling or hanging out with my girls. The pictures are beautifully taken.

Jesse stands near the back sliding door, his dark hair mussed by the ocean air. He's taken his suit jacket off, rolled up the sleeves of his shirt, his forearm muscles working as he clenches and unclenches his fists, shakes his hands at his sides.

"I'm nervous," he says. "I didn't want you to think I was a stalker. But I wanted to…" Jesse clears his throat. "I'm not good with words."

I can't find anything to say either.

"It's been you since before I understood what it meant to be in love."

"In love?"

"Yes," he says. "In love. Before I knew what it meant. But I know now." He comes forward a step. "I know what it means to be in love."

"What does it mean?" I ask.

Because I'm genuinely curious, even with tears spilling down my cheeks, even as I study the years' worth of pining for me. I want to hear it from his mouth. I need it like I need to breathe.

"It means… It means…" He scrubs his hand over the back of his neck. "It means I quit my job today. Because you taught me that I don't need to be like my grandfather to be good enough."

"Jesse."

He holds up a palm. "It means that the ring on your finger is real."

"Real?"

"Yes. It's real. The diamond is real. It's not a moissanite. I couldn't— I couldn't put a fake ring on your finger, Marci." He takes a break. "Love means that I will do anything to take away the pain others have caused you. That I will spend the rest of my life ensuring that you wake up to fresh coffee and pancakes. That I will carry you to bed when you are tired. I will care for you when you are sick. I will stand for you when no one else will. And I will accept you as you are. Now and forever, Marci Walsh."

"Jesse." The word is strangled.

"It means that I love you with the wretched, torn parts of my soul. And I hope that it will be enough for you to love me back." He drops to his knees in front of me, taking both of my hands in his. He kisses them and presses them to his cheeks. His eyes are fixed on me. Blue as the waves crashing on the beach outside our home. "Please, Marci, please be my *real* wife. You've helped me realize that I can love, and that I want to love, and that I was always worthy of love, and there is nothing in the world that I won't do to make you happy."

"Please stand," I whisper. "You don't deserve to kneel in front of anyone, Jesse."

Jesse gets up, and I throw myself onto him, wrap my legs around his waist, my arms around his neck.

"Yes," I whisper. "Yes, yes, yes. I want to be with you forever. Forever."

"You swear?" he chokes it out.

"I swear. I love you too, Jesse Taylor. I love you more than anything."

He cups the back of my head in his hands and brings his lips to mine, claiming me completely. He walks me back to the bed, and we fall onto it together, kissing, crying, and laughing. Because this is it.

This is us.

We've taken each other's wounds and helped each other heal. There's nothing fake about who we've become or our future together. Especially when we'll be spending every second of it in each other's arms.

Mr. Skitters meows from the bedroom door, and Jesse and I quit kissing, sharing an amused look.

"We'd better feed him," I say. "He'll never give us any peace."

"This is what we get for being cat parents," he replies.

Jesse and I head into the kitchen of our cute cottage, Mr. Skitters' purring, his little ginger tail shaking as he follows us, and I capture the moment in my memory. Like a photograph.

Epilogue

JESSE

"IT'S HAPPENING," I say, slapping down the newspaper on the counter in the Heartstopper.

Marci leans her palms on the counter, popping one of those delicious fucking hips as she studies it. She covers her mouth with one hand, but she can't hide the joy that shines past her fingers, the smile, the tears.

"Oh my God, Jesse. Oh my God."

"It's happening," I repeat, triumph in my tone. "Come here, Angel."

"Baby!" She squeals it out, and Hannah makes a gagging noise from the stool nearby.

We ignore my sister as Marci rounds the counter and runs to me. She throws her arms around my waist and squeezes me hard.

"Oh my God. Oh my God."

She says it over and over again.

I hold her tight. It's not right to laugh or lift her, because the fact is, she should never have lost her father.

But the news that Sheriff Oakes is making good on her promises is uplifting. The case against that asshole ex-sheriff is being built as we speak.

"Congratulations, Marci," Hannah says, and jumps up to hug her too. She squeezes her then sits down again, watching us with a broad smile.

"Are you ready for this?" I ask, cupping Marci's cheeks in my palms, my thumbs wiping away tears. "They're going to contact you to testify."

"I'll do whatever it takes to see justice served," she replies.

"And I'll be with you," I murmur, brushing her hair back from her face.

I kiss her beside the ear, gently, and enjoy the way she leans into me, clutching my shirt.

"Jesse."

She tilts her head back, her breath chasing across my lips.

I tug down on that soft bottom lip, hungering for her.

"Guys, seriously," Hannah says. "It's been six months. When is the honeymoon phase going to end, because this is out of hand. You two are practically eye-sexing each other in public."

"Eye-sexing?" Marci and I ask in unison.

Hannah sticks out her tongue at us and then takes a bite of her burger.

"Whatever. I need more jalapenos."

"Still preparing for the pepper-eating contest?" I ask.

"Hell yeah, I am," she says. "I've got to have a stomach of steel if I want to win. You think it's the burning tongue that gets ya? Wait until it's on the way out. The other end."

Marci grimaces and returns to her spot behind the counter.

"Grant, you got the jar?"

"Again?"

"Again."

The cranky chef slaps down a jar of pickled peppers in the kitchen window. Marci takes it, hands it to me, and I pop the lid off, then place it in front of my sister.

Hannah removes a pepper by the stem and lifts it.

"They're packed with vitamin C. Great way to fight off the cold."

"And kill your tastebuds," I say.

"Can't take the heat, get out of the pepper-eating contest," she replies and crunches down on the jalapeno.

Marci's gaze is on the paper, the bold print headline declaring the audit and the breaking news about the last sheriff.

"I can't believe this is happening. I can't believe he's finally going to pay for what he did. Jesse, this is because of you. This is your doing."

"It's us," I say. "Not me. We're a team."

Marci beams at me, beautiful as ever. Perfect. It's like I can see her soul shining through, and it glimmers so bright, it's the only thing I can see.

Hannah leans over and peers at the newspaper headline.

"Still can't believe he got away with it for so long. Did you hear about Nate?"

Both Marci and I snap our attention to my little sister.

"What about him?" Marci asks.

"We haven't been keeping track," I add in.

"Yeah, well, you've both been preoccupied with each other."

"And the diner," Marci adds. "And setting up Jesse's new business."

I've been taking photos. Weddings, kids, pets, anything I can. I don't need the money, but I want to do it, and it brings me so much fucking joy, I don't give a fuck what anyone thinks.

"Nate Davis is leaving Heatstroke," Hannah says with a devilish smirk. "That asshole got what he deserved. His wife left him. Caught him cheating, apparently."

"I want to be happy," Marci says. "But I'm over it. I don't care."

I love this woman so damn much. I sit down on a stool in the diner, reach into the pocket of my jeans, and place an envelope on the counter between us. It's unmarked.

"What's this?" Marci asks.

"A celebration," I say.

She opens it and removes two plane tickets. Marci starts shaking, and Riley, her server, stops nearby with her tray.

"What's going on?"

"It's our honeymoon," I say. "We never got a real one. We're going to Rome."

"Rome?" Riley perks up. "Oh my gosh, that is *amazing.*"

Hannah gasps. "Jesse, that's so thoughtful."

Marci practically dives over the counter again, trying to wrangle me into a hug. I laugh and lift her into my hands.

"I think," Riley says, "you should take the rest of the day off, boss."

And we do.

I take my wife home in our new silver Audi, park outside the cottage, and lift her into my arms. I carry her into the cottage, over the threshold, and into the bedroom. I lay her down on the bed, her splash of red hair spread on the white sheets.

My woman. My forever. My home.

I lie down beside her, draw her into my arms, and keep her, the broken pieces, the whole ones, and everything in between.

"I love you, Jesse."

It's all I've ever wanted to hear from her perfect lips, and as I capture them, I know that for the first and last time, I have found it. The real thing.

"I will love you," I whisper, between kisses and caresses, "for the rest of our lives. And when we die, I will follow you, wherever you go, Marci Walsh."

———

Join Bailey's mailing list and read more of Marci and Jesse in a **bonus epilogue! Scan the QR CODE below to get it.**

Read Hannah and Savage's story in Savage Love.
Hannah's trapped with her brother's best friend during a storm.
Savage swore he'd never touch her. Can he resist breaking his
promise?
Scan the QR CODE below to get it.

About the Author

Bailey Hart writes small town swoonworthy romance that leaves readers with all the tingly feels. She loves wearing her nails long, eating Mexican food, and dancing like nobody's watching. When she's not writing, she's at dance class, spending time with her son and husband, or daydreaming about her next story idea—spicy scenes included. She lives in Cape Town, South Africa, and desperately wants a cat in the near future.

Come visit her at www.baileyhartromance.com

Bailey's Babes

Come join Bailey in the Facebook Group and hang out with other romance babes just like you! You'll get sneak peeks from new books, access to giveaways, and bookish conversations that will make your reader heart sing.

Acknowledgments

Writing *Fake in Love* brought me so much happiness, but I wouldn't be writing if not for the amazing people who surround me and support me. Thank you, thank you, thank you.

My husband/fiancé/partner/person who is there for me when my ideas dry up, when my cheeks are wet, and when I need inspiration. I love you.

My intelligent, feisty son who puts a smile on my face every day and is basically a meme factory at this point.

Claire, my assistant, who proofreads for me, is always available when I need her and has been so kind and understanding through the ups and downs.

To Echo, you design the best covers. Period. I'm so lucky to have you, and I can't wait to see what you come up with next.

To the influencers on my influencer team. You have put a smile on m face every single day since the launch of my debut novels. I'm so lucky to have you. Thank you, Erin, Rickie, Alexandraa, Monica, Sydney B, Amila, Paige, Brit, Fatima, Alex, and all the other ladies who have been so supportive.

To my ARC readers! Thank you for reading Marci and Jesse's story. I'm honored that you want to read my work and support me. You are amazing!

And to my readers, the ones who read, who tag me,

who message me, who spend all night reading when they shouldn't, who squeal, giggle and kick their feet. You're the reason I started writing in the first place.

FYI My two favorite scenes to write in this book were the "armchair" scene, and Jesse's love confession with his pictures. I can't wait to see these characters in the next story. I'm going to miss them.